C000271550

THE LOVE TRAP

CAROLINE GOLDSWORTHY

Copyright © Caroline Goldsworthy, 2020

Gordian Knot Publishing Ltd, December 2020

ISBN: 978-1-9161221-7-8

Paperback Edition

All rights reserved.

The right of Caroline Goldsworthy to be identified as author of this work has been asserted by her in accordance with sections 77 and 78 of the Copyright, Designs and Patents act 1988.

All rights reserved. No part of this publication may be reproduced, stored in retrieval system, copied in any form or by any means, electronic, mechanical, photocopying, recording or otherwise transmitted without written permission from the publisher. You must not circulate this book in any format.

This book is a work of fiction. Names, characters, businesses, places, events and incidents are either the products of the author's imagination or used in a fictitious manner. Any resemblance to actual persons, living or dead, or actual events is purely coincidental.

Cover design copyright ©Caroline Goldsworthy

❀ Created with Vellum

CHAPTER ONE

Lily

A sudden scream from the garden pierced the air. I dropped the tray of chicken drumsticks I'd been taking from the oven. My pristine kitchen floor, which I'd cleaned first thing that morning, a jumble of sizzling chicken, as fat and greasy liquid oozed across the marble tiles.

For a moment I was conflicted. Run outside or stay and clean up? But my maternal instinct had taken over and I raced into the garden before my brain caught up. Guests turned to stare at my sudden arrival. Some stood open-mouthed, hugging themselves. Others were turning away from the tableau in front of them. Roxy, Darcy's rabbit, was lolloping across the garden and Topher, my husband, had a shotgun trained on it. Our five-year-old son, James, was mimicking his father's actions and shouting, 'Rabbit pie! Rabbit pie!' His little sister toddled after the rabbit but was too slow to catch it.

'Topher, what are you doing?' I yelled at him, before I thought of the consequences. I chased Roxy to pick him up.

Grasping the rabbit by the scruff of his neck, I scooped him into my arms and tried to calm him. Totally oblivious to the danger he was in, he wriggled to escape from my grip.

'Open the hutch, please James.' My son stomped over to the hutch and, pouting, he opened the door. It ricocheted off the side of the hutch, catching me on the elbow. I grimaced. Glaring at Topher, I put the rabbit back in his hutch and, once Roxy was safe, I marched over to my husband. I held my hands out and, laughing, he dropped the shotgun into my arms. I winced at the weight of it on my sprained wrist.

'It was just a bit of fun,' he laughed, glancing at our wide-eyed guests. Not one of them could meet his gaze. 'You're overreacting, darling.' But I shook my head and refused to look at him.

How could he humiliate me like this? Our guests' silence was oppressive. Their horror tangible, like a cloak of mist hanging over the celebrations. It was as heavy as the smoke from the sausages he'd left to burn on the barbecue. My eyes watered; I was queasy, but whether that was caused by the charring sausages or my embarrassment I didn't know. I wanted to run. To hide and cover my shame. My face burned as I focussed my attention on pushing the top lever to break the gun as Topher had shown me in the past. The brass bases of the cartridges glinted in the summer sun. Aghast, I glanced up at him. *This was his idea of fun?*

I wedged it under my right elbow and took Darcy's hand. We dashed into the house; I dried Darcy's tears and put her in the highchair. Running upstairs, I locked the shotgun in the hidden eaves cupboard in our bedroom. You'd hardly know it was there, but having a loaded gun so close to where we slept made me shiver. Topher and I had argued about it many times, but he was convinced we needed to be prepared for possible intruders. I disagreed, believing that intruders could turn the gun on us. He knew better. Topher always knew better.

Returning to the kitchen, Darcy was happily banging a plastic spoon on the highchair's tray, and I remembered the chicken catastrophe. I kneeled to collect the dropped drumsticks together, wincing as I put weight on my right hand. Hearing the familiar click-clack of heels on the newly laid Italian Calacatta tiles, I hoped she didn't mark them. The heels clacked closer into my line of vision, and I recognised the slim ankles of Stephanie Silcott.

'Lils, what are you doing down there?' She reached down and grabbed my right hand, pulling me to my feet. I couldn't help myself and I squealed with the pain. She dropped my hand and I sank to the floor.

'What have you done?' She reached out to me, catching my gaze as I snatched my hand back.

'I trapped it in the door. You know how clumsy I am. It just slammed back on me.'

Stephanie pursed her lips, brushing a strand of dark blonde hair behind her ear. 'Of course it did.'

I forced brightness into my voice. 'What are you doing in here? Why aren't you outside with the rest of them?'

Stephanie sighed. 'Topher was extolling your virtues to everyone after the rabbit rescue. I thought I'd come and talk to the real thing. He said you've got another part-time job teaching music?'

I nodded. 'Yes, I started a few weeks ago,' I told her. 'The head is nice and the children seem to want to learn.'

'Don't you miss it?' She twirled her empty wine glass in her fingers, which gave me the chance to walk to the fridge so she couldn't see my face. Naturally, I opened the door with my right hand, flinched and used my left. I retrieved the bottle of white Rioja, trying to ignore her question.

3

But it was no use. Of course I missed my other life. Who would not? I closed my eyes, transporting myself back to another time.

Arms aloft, bow in one hand, violin in the other, I acknowledged the Lincoln Center audience. Sweat tricked down my face, down my back. I was exhausted and elated at the same time. My body vibrated in time with the cheers and the clapping. Another standing ovation. I quivered as goosebumps rose on my body. Lowering my arms, I gathered violin and bow in the same hand and curtsied to the crowd. They'd want an encore; they always did. I glanced at Phillip Trevelyan, the conductor. He smiled at me, nodded, and we resumed our positions for the encore.

But that was before. Before marrying Topher Gundersen. Before my accident.

Stephanie took the bottle from my hands, dragging me out of my reverie. She unscrewed the cap and poured herself a generous slug. Looking around for my wine glass and not finding it, she took one from the cupboard.

I smiled at my oldest friend, who knew her way around my kitchen almost as well as I did.

'Well?' she said, passing the glass to me. 'Do you miss it?'

'No, of course not.' I saw the slight rise in her eyebrows, her head angling to one side. We had been friends since meeting at university during Freshers' Week fifteen years ago. She knew when I was lying. But she also knew me well enough to know when to push the topic and when not to.

I raised my wine glass to Stephanie and she returned the toast and sipped from the glass, leaving a hint of pale pink lipstick on the rim.

I found I'd drunk half of my wine in one mouthful and, horrified at my lack of control, I checked I'd collected all the drumsticks. I rinsed them under the tap, slamming each one back into the roasting tin as I watched my guests wander around the garden. I bit my lip, holding back the tears that threatened to overwhelm me. Today was supposed to be a celebration and all I wanted to do was cry. I tried to swallow, but my mouth was too dry. *Where's my wine?* But all the same, I hesitated; Topher would be angry if I drank too much.

As if on cue, he walked in from his duties as barbecue chef. 'Lily, where the hell is the chicken and the steaks?'

I whirled to face him, my heart beating a little faster as my body tensed. Once, seeing him would have created such pleasure. But no longer. Now all I could see was the man he'd become. I gasped for air, panting, my mind whirling. *What was I supposed to be doing?* I clutched my hands to my sides to stop them shaking.

'I dropped the drumsticks.'

'Well, wash them off and bring everything out. No one will notice after I've saturated them in barbecue sauce.'

'What do you *think* I'm doing?' I retorted. He smiled at me and, although Stephanie couldn't see that the smile never reached his cold, ice-blue eyes, I could.

CHAPTER TWO

Lily

I took the cooked chicken and the raw steaks to Topher. He greeted me with a huge smile and compliments as I approached him.

'My beautiful and talented wife!' he declared to everyone.

I blushed at his tributes to me; it was as if the gun incident and the tantrum in the kitchen had never happened. *Perhaps he can change? He's promised so many times.*

'Rabbit rescuer and outstanding cook. A round of applause, people. Happy anniversary, darling.' He raised his glass in salute and I smiled back at him. What else could I do?

'Happy 'versree, Mummy,' said James, holding his plastic tumbler in the air. 'See, I'm being just like Papa.'

'You're going to be exactly like Papa when you grow up, aren't you James?' said Topher.

The *ah* sound resonated around the garden. I covered my lips with my left hand, the bile burnt the back of my throat.

Topher gave me a nudge and I winced with pain. 'Return the toast, darling,' he said, tracing his fingers lightly down my arm. 'I like the long sleeves. It reminds me of New York.'

'No glass,' I shivered, snatching my arm away. It was our anniversary and he was reminding me of *that*? No, he was never going to change. Someone rushed forward with a flute and something bubbling within. I raised the glass to him, took a sip and shuddered. It was lukewarm. 'I must get back to the food.' It was a well-worn excuse, despite wanting to spend time relaxing with the guests. I toasted everyone and pretended to take another mouthful. I left the glass on the buffet table as I passed. I'd collect it later.

Back in the kitchen, I found Stephanie perched on a barstool. The way she was rocking her Jimmy Choo's on the toes of one foot reminded me of the first time we met. She was sat on a bar stool then, although the shoes were purple Doc Martens. She had filled out and was sleeker than she had been — the cat that got every single last drop of the cream.

Pushing my refilled wine glass towards me, she said, 'Are you going to show me what else you've done since I was last here? This extension looks fabulous, but I want to see the rest of it.' She raised her glass in a toast to the new garden room and the lantern roof-lights, which allowed the daylight to flood into the kitchen and dining areas.

'Come on,' I replied. We went out into the long, shadowy hallway and I wondered about whether the second set of doors should be kept open. Topher preferred them closed, keeping the front door area separate. It was another source of contention, but I had learned to pick my battles. All the same, it was rather dark and dingy. Perhaps I should find a lighter paint, which would bounce light back?

'Here,' I announced, pushing the door open. Stephanie stepped over the threshold ahead of me and gasped.

'Oh, Lily! It's beautiful.'

7

'Thanks,' I said, as I stood beside her. I was proud of what I'd achieved in this room. The house, a substantial old vicarage, was early Victorian, with 1930s renovations. I'd spent time researching and sourcing the light fittings and a cast iron fireplace to replicate what had been stripped out by the previous owners. The trellis wallpaper, a copy of the Arts and Crafts era, wasn't strictly correct for a Victorian house but I had always loved the designs of William Morris. I'd restricted the paper to the fireplace wall, picking out a salmon pink paint for the rest of the room. Stephanie strolled around, touching things. The music stands, cushions, even running her long fingers over the wallpaper, whilst she sipped her wine and sighed happily.

She turned to face me, and I was surprised to see tears in her eyes. 'You've worked so hard,' she said. 'I love it.'

'Thank you.' But *thank you* seemed inadequate. I frowned. It was odd that Stephanie was crying. She hardly ever cried.

The last time I'd seen her cry was when we'd met after my fateful trip to the States. She'd come with us for the initial house viewing. That was nearly five years ago. I'd had a small baby on my hip and my fingers were still strapped up and sore. I'd taken one look at the house — the rambling garden and weed-strewn drive — and had been sure it would be too much work. Topher had convinced me the house was calling out to me, that it needed my help.

'You need this project,' he'd whispered to me. 'I can see you're entranced by it. Think what it could become. Plus, it will help you get over the accident.'

I'd clenched my jaw and squeezed my eyes shut, but that only brought the memories back. *Exquisite pain, as if my fingers were on fire. When I dared to open my eyes, my mangled digits were twisted and bloody before me. Bent like broken twigs, the vison of my lost future swam before me. My stomach clenched and I wanted to retch. Nearby, I saw the root cellar doors where my fingers had been trapped, lifting, and crashing down in the tornado, and I wondered how I had been so stupid.*

Deep down, I knew Topher was right. He'd supported me through my accident and coming to terms with giving up my career, and I felt indebted to him. A short while later, the Old Vicarage was ours. 'It's a labour of love,' I told Stephanie. 'I spend a lot of time in reclamation yards.' In fact, the battered old Volvo Topher had bought me had become a familiar sight at most of the yards locally, but I thought of Stephanie's glamorous sports car and I didn't mention this to her.

She tiptoed across the room to look at the photographs and certificates lining the wall opposite the fireplace. 'Oh Lily,' she said, 'Are you sure you don't miss playing in front of all those people? I know I would.'

I fixed my smile in place and shook my head. 'It was never going to work with a baby, in any case,' I replied. 'Then...' I shrugged and held up my hands. She looked at my poor fingers. They'd recovered better than I thought they would, but I still couldn't flex them as I used to be able to do. It was hard to grip the neck of a violin, but I could do it well enough to show students what they needed to do. I could still play a little, but I'd lost my touch and the sounds I produced were nothing more than an annoyance.

I followed her gaze to the many photographs of me playing, eyes closed and lost in the music, bowing to the audiences. I traced my fingers over my violin case. My thumb rested on the clasp, rubbing it gently. For a moment I thought about what lay inside. I didn't open the case. It was too distressing. Who wouldn't miss the adulation and the foreign travel? But it was not always glamorous. One hotel looked pretty much like another, and we rarely got to see much of the cities where we played.

I glanced at Stephanie. 'Are you okay?'

She nodded, downing the rest of her wine. 'Just bloody John again…'

But before she could say anymore, there was a clatter in the hallway and my mother burst into the room. Her face was flushed from alcohol and her eyes flashed fire. A visage I remembered so well. 'So this is where you're hiding yourself, Lillian,' she said. 'You do know you have guests waiting outside?'

'Yes, Mummy,' I replied. *How does she always make me feel like a naughty child again?* Stephanie's eyes narrowed as she stared at my mother. But before either of them could say anything else, I scuttled back to the garden to ensure everyone had seen the plates and cutlery I'd laid out earlier.

Outside, all was under control. There were no guests milling around without food, a drink, or a place to sit.

'I've sorted everyone out,' Mummy said. 'I knew I couldn't rely on you to do it.' She strode away to berate tardy guests who weren't lining up for food in a manner she saw fit.

'Your mother is still on form, I see.' Stephanie appeared by my side. She'd gathered my wine glass again and placed it in my hand. 'But it looks like any crisis has been averted. Now come on, drink up. I know there's more where this came from.'

'I can't,' I replied. 'Too much to do.'

'Lily,' she told me, 'This is your wedding anniversary too. Let Topher do some of the work.'

I looked over to the gas barbecue where Topher was serving charred lumps of meat to people. He caught my eye and indicated the table with his head. Instantly I saw the salad bowl was empty and I jogged inside to find the other one. I returned to the garden and swapped the bowls. Turning to smile at him, he simply nodded at me, his mouth in a thin line.

'Would you like a beer, darling?' I called to him.

He nodded, and I returned to my kitchen to fetch him a chilled beer from the beer fridge. I held the cold bottle to my forehead and suppressed a whimper. Despite what the divorce lawyer had said about maintaining possession of the marital home and getting evidence of his behaviour, I wasn't sure how much more of this I could take.

CHAPTER THREE

Stephanie

Tired of watching Lily flit about, making sure everyone had everything they needed, I wandered back inside and took a seat at the breakfast bar, my fingers caressing the black marble worktops. I wondered where she'd sourced them and for a moment I was envious that she had a husband who would buy her anything she wanted. But then, I'd often found myself envious of Lily. My entire flat would fit into her kitchen and garden room area alone. Plus, she had the man I'd wanted for myself. Although I would never have given up my work to have children as she did. In fact, I was pretty sure I would never have had the children in the first place. And there was the difference between us. Lily had always been a people pleaser, and we'd become friends in spite of it rather than because of it.

In part, I sometimes wondered if I befriended Lily so I could stay close to Topher Gundersen. Perhaps I did and, if so, what kind of a friend did that make me? But I knew I had always looked after her. Helped her stand up to her dreadful mother, for one thing.

It was at my insistence that she used the name Lily rather than Lillian. It was what her father had called her. I was still thrilled to see Lillian Stanton still hadn't forgiven me. I caught a glare from her as she stalked around the garden looking for some excuse to berate Lily for an imagined slip-up. I raised my glass to her and was rewarded by a scowl. I grinned back.

I resumed my study of the kitchen and the garden room extension. It was very tidy, and I sensed another hand was at work here. I was no neat freak, but I was still amazed that the two years sharing a house with Lily hadn't wrecked my nerves. Every so often her mother would descend upon us with mops and dusters. We'd run to the nearest pub and afterwards spend weeks unable to find anything.

My phone bleeped and I pulled it out of my jeans pocket. Denise.

How's it going? she'd texted.

OK, I guess. Wish you'd come with me, I replied.

Sorry, duty calls and all that. How's Lily?

Pale. Clumsy. I'm worried about her.

I'm not busy right now. Why don't you call me? she messaged.

I looked around before deciding the music room might be the best place to hold a private call about my hosts.

Denise answered at the first ring.

'What's up?' she said.

'Hmm,' I said. 'She's really not herself. She's sprained her wrist. Do you think there could be a health problem?'

'Was she clumsy when you knew her at uni?'

'Nope, not that I recall. And certainly if she'd been this bad I would've remembered. It's like she's become a complete klutz.'

'Can you suggest she sees her GP?' Denise said.

'I dunno. I can but try. She looks terrified. We were in her music room,' I gazed around at the photos and certificates. Lily had always had something of a charmed life, apart from the accident. 'Oh Denise, you should see it, it's so beautiful. Anyway, her mum came to find her and she was petrified.'

'Perhaps you should tell her about your therapist?'

'One thing at a time, hey,' I said. 'But she does seem so timid these days. Especially with Topher.' I heard a phone ringing in the background.

'Gotta go,' said Denise. 'Talk later?'

'Sure,' I said, and rang off.

I strolled back to the kitchen and to the fridge to pour myself another glass of wine. I was glad I'd booked a taxi and left my car at home, but at this rate I wasn't going to be safe to drive in the morning. I decided I should head out into the garden to make small talk with Topher's friends. Why was I the only one of Lily's friends who'd made it to the party?

At university we had always been part of such a large crowd. Even after we all left, we'd kept in touch, often getting together just to see Lily play if we could. I remembered the trip to Paris the best. Kate, Justine, Emma, and I had dragged Lily out for dinner after the concert and we'd drunk wine in a cafe on the edge of the Seine.

'Lily, I've been waiting for you at the hotel.'

We all looked up to see Topher leaning against a lamp post with his hands in his pockets. He was wearing a black bow tie with a cream silk scarf around his neck which matched his dress shirt.

Lily rose to her feet and wobbled. She grabbed the table for support, sending wine glasses and the bottle flying. Two waiters rushed over to clear the mess and right the table.

'What are you doing here?' Lily slurred, still unsteady on her feet.

Topher, oblivious to the broken glass, dropped to one knee and opened a small box. Kate and Emma squealed, clapping their hands and jumping up and down. Justine and I simply exchanged a glance, but I looked away quickly. The scenario was my dream, except in my dream he wasn't proposing to Lily.

Lily tottered towards Topher, placing one hand on his shoulder. She reached out for the box, tentatively, as if she expected it to be snatched away. She bowed her head towards him. 'Yes,' she whispered. 'Oh yes.'

He stood, towering over her, and scooped her into his arms. Then they stepped away from each other and he placed the ring on her finger, before kissing her hand.

After the Paris trip, one by one, the band of sisters had fallen apart. Everyone was married now and most had children, but it was no reason for Lily not to invite them to this gathering. I hadn't seen Kate since Lily's wedding.

I drifted into the garden and nodded at some shared acquaintances from the legal circles Topher and I both move in, but I was lost in my thoughts about Lily and our old friends. Perhaps it was just natural, I thought. Simply the way of things. Children, I was told, move you into different social groups. You became friends with the parents of children at the same nursery. Of our university troupe, I was the only one who was not married. I had no children. I didn't even have a plus one. Someone had come into my life. I'd thought he was the one, but he wasn't. Since I'd told him it was over, he'd plagued me with calls, flowers and, when that didn't work, he'd progressed to following me everywhere I went. It was how I met Denise.

Him I'd met at some dreadful works do. Grainger's and

Didcot Solicitors had always insisted on having their Christmas party in January. They said it was to buoy up our spirits in the worst month of the year. I think it was mostly to save money by not splashing out on a Christmas menu. John's insurance firm were doing the same, and we'd met sneaking down the stairs, both trying to escape without being seen.

We'd gone to a bar and exchanged work-party war stories. He'd made me laugh and so I'd invited him back to my flat. We'd only left my bed to forage for food throughout the rest of the weekend. Unexpectedly, he'd wanted to see me again and, although I'd seen no future in it, I'd continued to see him. He'd made me laugh out of bed, and in bed he'd made me scream. But it wasn't enough to base a relationship on. Now I was in danger of being the last one without a husband.

Who was I kidding? I *was* the last one without a husband, but even that idea didn't make John a contender. I didn't need a man to make my life complete, but sometimes, just sometimes, it would be nice to have someone.

I suddenly realised the group I was standing with were expecting me to answer some question or other. I'd not been paying attention and I made an excuse. As I stepped away, I caught Topher's eye. We exchanged a smile, and I knew. There would only ever be one man in this entire world I really wanted.

But he was married to Lily.

CHAPTER FOUR

Lily

The last of our guests left in the early evening, which gave me, Topher, and the children time to relax ahead of the working week. Loading the dishwasher, I made sure everything was arranged exactly the way Topher liked it. I ran the rinse programme then wiped the marble worktops and polished them with a dry cloth. The hairs on the back of my neck rose; I knew he was there even before he spoke. My heart pounded, my vision blurring, and I fought to bring my breathing under control. Mentally, I went through every item in the dishwasher, and resisted the urge to rush to the machine and make sure I'd stacked it the way he preferred.

The rinse programme ended, and he opened the machine to check it. I closed my eyes and tensed.

'Well done,' he said. 'That's almost perfect. But, despite what I said this morning, you've still left empty cartons in the fridge.'

I twisted around to stare at him, narrowing my eyes. I'd made sure the fridge was perfect, I knew I had. I rushed across the room and snatched open the door. Picking up the first carton from the bottle shelf, I shook it. Empty. And the second, and the third one. *No! How could this be happening? I had emptied them. I remembered doing it!* I'd thrown them in the bin and I'd marked them with a black permanent marker. He was playing tricks on me. I took the cartons to the sink and emptied them out. Damn! Juice. Milk. Not water as I'd expected. Trembling, I turned the carton upside down. No mark. I tipped the second carton over, and the third. No marks. Where were the marks? I'd put them there before I put the cartons in the bin. I ran to the junk drawer where I'd left the permanent markers. I yanked the drawer open. The marker wasn't there. Where was it? I'd left it on top of the rolled-up carrier bags and old envelopes I used for shopping lists. I knew I had. It must be there. It must be somewhere! I pulled out the drawer and tipped everything onto the island.

'Lily, sweetheart.' Topher reached over and grabbed my hands. 'What are you doing? What are you looking for?'

'I put marks on the bottom of the cartons. I know I did. Like the ones I showed you this morning.'

'Which ones this morning? What are you talking about?' He stepped back, dropping my hands, and a look of horror crossed his face. 'Lily, darling Lily. We didn't talk about cartons this morning. That was last week. Don't you remember?'

'No, it was this morning. You just said it was this morning, I know you did. You did this to me.' I pulled back my sleeve to show him the bruises on my wrist. 'I know you're playing tricks on me, so I've been marking the cartons.'

'Marking the cartons? Are you mad? What have you been marking them with?' He sighed and prodded the pile of junk on the island.

'I had a black permanent marker.'

Topher laid the drawer on a tea towel and began replacing everything in the drawer. 'There's no marker pen here,' he said. 'Are you ill again, Lily? Perhaps we need to make you an appointment with Dr Naseby?' He cocked his head to the side, his eyes filled with tears. He brushed them away and stepped towards me, holding me close and stroking my hair. When he pushed me back to kiss me on the forehead, there were fresh tears in his eyes.

'I love you so much,' he said. 'I hate seeing you like this.'

'I'm not like anything,' I said, pulling away from him. I closed my eyes and replayed the images of myself marking the milk cartons and the orange juice one before I'd put them in the kitchen recycling bin. It was as clear in my mind as if I had just done it. I snapped my eyes open and strode across to the bin, expecting to see the cartons in there, but it was empty.

'No!' My vision blurred and dizzy with panic I staggered towards one of the bar stools.

Topher grabbed me before I fell over, hugging me and whispering. 'It's all in your head, Lily, darling. It's all in your head.'

'It's not,' I protested, but in all honesty, I no longer knew.

He sat me down, cleared away the drawer and the detritus on the counter-top, made me a warm drink and walked me upstairs to bed. He undressed me and put me into bed as he would have done with one of the children.

While he was so calm, I asked the question that had been nagging at me all afternoon. 'Why was the shotgun in the garden?'

'I was trying to get rid of the rats before our guests arrived. I did tell you,' he sighed, stroking my cheek with gentle fingers.

'Rats?'

'Yes, the ones in that compost heap you insisted on having. It'll have to go, Lily. I don't want rats near the children.' He kissed me on the forehead and tucked me in, putting the herbal tea within reach. 'You didn't take the cartridges out of the shotgun before you put it away, did you?'

I shook my head.

'Good,' he said. 'I want to have it ready for action should we ever need it. Anyway, I'll sleep in the guest room. You get some rest.' At the bedroom door, he paused, leaning his head against the frame. His smile was so sorrowful, an overwhelming rush of guilt flooded my senses.

If I didn't ask now, I'd never ask. 'Can we go back to couples' counselling?'

'Of course, darling. Just as soon as you're well enough. We don't want a repeat of last time, do we?'

I tucked my chin into my chest in shame. I'd told the therapist about Topher's behaviour, but it had backfired on me. It was all in my head, they'd both told me.

'Goodnight, beautiful,' Topher said. 'Sleep well.'

Once he'd closed the door, I waited for the middle stair tread to creak. Good, he was gone! I sat up in bed and reached under the mattress for my journal. I needed to write down everything that had just happened.

CHAPTER FIVE

Lily

'What are you still doing here?' I asked Topher as I rushed into the kitchen. I'd overslept. I still felt woozy, as if I'd taken sleeping tablets. 'Shouldn't you have left?'

'Manners, darling,' he said. 'Good morning. Did you sleep well?'

'Er, good morning; yes, fine,' I said. 'Why are you still here?'

'My first case isn't until mid-morning. I did tell you,' he replied. 'I don't have to be at court for a couple of hours. Where are you going?'

'To work, of course. Where do you think I'm going on a Monday morning?' My body stiffened as I heard the first notes of Albinoni's Adagio. *Where's that coming from? Was it in my head?* But no, I saw him smirk as he placed his newspaper on the breakfast bar.

'No need,' he said, frowning as I turned the music off.

I glared at him and continued looking frantically for my keys. 'What do you mean?'

'I called in sick for you,' he told me. 'I thought you needed some extra time to tidy up after the party yesterday.'

'And they believed you?'

'Yes, I think so,' he smiled. He picked up the paper and folded it so he could bring the article he was reading closer to him. I wished he'd get his eyes tested and wear glasses. 'I emailed them from your account last night. I thought you would have a bad head after all you drank at the party. That headmaster of yours just replied it was okay and he hoped to see you soon.'

I put my handbag next to the detritus of plates and dishes. 'You hacked into my email account and told my boss I was too ill to come into work?' *How could he think this was acceptable behaviour?*

'Hardly hacked, darling,' he replied. 'You need a stronger password if you want to call it hacking. Anyway, look at the mess this place is in. It's no wonder you can never find anything. What have you lost now?'

'Car keys,' I replied, head down, avoiding his gaze. *Where the hell are the keys? I put them in the bowl on the Welsh dresser yesterday so I could get to my meeting with the therapist. I'll have to get Heather to help me look for them again.* I bit my lip, thinking about all the times my mother and Topher had teased me about "Lily Standard Time". *Is it getting worse?*

'Well, fortunately you don't need them now. So you can go and get changed and then come back down and clear up this mess. I don't know why you insist on working. You want for nothing. There's plenty to do here. After all, it's not as if we need the money from your little job.'

But I love my job, I wanted to tell him. I love the freedom and the sense of my old self. But all I said was, 'Heather will be here soon. She can help me.'

'Oh, I called her and told her to take the day off.' He

placed the paper on top of his breakfast bowl and pushed away from the marble counter-top. 'You don't mind, do you? Since you're going to be here anyway. You can spend some quality time with the children.'

I sighed. Why did he always do this? I looked at my bruised wrist. It was still sore from arguing with him yesterday. Choosing to protect the children from yet another set-to, I decided I'd call Heather later and explain that there had been a misunderstanding. I smiled at him, one of the loving smiles he expected. He kissed me on the top of my head before he sauntered out of the room. He ambled upstairs and I heard cupboards open and close. The children came racing down the stairs. James was the first into the room and I heard Darcy sliding down on her bottom. I rushed into the hallway and caught her before she tumbled.

'James, you do need to make sure she's safe on the stairs,' I told him. 'That's why the stairgate is there. To stop Darcy getting onto the stairs on her own.'

'I was with her,' he told me, fixing me with his blue eyes, just like his father's. 'Silly Mummy. She was safe with me.' He looked at me, wide-eyed innocence, and I couldn't help but remember how he'd imitated his father yesterday. Don't be silly, Lily, I told myself, he's only a child. I ruffled his blond hair. He shook my hand away, moving away from me, and smoothed his hair down.

'I know, sweetheart,' I told him. 'But she needs watching every second.' I bounced Darcy on my hip. Unlike James, she was exactly the image of me. Elfin and pale with mousy brown straight hair.

'Okay, Mummy,' he said, but he had already made his way to the snack cupboard and clambered on a chair. He pulled a packet of crisps from the cupboard and struggled to open them. He stared at me and I popped Darcy in the highchair so I could collect some scissors. Once I'd snipped off the top, I passed the packet back to him.

'What do you say?'

'Fank oo Mummy,' he said, batting his eyelashes at me.

'You're welcome,' I replied, ignoring the baby talk. I turned my attention to Darcy and almost missed Topher's shouted goodbyes as he raced to the front door and East Finchley underground. I drove there if I needed to use it, it was easier with the children, but Topher always walked. His long legs would stride out and eat up the short distance in twenty minutes. Or so he told me. I needed to trot to keep up with him should I ever walk with him.

Barely had he left the house when I heard keys in the door. I froze. *What's he forgotten?* I swiftly looked around the kitchen. His briefcase was gone, so had his keys and wallet. Darcy's lip wobbled, her eyes wide in fear. Then I heard a shout.

'Only me.'

'Heather? What are you doing here?' I asked, as my home help bustled into the kitchen. I headed to the kettle as she swept Darcy into her arms and made my baby squeal with delight.

'Oh, what am I going to do with a day off?' she said. But she kept her eyes on Darcy as she spoke. And I wondered.

It wasn't the first time she'd turned up after Topher had cancelled her time with us. 'Heather?' I said, hesitantly.

'Look,' she said. 'I knew you'd got the party yesterday and I knew there'd be a lot to do. You can't clear it all up and look after the kids too. That's why you hired me in the first place.'

'Thank you,' I whispered, blinking tears from my eyes.

Heather looked away; I thought she might be embarrassed by my emotion. We began returning the house to a level of tidiness I find uncomfortable, but that Topher insisted upon.

At eleven a.m. Heather brought me a cup of tea in the garden. I was weeding the flowerbeds again, picking out the persistent ones that had grown since I'd spruced up the garden before the party.

'Don't you need to be off for your appointment?' she said.

I rocked back on my heels and smiled my thanks at her. 'I cancelled it. When I couldn't find my keys.'

'I think you should go,' she said. 'Call them back and you can take my car.'

I hunted around for my mobile phone but, still unable to find it, I used the landline. My appointment hadn't been filled, so I changed my clothes, grabbed my journal from under the mattress, and jumped into Heather's car. My heart pounded as I waited while the electric gates swung open, signposting freedom.

CHAPTER SIX

Topher

Topher Gundersen strode down the street towards the dishevelled café where he was meeting his client: Mark Brown, a small-time petty thief whose light fingers could never resist an opportunity. Stupid really, Topher mused, especially when the man could make much more money with his other skills and receive less attention from the police. Still, he knew that, as the man's advocate, it wasn't his place to tell him how to live his life.

Topher nodded at the waitress before making his way through to the back of the café where his client waited. Topher shook hands with the tall, skinny young man. Almost the same height as his barrister, Mark was frail-looking, lacking Topher's broad chest and shoulders. His skin was pockmarked and pale in stark contrast to Topher's golden tan. Even in the dull light from the overhead bulb, he was blinking like a mole unused to sunlight.

'Did you bring it?' he asked.

'Of course,' replied Topher. He took his laptop from the bag, typed in his password, and slid it across the table.

'And you did everything else as I told you?' asked Mark, tapping away at the keyboard.

'Naturally.' Topher leaned back in the plastic chair, resisting the temptation to place his feet on the chair next to him.

'Good,' came the reply. Low conversation hummed in the café, interrupted only by the loud clacks of the keyboard.

'There you go,' said Mark after a few minutes. He slid the laptop back to Topher, who stared at the new screen layout. 'You can change camera angles like this,' he muttered, pulling the computer closer and moving his finger from side to side on the mouse pad.

Topher watched. He could see his home, his wife and children, the mess that she still hadn't cleaned up. Movement in one of the bedroom cameras caught his eye. Heather! Why had she disobeyed him? He jumped as Heather moved closer to the camera. *What the hell was she doing there today? Had she seen the camera?* But no, she was just dusting the toys on the shelf. He would need to make sure the camera was facing the right direction again when he returned home.

'You've done well,' he said, biting back his anger at the housekeeper's insolence. He took a brown envelope out of his breast pocket. 'Is your mother going to be in court? I'll give this to her, shall I?'

'Yeah, that'll be great, thanks,' he said. 'Mum always comes and supports me.'

Topher nodded and replaced the thick envelope in his jacket pocket. He wasn't sure how he could pass the money to his client's mother, but what he had discovered with so many of his clients was how adept they were at subterfuge.

Although not sufficiently adept that they didn't regularly need his services as a defence barrister.

'What about the other thing and the phone?' Topher asked. He tutted. He'd almost forgotten the most important things.

Brown nodded. 'Sure,' he said, and slid a padded envelope across the table.

Topher slipped it into his laptop case.

'Have you got the phone with you?'

'Of course, she won't miss it. She's always losing it in any case.' Topher took his wife's mobile from his laptop case.

'Not 'ere! I got a mate you can send it to. Address is in the envelope. He'll clone it for you. The tracker not good enough any longer?' Brown said.

'It's been fine,' replied Topher, 'but I just want to keep an eye on her messages and phone calls. She's been getting some nasty texts and I want to protect her. If I have a copy of her phone I can delete them before she sees them.'

'Yeah, of course you can,' replied Brown.

Topher saw curiosity flash across the man's face, but Brown was being well paid. And Topher was not about to share the true reason for wanting his wife's phone cloned. The tracker had worked well. Well enough for him to see his wife had spent two hours in central London when she should have been at work. When he'd tracked the address down he'd been disappointed to discover it was a firm of solicitors. He was suspicious; if she'd wanted legal advice, why not ask him or Stephanie? The mystery was solved, however, when he'd found the letter hidden in the lining of her handbag. She was after a divorce. Topher was outraged. Of all the ungrateful women, he'd never encountered one as ungrateful as his wife. How dare she? He'd given her everything she needed. The house was refurbished exactly as she wanted it. And she was after a divorce. Again. As if their last conversation on the matter hadn't been enough to dissuade her. He was never going to allow her to leave him and take the children. Never. He would protect his family from breaking up if it were the last thing he did.

Topher rose, slipping the phone and laptop into his case. 'I'll see you in the courtroom,' he said.

Brown nodded, passing Topher a scrap of paper. 'The names you wanted,' he said. 'They should be able to help you.'

Topher took the note, ran his gaze down the list and placed it in his pocket along with his iPhone. 'Thanks,' he said.

'No problem. Just you make sure you get me off again.'

With a curt nod at his client, Topher left the café, taking the list of names and a battered looking Nokia out of his pocket. He rang a number on the list, smiled grimly as the call ended, and with a spring in his step, made his way to court.

Topher couriered Lily's phone to the contact Brown had given him and arranged for the original mobile and the new cloned phone to be sent to his chambers once the work had been completed. He could only hope that Lily didn't miss her mobile before he got home in the evening.

Pleading Brown's case took all his skill that afternoon. Watching the jury, he was sure they wanted to convict and go home. *Was the foreman asleep?* Topher couldn't be sure and not for the first time wished he could stroll around the courtroom as his American counterparts did. That would shock the dozing juror into wakefulness. He smiled grimly and continued to present Brown's case from his lectern in the centre of the courtroom.

CHAPTER SEVEN

Lily

When I returned from my appointment, Heather had completed all the housework and I was able to relax before Topher came home. He was never early. I had a whole hour of peace before I began cooking his evening meal. Even though there were enough leftovers from the party to feed us all for the rest of the week, Topher always wanted a hot meal when he came in. I'd learnt to make dishes that could stand waiting for a while, even for hours, until he arrived home.

I made my way back into the garden, continuing the search for more recalcitrant weeds that had made a reappearance over the weekend.

'Oh, I forgot to say…' Heather called out to me, 'I've left your keys in the wooden bowl in the kitchen.'

'Thank you. I was searching everywhere for them.'

'Did you look in the freezer?' Heather asked.

I frowned. Was she joking? But she wasn't laughing. 'The freezer?'

'That's where I found them,' she replied. 'I was making

space for some of the leftovers. Perhaps you dropped them when you were getting the meat out?' She shrugged and I returned the gesture.

'In the morning, then,' and she waddled down the hallway and out the house. I heard her car engine start and then a clang and thrum as the electric gates swung open. I rested on the grass, waiting to hear the gates shut, staring at the three stories of our house which towered over me.

As soon as I knew she'd gone I rushed over to the wheelie bin patio. The cartons Topher said I'd left in the fridge were in the recycling bin. But the ones I'd marked up yesterday were outside in the wheelie bin.

I pushed at the large bin, knocking it on its side, and pulled every last carton out onto the paving slabs. I sobbed with relief as the cartons each had a firm black blob scribbled onto the base. *But was I going mad? Had I forgotten to mark the cartons yesterday? Or had I left them in the fridge? Think, Lily, think!* I collapsed onto the slabs and hugged my knees, rocking myself backwards and forwards as I wracked my brains.

'Okay, Mummy?' I opened my eyes. Darcy had come to find me. I hugged her close, breathing in the smell of her fine hair, scented with baby shampoo, and used it to push away another smell. Another unbidden memory. The stench of my own hair, rank and greasy. Unwashed. It surrounded me as I lay on a padded floor in a cell where Topher had sent me for my own protection after my accident. My hands, heavily bandaged, were strapped to my sides. I shivered and loosened my grip on Darcy to find a tissue. Wiping away my tears, I stood and lifted her from the ground.

James hadn't appeared, and I strolled back into the

house to see what he was up to. Silence was never a good sound where my son was concerned. But I needn't have worried. He was sat at the small rattan children's table in the garden room, totally engrossed in colouring pictures of spaceships.

'Are you okay, James?' I asked, and he nodded his head without taking his eyes off the page. Orange and red flames shot out of the rear of the spaceship. I wasn't sure the crew would survive that particular flight. Darcy wriggled to be put down. I placed her on the floor and she toddled back to the garden and her sand pit. She sat batting the base of a small seaside bucket and, when the sand came out without forming a castle she squealed with anguish. I brought her some water to moisten the sand and we played quietly together. I could still see James from where I was sitting, and I relished these few moments of perfection.

All too soon it was six o'clock and I needed to begin preparing food for Topher. James stayed at the table, eating his supper and drawing. Darcy was in her highchair, chatting to me in baby talk as I prepared his meal.

My mind raced as I chopped vegetables. Where was my mobile phone? At least I'd got my keys back and wouldn't have to admit to Topher I'd been unable to find them. But I'd searched everywhere for the phone. Even Heather hadn't been able to find it. What if he'd been calling me or texting me and I'd missed the calls? He'd be furious.

As if my thoughts invoked his appearance, his key slid into the Yale lock. The metals scraped against each other. The door clicked shut and his precise footsteps echoed in the tiled hallway. I was shaking so much I cut my finger. I turned on the tap and rinsed the veg before he entered, so he wouldn't see blood on the food I'd prepared. I wiped my hands on the tea towel as he walked into the kitchen. James leapt up to greet him, but Darcy slunk low in her highchair. All baby talk silenced.

'Good day?' he asked.

'Yes, fine,' I said. 'Do you want to eat first or shall I get these two ready for bed?'

'I'll do that while you cook,' he said. James yelled in delight but Darcy whimpered. Topher yanked her out of her highchair. 'Come on, scaredy cat. Daddy's turn to do bath and story.' He strode out of the room. Darcy's thumb was in her mouth, her eyes filling with tears as he carried her away.

I gripped the tea towel in my hand tighter. I put a plaster on the cut and began to cook his dinner. I was on high alert for Darcy's cries.

'She's getting better with me,' he said, strolling back into the kitchen. 'Red or white?'

'Red. Pork schnitzel. Two minutes.'

The plop of the cork coming out the bottle made me jump, but he pretended not to notice. I brought the food over to the table, nearly dropping it when I saw my mobile peeking out the top of my handbag. How did it get there?

'Problem?' said Topher, pouring me a glass of wine.

'No,' I said. 'I don't remember leaving my mobile there. I was looking for it earlier.'

'Perhaps it slipped into the hole in the lining, darling.'

I froze. How did he know about the gap in my handbag's lining?

I placed his dinner in front of him and sat opposite. Surely he must be able to hear my heart beating. My hand shook as I returned his toast over the meal. *If he knows about the handbag, what else does he know?*

'There's a pattern,' my therapist had said. 'Watch for the patterns. After the explosion he can go back to the honeymoon phase. To remind you why you're with him. Hearts and flowers, I call it. Log it in your journal and don't get taken in.'

Raising my glass to sip some, the wine slopped over the rim. Topher tutted at me and I ran to the kitchen to fetch a damp cloth. I mopped the wine, hoping I'd be able to get the mark out of the tablecloth, while he continued eating. From the outside it would seem like a perfectly normal marriage. After I'd returned the dishcloth to the kitchen and put it in cold water, I sat at the dining room table and tried to eat. The breadcrumbs on the pork were like ashes in my mouth but I didn't trust myself to raise the glass to my lips again.

'You didn't finish telling me about your day,' he said. 'I see there are a few things you've missed. Shall I write a list for Heather?'

'No, it's fine,' I said. 'I can do it.'

'Just make sure you do,' he said. 'I don't want to come home to a mess again.'

CHAPTER EIGHT

Lily

The following day there were no dramas and Heather had arrived and taken over by eight o'clock. Topher seemed to be in a good mood that morning, but I had been careful to get everything ready the night before so I had no last minute problems finding keys or ID cards or anything like that.

For a change, he asked for a lift to the underground station. Although I was conflicted, I complied happily as there was no telling how quickly his mood might change. He kissed me warmly before he jumped out the car and strode away into the crowd. I stayed watching for a moment. He was a head taller than everyone else and his gold hair shone like a beacon. I sighed, remembering more loving times.

There was no time for coffee and a chat in the staff room before my first class and so I made my way to the music rooms, hoping that perhaps I could grab a hot drink before the first students arrived. I stayed in the music room referring to the teaching plan and selecting the sheet music for the day's lesson, then I went to make myself a coffee in the small kitchen behind the stage in the main hall. When I returned to the music room it was still empty. None of the students had arrived. I looked at my watch to discover that it was a quarter past nine. Perhaps the students had been sent elsewhere because I'd been ill the day before? I decided to go and see Miss Keeble, the school secretary. She frowned at me when I walked into the room. Surprised and a little embarrassed. I smiled warmly at her, although I feared something was wrong.

'Hello Joan,' I said. 'I was waiting for my class in the music room, but no one has turned up.'

Joan flushed and pursed her lips at me.

I waited patiently but I was astounded, as I'd never seen Joan lost for words.

'The headmaster wants to see you,' she said finally. 'There was a note in your tray in the staff room.'

'I'm so sorry, Joan. I was running a little late so I went straight to the classroom. Is there a problem?'

'You could say so,' Joan sniffed. 'If you just wait here and I'll let Mr Jacobs know you're waiting to see him.'

I flopped into the chair opposite her desk. I wondered if David Jacobs, the headmaster, wanted to discuss my absence yesterday. It wasn't the first time Topher had called in sick for me. Much as I found it irritating, I believed him when he said he was doing it for the best reasons. *The divorce lawyer I'd spoken to had another word for it, however. Controlling.*

Joan returned to the office, her face still flushed. 'The headmaster will see you now.'

There was a sharpness to her voice I'd not heard before, and I quickly made my way to David's office. In the past I'd just knocked on the door and walked in, but today something felt different, so I knocked and waited.

'Come in.'

I pushed the handle down and peeked around the door. He didn't smile as he normally did. *What the hell was going on?*

'Come in. Sit down, Mrs Gundersen,' he said.

David had never been so formal with me but, following his lead, I greeted him in the same formal manner.

'You're probably aware of why I have called you in today,' he began.

I shook my head. 'I've no idea, David. Am I in some sort of trouble?' I sat in the plastic chair opposite his desk and waited for him to continue.

'There have been complaints, Mrs Gundersen.'

'What sort of complaints?'

'Serious complaints, Mrs Gundersen.'

'David, I'm sorry, I don't understand. What kind of complaints? And please call me Lily as you've always called me Lily. Why are you calling me Mrs Gundersen today?' My nails dug into the palms of my hands as I clenched my fists in my lap. I looked down. Twisting my hands had made my knuckles white. I quickly released my fingers and stretched them out, massaging first the right hand fingers and then the left. Although many years had passed since my accident, too much clenching still made my hands dreadfully sore.

David had been extremely quiet during this time, and I looked up to see him watching me massaging my fingers.

'Lily…' He coughed. 'Mrs Gundersen. There has been a complaint that you assaulted one of the students.'

I stared at him, but he couldn't meet my eyes. 'You're seriously suggesting I would hit a student?' I stood and started pacing behind the chair. 'David, I implore you, please tell me who is saying this?'

'I'm sorry,' sighed David. 'The full accusation will be put into writing and be sent to you in the post. In the meantime, I must ask you to give me your identification card and any

37

keys you have for the school. I will arrange for someone to escort you from the premises. You may not return to the school unless invited for interview, but it is highly likely any conversations will take place in the council offices, rather than at the school.'

I stopped pacing and I hung onto the back of the plastic chair, trying to maintain an upright position. My legs no longer seemed strong enough to hold me. David picked up his phone and asked Joan to join us in his office. I opened my handbag and gave him the keys and my ID card. Joan took me gently by the elbow and propelled me back to my car.

'Will you be okay to drive home?' she asked.

I nodded. I no longer trusted myself to speak without bawling, releasing the hot tears stabbing at my eyes. She pushed the driver's door shut. I sat in the car park, eyes closed, brushing the tears away, waiting until my heart stopped pounding and I could drive home safely.

Recovering my composure, I turned on the engine and connected my phone to Bluetooth.

Stephanie sounded really excited when the call connected. 'Hello, you!' she said. 'I was just thinking about you. That was a great party. How are you?'

'Not good,' I replied. 'I've just been fired. They're accusing me of hitting a student.' Even as I said it, still couldn't believe the words coming out of my mouth.

'What?' Stephanie sounded as shocked as I was. 'Did they say who'd made the accusation?'

'No, they wouldn't tell me.' I bit back a sob and blinked away tears, which were still forming. 'They said they would send it all to me in the post.'

Stephanie's howl of laughter took me by surprise, until I

remembered it was her habit to laugh when she was embarrassed. 'You are joking?' she said.

'I'm really not.'

'So, if they've fired you they have to give you good reason,' she said. 'They can't just say they'll provide the evidence later. Have they told you that you need to talk to the police?'

'No, nothing like that. Oh God, I'm going to have to tell Topher. If he thinks this will reflect badly on him, he'll kill me.' Fresh, hot tears ran down my face as I envisaged the conversation with my husband.

'Where are you now?' asked Stephanie, ever practical.

'I'm still at the school,' I told her.

'Have you got the car?'

'Yes, I'm sitting in it now. I'm still in the car park.'

'Okay,' she said slowly. 'Go home. Drive carefully, but just take yourself home. Have a cup of tea and a good cry. I've got a couple of meetings this afternoon, but I'll put them off and come round and see you after lunch.'

'Okay,' I said, disconnecting the call. I put the car in gear and pulled slowly out of the car park.

'Call Heather,' I said, and the technology did its thing.

'Hi Heather,' I said, when I heard her answer. 'There's been a bit of a mix-up at school, so I'm on my way home.' I couldn't bring myself to tell her the truth, although I knew she'd have to know at some point. We chatted for a few more minutes and she told me she was taking the children to the park. Did I want her to wait until I get back?

'No,' I told her. 'I've got a bit of a headache so I think I'll have a lie down when I get in. Listen, Heather, there's a guy trying to undertake me in a Range Rover. I think I probably need to concentrate until he's out of the way.'

'Okay,' she said. 'Catch you later.'

The black Range Rover was completely filling my rear-view mirror. I didn't know what I'd done to annoy him, but he was weaving around, headlights flashing.

I pulled onto the North Circular and moved to the inside lane, but instead of overtaking and passing me, the Range Rover stayed behind me, flashing lights inches from my tail.

CHAPTER NINE

Lily

I had no idea what to do. When I slowed down, the Range Rover slowed down. When I sped up, the Range Rover sped up. Even though he was close enough that I should've been able to see him in the rear-view mirror, the windscreen was so dark I couldn't make out a face.

Up ahead I saw a garage and I put my indicator on to let the driver behind know I was pulling off. As I reached the slip road to ease onto the garage forecourt, the Range Rover nudged my car and pushed me past the exit lane. I clenched the steering wheel as hard as I could to stop my car being pushed into the outside lane.

I twisted in my seat and waved at him with my right hand to beckon him past. But he just flashed his lights at me again. I maintained the speed limit and he sat on my rear bumper. *Why was this happening to me?* I didn't believe I'd pushed in front of him or cut him up. I couldn't understand what was making him behave this way.

I shook. 'What do you want from me?' I whispered. My

mind raced as I flicked from watching the road ahead to looking in the rear-view mirror. I want to go home, I muttered. *But you can't leave the dual carriageway*, another voice in my head hissed at me. White knuckles gripped the steering wheel. I grimaced with the pain but it was nothing compared to the pain in my chest where my heart pounded. My mouth was dry. My head aching with the noise of blood hammering through it.

Ahead I saw a lorry, the blue curtains on the trailer swollen, beating time with the breeze. It swayed from side to side. *You're going to have to get past it.* I peeked in the rear-view mirror. *Yes! He's dropped back. Perhaps he's calmed down?* Still unsure what I had done to cause his annoyance in the first place, I pulled out and, miracle upon miracle, the Range Rover remained several metres behind me.

I breathed a huge sigh of relief, overtook the lorry, and indicated to pull back in. The lorry driver pulled on his air horn. Confused by the cacophony of sound, my blood curdled. I lunged forward as the Range Rover crashed into the rear of my car. I tensed my arms, bracing myself before hitting my chest on the steering wheel. The Range Rover shunted me from behind again. My hands throbbed with pain as I clenched the steering wheel, wrestling it to keep the wheels straight. I tried everything I could think of. Everything I had ever been taught, just so I could keep my car on the road. *What if the car span? I couldn't remember how to correct a spin!*

Then it happened. My Volvo hit the central reservation barrier, but bounced off. I braced myself for the collision with the lorry, but the Range Rover shunted me again. My car lunged forward once more. The whole car shuddered as we left the ground. The collision with the barrier launched us into the air, over the central reservation and into oncoming traffic. Still I held onto the steering wheel, this time to stop myself from hitting the roof, which was now below me. I hung upside down. The seat belt cut into my shoulder blade, flattening against my crushed ribs, and constricting my hips. Every loose item in the car — sweet wrappers, tissues, crayons, crisp packets — swirled around my head. *I must have a clear out*, I thought as the car flipped over and rolled again, miraculously landing on its wheels.

Horns. Squealing tyres. Burning rubber. Crunching metal. The nauseating stench of diesel and petrol. A car hit the Volvo's rear, twisting the car around. A people carrier coming towards me. A glimpse of a child cocooned in a car seat. *It's the same one as I have for Darcy.* The last thing I remembered were the horrified faces of the parents before I hit the vehicle head on.

Then, there was silence.

When I came to, an oxygen mask covered my mouth, pressing on the bridge of my nose. I tried to raise my hand to remove it, but my fist remained, clenched and frozen at my side.

'Stay still,' I was told. The calm demeanour of a paramedic but she looked worried, as her eyes skimmed the condition of my car.

'What's your name?' she said. 'I'm Katie. Can you tell me your name?' All smiles and professional optimism as she held my hand. She shifted to one side and I saw a fire-fighter approach with a machine which looked like oversized bolt cutters.

Katie covered me with a blanket. 'To protect you from the glass,' she whispered and then stepped back.

The fire-fighter began to cut away at the upright around

the shattered windscreen. I felt the small squares of glass fall on the blanket, but I was protected underneath.

As he worked, I drifted in and out of consciousness. It was a relief, as the noise from the machine was unbearable.

As he prepared to pull the final sections of crumpled metal from my legs, I screamed in agony. I remembered the pain from the night I mashed my fingers, and yet I couldn't envisage how much pain there would be from my crushed legs. I needed not have worried, as Katie changed the mix in my breathing mask, and I drifted into unconsciousness.

I woke again as the trolley was pulled from the back of the ambulance, yelping as the wheels hit the floor, jarring my body. I couldn't avoid the view of the bright fluorescent lights overhead as I was raced into accident and emergency.

Memories of another emergency room flooded my mind. *Squeezing my eyes shut and clenching my jaw, I held my breath, trying to compel the pain to shift, but it wouldn't leave. My fingers were aflame. Exquisite agony. Nausea threatened to overwhelm me but lying flat on my back on the trolley would have made me choke. Opening my eyes, I saw my fingers were mangled. Twisted and bloody. Misshapen.*

Bright lights in front of my eyes, which I squeezed shut again. Obediently though, I tried to open them when told. I bore the probing white light on my pupils. Then a mask was placed over my nose and mouth. Cool air, gas, and then, sweet oblivion.

Stern, determined faces surrounded me, rushing my trolley to a side room for intensive treatment. I whimpered at each jolt to the trolley as it crashed into the double doors closing off sections of the emergency area.

I knew nothing of what happened next, although later Topher told me everything. My right leg was broken, with significant damage to the knee. He told me he hoped I would be able to walk again. I sent up a silent prayer of thanks that the children hadn't been in the car as well.

The next few days passed in a blur of sleeping, groggy from the pain medication, forcing myself to open my eyes so I could stare at the small bright light, and watching the path of the doctor's index finger to prove I wasn't concussed.

Once again, my mind went back to a different accident and the same promises of a full recovery.

Another of Topher's lies.

CHAPTER TEN

Lily

I woke one morning to find a diminutive dark-haired woman sitting in the visitors' chair.

'Hello,' she said. 'My name is Detective Constable Denise Jones. I'd like to ask you some questions about the road traffic collision.'

'I can't remember anything clearly. It's all such a muddle.' I shook my head, an action which I instantly regretted as pain reeled around my head and neck. I closed my eyes and allowed my head to sink back on to the pillows. Pictures flashed through my head, the images whirling around, but I couldn't make sense of any of it.

'Mrs Gundersen,' she said, 'when you crashed your car, four people died.'

Unbidden, a small face came back into my mind. My vision fixed on her car seat logo. The same car seat as Darcy's. 'No!' I screamed.

A nurse rushed into my private side room. 'You'll have to leave,' she said to the detective constable. 'I can't have you disturbing Mrs Gundersen like this. She's still extremely ill and she needs to recover.'

Detective Constable Jones stood, slipping her notebook and pen into a small black bag. 'I do need to talk to you, Mrs Gundersen. I will come back tomorrow and see if you are any better. Four people were killed. I need to speak to you about that and interview you under formal caution.'

'Out!' demanded the nurse. 'Out now. You were told quite clearly not to upset my patient. Have you even got permission from Dr Sanders to be in here?'

DC Jones backed away, giving me a short, sharp nod.

As she turned to go, she collided with Topher. The top of her head barely made it to his chest. He placed his hands on her shoulders and pushed her back.

The detective stiffened and glared at him. Taking a deep breath, she drew her shoulders up and back, thrust her chin out towards him. Part of me admired her bravery. If only I could be that brave.

'You,' he said. 'I thought I made it quite clear that you couldn't interview my wife without a solicitor present. Since I can see no solicitor here I must ask you to leave.'

He turned to the nurse. 'Has Dr Sanders said my wife is fit to be interviewed?'

The nurse shook her head. 'I've already made it clear to this police officer, but she refuses to leave Mrs Gundersen alone.'

'I'm a Detective,' Denise Jones said. 'Not a police officer.'

Topher looked down at both women. He then fixed DC Jones with a steely gaze. 'Do we need to add harassment to your list of misdemeanours, Detective? My wife will talk to you when the doctors deem she is fit to do so, and not before. Now leave.'

He held the door open for her, and she gave me one last

penetrating stare before, chin held high, she departed. Through the mesh window, partially obscured by a Venetian blind, I saw her speak to a uniformed officer. Was I under arrest?

'What the hell have you done this time, Lily?' Topher rounded on me as soon as we were alone.

I tried to raise myself on my elbows and push myself into a sitting position. It was no use, and I flopped back onto the pillows. With a grunt, Topher threw a device onto the bed. Lifting it, I saw that it raised the back of the bed. I pressed the button and waited whilst the bed whirred me upright.

When I sat facing him, I told him everything that I did remember: the conversation with David Jacobs at school, how the accident appeared muddled, disjointed, but I remembered the lorry, its loud horn, and being shunted. Had the lorry hit my car? Topher paced the room, occasionally batting the back of the chair. I was terrified. Expressions of disgust, anger and disbelief crossed his face.

'Are you sure?' he asked, placing his hands on his hips. 'Are you sure someone tried to push you off the road? Why would anyone do that? Why would *anyone* want to do that to you? Are you sure that you didn't do this to yourself?'

'Topher, I'm not guilty of any of these things. I've never hurt a student. I've never put a hand on one. Not even a hand on their shoulder. And I did *not* try to kill myself! I'm mortified you think I would.'

Topher glared at me. I knew that look. He was working out the best course of action for him. How he could best protect his own interests. My needs were unimportant to him.

'You have to tell the police what happened. I have to tell them the truth,' I told him, but he shook his head.

'No, you're not well enough. Leave it for a little while. Wait until things calm down.'

'Topher, this isn't going to calm down. Four people are dead, two of them children. This is never, ever, going to calm down.'

'We'll get you a good solicitor,' said Topher. 'Don't worry about the assault case. I'll get Peter Robinson to help. He'll come in and take care of the car accident part of it and the potential manslaughter. We'll do our own investigations. Oh, Lily,' he sighed, 'You know, you could go to prison for this?'

I bit my lip. Tears fell steadily down my face and I closed my eyes, trying to hold back the sobs that were trapped in my throat. My heart was pounding, threatening to leap from my chest. Making me dizzy from the images whirling through my mind. If only I could slow them down. Review them one by one. I couldn't think. I needed to think. I needed peace to gather my thoughts. What was that noise? I snapped my eyes open. I was still connected to the heart rate monitor. I snatched at the sticky tabs on my chest, pulling them off. Gasping at the pain as the adhesive tugged at my skin. The machine squealed and the police officer at the door peeked in. Topher pulled the plug out and the machine fell silent.

Would he disconnect the machine so calmly if I were dependent on it?

Topher came over and grasped my hands. I squeaked with the pain. Was he so stupid he'd forgotten about my hands?

'I'm sorry, I'm sorry,' he said, releasing his grip.

For once he really did look sorry. I met his gaze with something bordering disbelief. 'I'm not guilty of anything. I'm not guilty of hitting a student and I'm certainly not guilty of causing the accident. You must believe me, Topher. You really do have to believe me.'

He slipped off the bed and looked at me. 'I don't know what to believe anymore, Lily. You said a Range Rover ran you off the road, but where's the evidence? Have you got any witnesses? I don't want to believe you would be so cruel as to hurt me this way. You know how my parents died. I don't want to think that you would try and punish me by killing yourself in a car crash.' Tears were falling down his face and he wiped them away with the back of his hand. 'Could you be so wicked as to harm our children in the same way and leave them without a mother?'

Of course I hadn't forgotten that his parents had been killed in a motoring accident. Their car had lost traction on an icy road and hurtled through the crash barrier. I covered my face with my hands. Now I knew the gut-wrenching fear they must have felt as their car careened down the slope. Did they pray? Did they hold on to each other? Did they declare their love for each other? Did they think of their son?

There was no hope for the occupants after the vehicle careered down a mountainside. Topher was just nine. It had happened long before I met him, and he didn't tell me the full story until I was in hospital in New York. Through sobs and tears, he'd lain beside me on my hospital bed, stroking my tummy where James was growing, and he'd told me how much family meant to him. That he'd do anything to keep our little family together.

I'd thought that since the birth of James and Darcy he had recovered from losing his parents. I thought he had put his grief behind him. Now I saw it was as raw today as it had been on the day of their accident.

'I'll do my best, Lily,' he said, as he prepared to leave. 'I'll do my best to keep you out of prison.' At that point, I realised he'd not been listening to me at all. He didn't believe me. He wasn't on my side.

There was only one person in the world I could possibly rely on. And that was Stephanie.

CHAPTER ELEVEN

Lily

It took some effort, but finally I got the nurse to agree to call Stephanie.

I relaxed back on the pillows and tried to doze but my mind raced, reliving everything: David firing me, the accident. I drifted into consciousness as I heard her Jimmy Choo's click-clacking down the corridor, long before I saw her striding into my room.

'Oh, I'm so glad to see you,' I sighed.

'Well, I'm glad to see you too,' she said. 'You had me worried. I left work early for our lunch date. I got to your place. Heather let me in and we sat drinking tea together but you never turned up. I even went to the park with the children.'

'I'm so sorry,' I replied. 'I really am deeply sorry, but it's been terrible. I have to tell you what's been going on.'

Stephanie sat down in the chair where Topher had just been. She put her handbag on the floor and crossed her long legs.

'Okay, tell me,' she said.

'So, we had our call and I told you I'd been fired and why,' I began.

Stephanie nodded. 'Yes, I remember the one. I'm hardly likely to forget it,' she said. 'What happened after that? Heather told me when you spoke to her there was a Range Rover tailgating you.'

'I've been going through what happened afterwards. Again and again. I've been trying to make sense of the pictures in my head,' I said, closing my eyes to shuffle through my memories. 'I remember driving away from the school and — you're right — suddenly, there was this guy on my tail. It's coming back to me now. In a big vehicle. It was all blacked out. The car was black. The windows were black. I couldn't see anything, but I'm sure it was a man. And he was flashing his lights at me, but he wasn't hooting. Don't you think that was odd? He kept flashing his lights and I pulled onto the North Circular to come home and I thought he'd just go past me and maybe hoot or wave a fist as he went past. But he didn't. He just stayed behind me on the inside lane and he kept flashing. I tried to pull off into a garage and he nudged the back of the car, so I shot forward. Oh, Stephanie, I was so terrified! I was absolutely petrified.'

She leaned forward to squeeze my hand. She hesitated momentarily, withdrew her hand, and reached over for my left hand. I wondered briefly if she'd remembered the last set of bruises. She'd not asked about it and it was good not having to lie to her again. 'How do you know what type of car it was when I can't remember?' I rubbed my head with the heel of my right hand. I couldn't quite open my right eye, and when I did the room refused to stay still.

'Like I just said, you called Heather and you told her it was a Range Rover. Do you remember that?'

I shrugged. 'Everything is still a bit hazy. I seem to remember trying to work out what I'd done to upset him. Then there was a lorry up ahead and I had to overtake it because it was going so slowly and so I indicated and pulled out into the outside lane. When I looked in the rear-view mirror, I saw the black car — the Range Rover — way, way behind me. I thought he might have calmed down. But then I indicated to pull back in again and the lorry hooted. I panicked. Then I was shunted forward, and I looked in the rear-view mirror and he was right behind me. That bastard hit me. My car hit the barrier!' I gasped for breath and Stephanie passed me some water. I took a sip and carried on.

'I'm trying to hold onto everything and trying to keep calm. Keep the car under control, you know? Then as I'm about to pull back into the inside lane the lorry edges closer and I think I'm going to hit it, but that doesn't happen because the Range Rover shunts me really, really hard and my car hits the central reservation again and the car just flips. I remember everything swirling around inside the cab of the car and I was hit with the whole lot of stuff I leave in there: coffee, random pens, pencils, crayons, and empty crisp packets. All of the shit I leave in my car. It was all just whirling around my head. Then I remember the jolt as I landed on the other side and was upright and I remember feeling relieved I was upright. But there was so much noise. It was deafening. I'd never heard noise like it. I couldn't believe I was okay, and I just opened my eyes and that was when I saw the people carrier. Just before I hit it, I saw a little girl in the back. She had a car seat like Darcy's.'

I pulled my hand away from her, so I could raise both to my face to cover my sobs. 'I hit the people carrier,' I repeated, 'And they're dead. Everyone was killed.'

Stephanie paused before speaking and took a deep intake

of breath. 'Yes,' she said. 'It was in the papers. A family of four. I'm sorry, Lily...'

I dropped my hands and looked at her. 'Topher doesn't believe me,' I told her. 'He thinks I've done this on purpose. He thinks I tried to crash the car. To be honest, I've actually no idea what he thinks, but I know he doesn't believe me. He doesn't believe me about the assault. He doesn't believe me about the crash. And now I've got this detective chasing me. She wants to interview me. She wants to interview me under caution.'

'Yes,' said Stephanie, 'but that's standard practice. Who is it?'

I nodded to the bedside cabinet where the detective had left a card.

'Ah yes, Denise Jones. Oh, well, there's nothing to worry about. I know her. She's been helping me with the John issue, and we've become friends.'

I watched Stephanie tap the card against her beautifully made-up lips, wondering why she'd not told me about this new friendship.

'You can trust her,' she continued. 'Why don't we get her to come in here and you can have an off-the-record chat? In any case, I can sit in on the chat and I can give you the benefit of my legal expertise. We'll make sure Denise realises it's off the record. You can just tell her everything you've told me. To be honest, she can even start looking into the assault allegations if they're taking it to court. If they sacked you then they are going to take it further. Therefore, someone in the police must have been aware of it. I'm sure it's not something they will keep private and tucked away within the school.'

'I don't know. I really don't know. David Jacobs said there would be something in the post, but I haven't seen anything so far.' Briefly I wondered why she'd not mentioned this Denise before, or why she'd not brought her to the anniversary party, but my head was still pounding. 'I've asked my mother to bring my post in, but she's not done that yet. Topher said there's nothing there for me.'

'Okay,' said Stephanie.

I gave her a weak smile as I saw her mind whizzing, working out all the options. I loved her practicality. I'd never ever known anything faze her, ever. It was one of the first things I loved about her.

'Okay, I'll call Denise and get her to come in and talk to you. I'll sit with you while it takes place.'

'And Topher?' I asked.

Stephanie gave me a strange look. 'I think we will manage this without Topher,' she mused. 'I think it would be the best thing all round. When you're out of hospital, you can do the formal interview with Detective Jones and with the solicitor Topher arranges for you, but in the meantime, it seems to me it would be better for you to have a chat with her woman to woman and see where it goes from there. Okay?'

'Okay,' I sighed, resting my head on the pillows again. 'Thank you.' Despite the amount of trouble I found myself in, I was feeling much more at peace. I knew I had called exactly the right person.

CHAPTER TWELVE

Lily

I have no idea how Stephanie managed it, but two days later, Dr Sanders had given the all-clear for an interview and Detective Constable Denise Jones was ushered into my hospital room. The two women greeted each other warmly with a hug. Stephanie called a nurse, and an extra chair was brought into my room. Stephanie put it in the corner and sat there, briefcase by her side and legal pad on her knee.

DC Jones took the chair nearest my bed. 'Hello again,' she said.

I gave her a quick smile.

'Okay,' she continued, 'I'm going to have to caution you. I know Stephanie said this would be just an informal chat between us but I'd lose my job if I were to do that. Stephanie has agreed to act as your legal representative, so this will be a voluntary, preliminary interview, and both she and I will be taking notes. You'll have to come to the station once you're released from hospital for a formal interview.'

I nodded, grateful for Stephanie's intervention. We've had

our differences in the past, but she was proving to be a better friend than I could have hoped for.

'Now,' said DC Jones, taking out her own notepad and sitting with pen poised, 'tell me in your own words exactly what happened.'

I sat back and I related to her my journey into work, my confusion over the lack of students in the class, and my conversation with David Jacobs.

'Let me stop you there,' she said. 'You were accused of assaulting a student at the school?'

'Yes,' I said, 'but I've not seen any evidence. They promised to send me details of the allegations in the post. It's been a week and Topher says that nothing has arrived from the school.'

'Okay,' DC Jones nodded.

'Will you look into it for me, DC Jones?' I asked.

'Call me Denise,' she said, breaking into a smile that transformed her face. 'Most people call me DJ. But yes, I will look into this for you. I'm surprised it's not been raised with the police already. With the facilities and the computer systems we have nowadays, the two cases should be linked via your name and date of birth.'

'I'd be grateful if you'd check up on it for me. I'm going out of my mind. Obviously at this stage, I haven't had a chance to put across my side of the story or prepare a defence.' I was stuttering. I couldn't even bring myself to consider that anyone could possibly accuse me of such a thing. I'd enjoyed teaching my students. Plus, I'd been slapped too many times during my own childhood to ever do that to anyone else.

'Tell me a little bit about your background. How did you come to be teaching at the school?'

'Before I married, I was a concert violinist. I had an accident when I first became pregnant and I've not been able to play properly since. I mean, I'm good enough to demonstrate what needs to be done, but...' I laughed self-deprecatingly. 'Those who can't do, teach. Isn't that the saying?'

DC Jones raised her head, tilting it to one side, looking at me with sympathy in her deep-set, dark eyes. 'It must be awfully hard for you.'

'It is, but I have my children and my home to keep me going,' I replied.

'And your husband,' said Stephanie.

'Oh yes, and Topher. How could I possibly forget I have Topher?' I tried to ignore the frown Stephanie shot in my direction.

'So, the day of the accident, you drove home? You were upset?' said Denise.

'I think I was in shock. I talked to Stephanie briefly on the phone before I drove away. I did some deep breathing meditation-type exercises I used to do before I went on stage. I calmed myself. I calmed my breathing. I phoned my housekeeper to say I was on my way home. As I was driving, I saw a large black Range Rover in my rear-view mirror. He was flashing at me. He followed me onto the North Circular and then when I was trying to overtake a lorry, he hit me.'

'Let me get this straight, you're telling me somebody used their vehicle to propel you off the road? You didn't mention a Range Rover when we spoke before.' Denise Jones's eyes reduced to slits.

'I couldn't remember anything at first. It's come back to me. I was overtaking a lorry — actually hasn't... didn't he come forward? Did he not see something? He hooted at me. It was the horn which alerted me to the Range Rover trying to mow me down.'

Denise looked at her notes. 'I can't see anything about a

lorry driver in here. I'll have to look into it. Leave it with me,' she said. 'So, is that the last thing you remember?'

'Yes, pretty much. I think the car rolled. Or at least I'm assuming it did. I just remember everything in the car flying around my head.'

Again, she flicked back to her notes. 'Yes, that can happen. You were lucky to escape.'

'Good old Vanessa,' I said. 'She's always kept me safe.'

'Vanessa?' Denise stopped writing and looked up.

'Yes, Vanessa,' I replied. 'She's my Volvo.'

'Was,' said Denise. 'She was your Volvo. You'll be needing a new one.'

A tear trickled from my eye and I brushed it away furiously. *How could I possibly be crying over a car when I've killed four people?*

Denise looked at me. 'Okay, I've made some notes. I'll take this away.' She turned her head towards Stephanie. 'You'll be doing the same? You'll do your own background checks on this new evidence?'

'I most certainly will,' said Stephanie. 'We need to keep each other apprised of what's going on.'

'Agreed,' said DC Jones. 'I'll leave it there for today, but I will do some investigating to see what CCTV there is. I'm surprised no one has come forward so far. I'll look into the lorry driver as well and then I will get back to you. Now your doctor has agreed you can be interviewed I would expect that, once you are released from hospital, you'll be called in for a formal interview.' She looked at Stephanie. 'Will you be the solicitor again?'

Stephanie let out an indelicate snigger. 'No, I don't think so. I think Mr Gundersen has someone else in mind for his wife's representation. Plus, since I'm a personal friend, it's a conflict of interest for me. I was happy to sit in today.'

DC Jones nodded. There were more air kisses with Stephanie, then she waved at me and headed off.

'Feel better?' asked Stephanie.

'I do,' I replied. 'Thanks for helping me get that off my chest. What happens now?'

'You'll need to do a recorded interview at the station,' Stephanie said. 'They may charge you with death by dangerous driving at that point. If so, we'll get a court date and try to get you out on bail before a court hearing.'

'And if I can't get bail?'

'Then you'll be put on remand.' Stephanie turned away from me. Her shoulders shook.

'What about my children?'

'I'm sure they'd be able to visit, but with the assault charge too, Social Services could be involved.' She came and sat in the chair Denise had been in. Her eyes were red.

'I didn't assault anyone,' I said. My jaw ached from clenching and I wriggled my lower jaw around, rubbing the sides with my hands. This couldn't be happening.

* * *

Denise

I went back to the station and started looking into the background of Lily Gundersen. I knew from Stephanie what a talented musician she had been and about the terrible accident she'd had in New York State — not the city, I discover; still, I supposed that trapping your hands in doors could happen anywhere, but a part of me wanted it to be somewhere exciting and fantastical.

I wondered why she'd done it. Stephanie had told me she'd hurt her hands purposely. It seemed a strange thing to do, but then my mother had always told me terrible things about baby brain and how it made you act unreasonably, irrationally.

As I pushed myself back from my chair, DI Anita Blaine popped into the squad room. 'What are you up to, DJ?' she asked, although I suspected she already knew. Nothing much happened in this police station that Anita Blaine didn't get wind of.

'I'm just doing some background checks on Lily Gundersen.'

'Okay, but don't waste too much time on it,' she said, narrowing her eyes at me. 'That woman's still responsible for the deaths of an entire family. Don't forget it.'

'I won't,' I told her. 'But there are some other things which have come up, and I'd like to look into them.'

'Okay,' said DI Blaine. 'But as I said, don't waste too much time on finding justification for her. Dig up some dirt. She's a murderer after all.'

Although I knew I shouldn't ignore a direct command from the guvnor, there was something about Lily Gundersen that made me believe she wasn't a murderer. Call it gut instinct, but I was not convinced that someone who could produce such beautiful music could be evil at their core. However, if there was one thing I'd learned since joining the Met it was to never judge by appearance. If Lily hadn't caused the collision, then who had? I needed to request the traffic camera footage from the Highways Agency. I groaned inwardly. It could take forever, especially if I had to convince DI Blaine to request it. Her name carried more weight on a request than mine did.

CHAPTER THIRTEEN

Lily

A few days after DC Jones visited me, I was allowed to leave hospital. Unfortunately, this also meant that Mummy had come to stay, so she could help look after me.

I was still on strong painkillers and I spent a lot of time asleep, but I was hoping that once I got home and could sleep in my own bed, I would begin to feel more alert. Topher offered to sleep in one of the bedrooms on the first floor so he wouldn't disturb me or knock my leg during the night. I readily agreed. After his attitude in the hospital, I couldn't bear him near me.

Surgery on my knee had been postponed indefinitely. Even so, I couldn't put any weight on my right side until my leg was healed. I was going to be completely helpless.

Before leaving hospital, I was looking forward to seeing how much work on the house had been done in my absence, but was extremely disappointed to discover work hadn't commenced on the garage extension or Topher's garden office.

'What's happened?' I asked Topher when I got back to the house.

'Oh, I've got no idea,' he shrugged. 'The workmen just didn't turn up. You'll have to phone them, but leave it until you're better, hey?'

'But this was going to be your garden office. You said you needed this so you could spend less time at chambers. I thought that was the whole idea?'

'Yes, but it doesn't matter really, does it?' he said. 'I did tell you I can always work from chambers. After all, I've been doing it for years.'

'I guess,' I said. 'But it's a bit of a disappointment for the kids. I think they were looking forward to having you at home more.'

I let the conversation drop, but there was something amiss. Topher had been so keen to have a home office and now he was almost blasé about the workmen not turning up. However, I was going to have to deal with the builders later. Head throbbing, I reached out for the analgesics on the bedside table and swallowed them down with water that mummy had left in reach.

The following morning, I called the building company to discover that, far from not turning up, the work had been cancelled. Apparently, whilst I was in hospital, I'd emailed them to put the work off. I was very apologetic to Mr Yates, the builder, and tried to convince him there was no way I had been emailing anyone whilst I was in hospital. I didn't need a calculator to see that Topher's casual dismissal of their no-show and an email cancelling their services added up nicely. Eventually, I got Mr Yates to agree to come and see me and bring a copy of the email. I looked around for my laptop. I was going to have to change the password again, but since I kept forgetting them, I had to write them down. *Was that why Topher was so calm? Had he cancelled them?* I asked mummy to bring me my laptop, but it took forever for her to find it and bring it to me.

'Lily,' she said, 'Why are you always so untidy? I spent ages looking for this. Absolutely ages. You're always such a mess.'

'Thanks Mum,' I said, thinking of the constant nagging about the state of my room when I was younger. Sadly, it did nothing to make me any tidier. I supposed the untidiness was my small rebellion.

'Thanks for everything you're doing here,' I told her. 'Perhaps you could go home at the weekend? I'm sure we'll be fine without you. Heather can come in every day; she'll look after me.'

'Now, now, you're just getting depressed again, aren't you? It's like the time when you had your accident when you were depressed about being pregnant.'

'I wasn't depressed about being pregnant,' I retorted.

Mummy looked at me with one of her knowing smiles. Disagreeing with her would be pointless.

She patted my hands. 'Of course not,' she said. She looked at my damaged hands with a moue of disappointment across her face.

'What's wrong, Mum? What are you upset about?'

'Nothing,' she sighed. 'Absolutely nothing.'

'Mummy?'

'It's just all that money and time we spent on your violin lessons and taking you to competitions. All that time and money wasted on you, and then you go and ruin it all.'

'I know, I'm sorry, but it was an accident. I didn't do it on purpose,' I told her.

'No, of course not. If you say so. Now then, here's your laptop. Is there anything else you want? Otherwise, I've got things to do downstairs.'

'No, Mum. I'm fine,' I said.

She went to the bedroom door and leaned against the doorframe, staring at me.

'I would have given anything to have had the opportunities you've had,' she said. Her smile was sad; wistful, as if she wanted me to feel guilty again. Then she was gone.

I picked up my laptop, logged in and checked my email. After a while I found the email to Mr Yates the builder, cancelling the contract and telling them I would pay monies owed so far, but that was the end of it.

I checked the date. 5th June. The day after the accident. The day I was unconscious. I noted at the bottom of the email that it said sent from my smart phone. I scrabbled around on the bedside cabinet to try and find my phone, and yes, the email was there in my sent items, but I couldn't have sent it. Whilst I was online, I logged into my bank account and I saw I had indeed paid off Mr Yates. There was even a little bonus in there.

This was when I was comatose in the hospital. While they were trying to fix my leg. In fact, hadn't I been in the operating theatre all of that day? It made no sense. Nothing did anymore.

I dashed tears away from my eyes as the door handle was pushed down. Topher. What did he want?

'I came to make sure you're okay,' he said. 'Do you need anything?' He strolled across the room and perched on the side of the bed. He traced his fingers down my bare arm. It was all I could do not to snatch it away.

He pretended not to notice how I trembled as he lifted

my hand to his lips and kissed it. Turning my hand over, he held my palm to his face. His skin was always so smooth. I hung my head, thinking of earlier times. Times when I had loved stroking his face, his chest, making love to him.

He smiled, but his eyes were cold. He ran his hand back up my arm. 'I hope you recover soon, Lily. We don't want to make you wear long sleeves again, do we?'

I snatched my hand back. *Bastard! How dare he threaten me again?* All the same, I was afraid. Scared that he'd commit me again as he had done in the States. My hands had been too severely damaged to be forced into a strait jacket, but he still liked to goad me about it. And with it, the underlying threat. Disobey him and I would never see my children again.

'I'm getting better every day,' I said.

'Good to know,' he said. 'By the way, the police aren't getting anywhere finding your Range Rover.'

I frowned. 'Range Rover?'

'The one you claim ran you off the road.'

'How did you know it was a Range Rover, Topher?'

'You told me, Lily. When you were in the hospital. Don't you remember?' He gave me such a sad smile, I could almost believe his sorrow, but I hoped he couldn't hear my heart beating. I knew I hadn't told him about the Range Rover. It had come back to me when I'd spoken to Denise Jones and Stephanie, but I'd not mentioned it to anyone else. Had one of them told him? But if that were the case, why would he lie about it? There was only one reason I could think of for him to lie and it was too frightening to countenance.

Terrified by more of his threats and determined that he wouldn't beat me, I decided to create the plan my therapist had suggested. First of all, to make sure I had somewhere to go. I logged onto my credit card account and went through the items. There had been some spend, which was odd since it had been quite some time since I'd last seen the card. I hadn't dared tell Topher I'd lost it. I ran my eye down the list of items. Then I stopped at one. *What on earth was that for?* I looked at it more closely. That was an awful lot of money and not a company name I recognised.

I sighed and shut the laptop. I was exhausted. I decided I'd Google the company name later. No doubt it would all become clear then. It was probably the painkillers making me so tired, I thought. I pushed the laptop away from me, and then remembered Topher would be annoyed if it fell to the floor, so I placed it on the beside cabinet. I removed one of the pillows from under my head, put it onto the floor and snuggled down so I could rest.

CHAPTER FOURTEEN

Lily

Life continued in the same vein for a while. Not unhappily, but Mummy refused to go home and stayed to look after me. After a while even James, usually her favourite, had taken refuge in my bedroom and was asking when Granny would be going home.

'Soon, sweetheart,' I said, 'Granny will be going home very soon.'

There was a knock on the door, and it opened to reveal a bunch of expensive flowers. Roses, lilies; all my favourites. I frowned as the door opened wider. The flowers shimmied, pollen dropping to the carpet as the bouquet shook and the plastic wrapping crackled. Stephanie giggled, unable to keep up the pretence. James rushed to hug her, and she bent down to give him a kiss and a cuddle.

'Now you go and find Granny, darling,' she said. 'Auntie Stephanie needs to talk to Mummy.'

I patted the bed, and she came and squatted beside me and gave me a huge hug.

'I'm so pleased to see you,' I told her. 'I'm going out of my mind with boredom sitting here.'

'Yes, I've phoned a few times and I've been put off by your mother. How are things with Lillian, by the way?'

'I just want her to go, but she says it's her duty to stay with me as I'm injured,' I groaned. 'I'm sure she wants to torture me.'

'Yeah, I'm not sure I could have coped with my mum staying for longer than a weekend,' said Stephanie. 'When's the knee operation?'

'Good news on that front. I don't need one, apparently. They told me the leg is mending well. I might need an operation sometime in the future, as I get older. But for now, as soon as I can put weight on my leg again, I'll be back to my old self.'

'That is good news, and you're definitely looking better. More roses in your cheeks than at your anniversary party. Have you stopped taking those dreadful tablets?'

'Yes, yes,' I told her. Although in fact I hadn't. They seemed to help push everything to one side, and I'd spent most of the last few weeks asleep. Mother had been threatening to give me bed baths, which was an absolute nightmare, so I managed to hobble to the bathroom to wash. But life was continuing, and I'd managed to persuade the builders to come back. Work progressed in the garden. I could stagger over to watch their headway from the window. I could dress and Topher had organised a wheelchair for me, which meant I could get around up here, but I was trapped on the top floor. I'd tried the stairs but couldn't manoeuvre the steps and crutches. My jailers, as I'd come to see them, were furious when I threw the crutches downstairs and slid down on my bottom. Topher had insisted I stayed up in my room.

I sighed. I looked at Stephanie and said, 'I'm so bored! I've read all the books on my "to be read" pile. I'm just going out of my mind with boredom.'

Stephanie laughed. 'Well, you'll be pleased to see what I brought you then.' She dug into the bunch of flowers and pulled out two small cans of gin and tonic.

'You absolute star,' I told her. 'There are some glasses in the bathroom.'

'Oh goody,' she said, 'I did wonder if we would be drinking out of mugs like we did when we were teenagers.'

I laughed, thinking of the many times we'd sneaked out of lectures and gone to sit by the lake at our university, watching the geese and drinking gin and tonic out of plastic bottles, leaning our backs against the faux standing stones that were placed around the lake.

She returned my smile. 'Thoughts?'

'I was just thinking about university.'

She giggled. 'Ha ha, yes, I remember only too well. We did have fun, didn't we? Well, when you weren't going off to do yet more practice. You were always so dedicated.'

'It's funny you should say that. I had a similar conversation with Mum two or three days ago. She remembers it quite differently.'

'Your mother remembers everything differently. For what it's worth, I remember you being very focussed. You knew exactly what you wanted to do,' Stephanie mused. 'Still, I didn't come here to talk about the fabulous Lillian. I've got other problems, like a stalker.'

'What?' I gasped. 'Not John? Still?' Stephanie had been threatened once before but, when it was over, she resumed with her string of men. None of them lasted for more than a month or two. 'You didn't tell me how you met him,' I said.

'At a ghastly January Christmas dinner.' She pulled her mouth down into a sad face.

I laughed and gave her the sympathy she desired. 'So, what happened?' I asked.

'Well, we started seeing each other on and off through February and before Easter it was definitely on,' she sighed. 'Then he got too clingy and I ended it. Now, well...' She shrugged. 'Why can't they take no for an answer?'

'I don't know, darling,' I said. 'Perhaps because you're too beautiful?'

She laughed. 'That should show them I'm out of their league,' she sniffed, and looked out of the window. 'Tell me what's happening outside. You seem to have the workmen back again.'

'Yes,' I said, 'It's the last job. They finally came back and are building a double garage for our cars so we don't have to park out front or in the rear alley anymore. And then Topher is having a garden office built.'

'Oh, a garden office? Is that where he's going to hide all his porn?' Stephanie giggled again.

'I don't know if he's got any porn,' I said. 'He's Danish, not Swedish.'

Stephanie looked at me. 'What, you never go through his stuff?'

'No, never. I'm not that kind of wife. Everybody has to have some secrets.' I tried to turn my mind away from scouring credit card bills, but the curiosity was overwhelming. 'Stephanie, did you tell Topher about the Range Rover?'

'No, why would I? I assumed you'd mention it.'

My blood froze. Goosebumps flared on my entire body. I rubbed my arms to warm myself. Sweat beaded on my forehead. *If Stephanie hadn't told him, how did he know the vehicle's make?* It must have been Heather. That was the only logical answer. Or was it?

'I wouldn't be able to resist going through his stuff,' said

Stephanie. She turned away from the window to smile at me. 'I'd be in amongst everything he had. I wouldn't be able to stop myself.'

'Yes, well, you always were a lot nosier than me.'

'I don't know how you can't be. I just love to know everything about people.' Stephanie shrugged again and wrinkled her nose at me.

'Is that what why you became a solicitor?' I asked.

'Possibly,' Stephanie said, the tooth glass of gin and tonic halfway to her mouth. She took a sip and looked at me thoughtfully. 'I do know an awful lot about people's lives now,' she said. 'Some of it I don't particularly want to know. Anyway, I didn't come here to talk about me. I came to talk about you. So, you've got the builders back. Did you get to the bottom of how they got cancelled?'

'No, I didn't. I checked my emails. I don't remember sending the mail, but Topher said I was so out of it when I was in hospital, I could have sent anything and not remember it later.'

'That doesn't sound very plausible though, does it?' She cradled her elbow in her left hand, the glass tapping her lips. 'Go on, what else?'

'Okay, so, I managed to persuade the builders to come back, and Mr Yates comes and talks me every day before he goes home. I don't understand it. I've never ever worked on something as complicated as this. It just seems to be one problem after another. I placed an order for some of the stuff he asked me to and it didn't arrive on the day and, when we checked, the order had been cancelled. It just keeps happening. I don't know what's going on. I just feel like there's two of me. One's doing one thing and the other one is doing everything she can to mess me up. I'm going out of my mind!'

'Well, you've always had your fair share of problems, haven't you? I mean, trouble seems to seek you out,' said Stephanie, her brows furrowed. 'Remember the time you were so stressed out we skived off and went to Ibiza for a week?'

'How could I forget,' I said, but frowned, as there were some things from that week I'd rather forget. 'This is different, though. I remember ordering things. I don't remember cancelling the orders.'

'What more have you heard about the assault case?'

'Nothing.'

'And you're sure you stopped the medication?'

I swallowed, as she looked at me.

'You haven't stopped taking those bloody tablets, have you?' she said.

I bit my lip. 'No, I'm afraid I haven't.'

'Well, you need to stop, Lily. You do know how addictive they are, don't you?' she told me. 'You really must stop. It's no wonder you have no idea what you've been up to if you're out of your mind on drugs all the time.'

'I know,' I said.

'Where are they?' she said.

I nodded to the bedside cabinet and she opened it. 'These ones?' she asked, holding up the bottle.

I nodded again. I was surprised to see how few were left. I was sure I hadn't taken that many.

'You know, I'm tempted to take them with me, and make you go cold turkey.'

I sighed and glared at her. 'You know, you're such a bitch sometimes,' I said, but I raised my tooth glass to her in a toast and sipped some of the gin. 'But not all the time,' I grinned.

'It's for your own good, Lily. You're not going to get

better if you're drugged up all of the time. It just causes its own set of problems.'

'Yes, you're right,' I replied. 'I'll try to do better. Anyway, enough of me. What are you doing about your stalker?'

'Bloody man. I called the police as you told me to do. Now I've taken out an injunction against him and he still hasn't stopped. But he has got cleverer.'

'Cleverer how?'

'He's using burner phones to contact me. As soon as I block a number, he gets another phone.'

'Is he still following you?'

'I think so. I feel like I'm being watched all the time, but I've not actually seen him recently. I just feel like he's there. All the bloody time.'

For a long time after Stephanie had left, I stayed in bed, my head spinning. I needed to talk to someone, someone who would believe me. The same person who'd warned me about Topher and to whom I'd refused to listen. I picked up my mobile and scrolled to his number, and then scrolled past it and back again. Sod it! I muttered.

I hit the green icon and waited.

After a few rings, a voice answered. 'Hello?'

'Dad?' I said, 'I need you.'

CHAPTER FIFTEEN

Lily

I kept my promise to Stephanie and stopped taking the medication. I didn't ask the GP for a repeat prescription. My mind was clearer, and with that, the progress on the building in the garden made headway. There were no more delays, and Heather, with the help of Mr Yates, supported me on the stairs so I could see the finished work in the garden for myself.

Mr Yates held my elbow as I stepped into the room that was going to be Topher's new office. I was delighted by the standard of workmanship. I felt like giving him a huge hug for the work he'd done, but as I lumbered towards him, he stepped back in shock.

'I appreciate your faith in me, Mrs Gundersen,' he said. 'Especially after our little misunderstanding. Now listen, Mr Gundersen asked me to make sure there was only one set of keys to the office. He didn't mind about the garage, but he was quite insistent there was only one lot of keys for his office. But locks always come with two sets, so I'm giving this bunch to you for safekeeping should his key ever get lost or anything. That way you won't need to call out a locksmith. You can just keep them in the house tucked away somewhere.'

I nodded, thanked him, and slipped them into my jacket pocket. He helped me back into the house and supported me as I hobbled back up the stairs to my prison.

I did have a little excitement, whilst stuck in the house. The only day of escape I had was when I was called to the police station to give a formal interview with DC Jones and her senior officer.

She introduced herself as Detective Inspector Anita Blaine. She was a slim, fair-haired woman, who looked at me severely as I hobbled into the room. When I was settled, she read me the standard caution and took me through the day of the accident. I related my story to her as I had to Denise Jones and to Stephanie a few weeks earlier.

It was clear from the expression on her face that she didn't believe me. And when she brought the interview to a close, I asked if I could ask a question.

'Go ahead,' she said, one eyebrow slightly raised and a confused expression on her face.

'I wanted to ask about the allegations made against me on the day of the accident. The school have never come back to me with any evidence.'

She frowned at me and turned to DC Jones, giving her a quizzical look.

DC Jones said, 'Yes, Guv. Do you remember I was beginning to look into it whilst we were gathering evidence for the manslaughter charges?'

'Yes, I remember. What came of it?' DI Blaine snapped.

'Nothing, Guv,' replied DC Jones. 'I contacted the school and they told me they weren't going to press charges.'

'What?' I looked at my solicitor. 'Did you know anything about this?'

His eyes widened as he removed a handkerchief from his breast pocket and wiped his face before moving his chair a little further from mine. 'No, I've not been advised of anything related to the assault charges. I thought your husband was handling that himself, Mrs Gundersen.'

'First I've heard of it,' I said. 'So, you mean the entire case was… it was a lie? It was some kind of sick joke?' I put my hands on the table, wishing I'd been able to stand up and thump it loudly.

'I… I honestly don't know,' replied DC Jones. 'I haven't been into the school to speak to the headmaster to discuss it with him.'

'I see,' said DI Blaine. 'I think perhaps we ought to pay the headmaster a visit and find out a little more about these claims. However,' she turned to me, 'it would appear, Mrs Gundersen, that you have got off scot-free with it. Don't expect to get away scot-free with the manslaughter charge. We will look into your claims. Be assured we will be investigating them.'

She frowned and turned to DC Jones. 'DJ, did we get the CCTV footage?'

'I'm not sure, Guv. I'll have to look into it myself. I'm certain I haven't seen a report on it, though.'

'Okay,' DI Blaine said, 'Make sure you get onto it ASAP.' She glared at me. 'We'll be in touch, Mrs Gundersen.'

I held her gaze. 'And the lorry driver?'

DI Blaine looked sharply at DC Jones. 'Which lorry driver would that be?'

DC Jones looked troubled. 'Umm, this is from the preliminary conversation I had with Mrs Gundersen when she was in hospital. I did give you my report.'

My solicitor leaned forward. 'And which preliminary conversation would that be?' he said. 'There's nothing about this in the disclosure.'

I put a hand on his arm. 'Don't worry, Peter, it was all above board. I had Stephanie Silcott with me.'

'I see,' he said in a voice that expressed the fact that he didn't see at all. 'I did not realise Ms Silcott had been asked to be your legal representative. Will you still be requiring my services?'

'Of course, Peter. Stephanie was just doing me a favour. We had a conversation. Stephanie took notes. DC Jones took notes. It was to help her progress the investigation without an interview like this one. My doctor had just given the all-clear for a chat. I wasn't able to come into the station at the time.'

Peter Robinson sighed. 'I will expect DC Jones to have all of your notes from the conversation.' He then looked at me. 'And you, Mrs Gundersen, I will expect you to ask Ms Silcott to supply me with her notes too. Now,' he said, 'What about this lorry driver? I've heard no mention of a lorry driver before, so who are we talking about?'

'The one I mentioned just now. He saw everything. Have you been able to trace him?'

'Yes, he's called Vinnie Craycroft, but he's still in hospital,' replied DC Jones. 'When you crashed, his lorry went over, and it jack-knifed on the southbound side. He's been in a coma for a while and he still is. I am in constant touch with the hospital, just to see how he's progressing. They have promised they will let me know as soon as he wakes so I can interview him.'

'So, Mrs Gundersen,' DI Blaine fixed her baby-blue eyes

on me and for a moment I returned to my own school days when my headmistress was able to reduce me to jelly with one single stare, 'It would appear we don't have all of the evidence we need to charge you at this time, so you are free to go. Please don't leave the area without letting me know.'

'I'd like to visit my father.'

'How far away does he live?'

'He lives in Cheshire. He moved there after my…'

'Then no, you may not go to visit your father, unless you let me know in advance. When you're leaving, and when you will be returning.'

'Mr Robinson, your client may not leave the country either. I would suggest she surrenders her passport.'

'I don't think you're being reasonable, DI Blaine,' said Peter Robinson. 'You can't ask that unless you've charged her.' He made a note on his legal pad. As the recording device was switched off, he closed his folder and he looked at me too, reminding me again of my headmistress. I felt as if I was always in trouble. I was always disappointing someone.

I struggled to my feet. Peter Robinson helped me and held the door open for me. As I stepped into the corridor, I saw waiting for me the person I'd disappointed most of all.

Topher.

CHAPTER SIXTEEN

Lily

After the police interview, I remained trapped in the master suite. My contact with the outside world was limited, as Mummy insisted I needed to rest and not spend all my time online. However, she soon relented after she'd run up and downstairs with my phone and laptop a few times. It wasn't a huge victory in the grand scheme of things, but it made me feel better.

I exchanged a few texts with Stephanie, who promised to find out as much as she could about the assault allegations. If David Jacobs thought he could sack me and later withdraw the allegations without reinstating me, he had another think coming.

Topher was working more from his garden office, rather than spending late nights at chambers. James was delighted to have him at home as I wasn't mobile. Increasingly, Darcy wanted to be upstairs with me and had to be carried downstairs to play in the garden. Topher was less delighted, especially at the noise they often made.

When I could steer my wheelchair close to the window, I propped myself up so I could see his office. He kept the blinds down and I couldn't see in. Stephanie's words began to haunt me, and I started to wonder what he was up to in there.

As I eased myself back into the chair and I did the wheelchair version of pacing the room, Heather popped her head around the door.

'I've brought you a coffee and the post,' she said. 'How are you getting on up here?'

I twisted in the chair to face her, and spread my hands palms upwards to indicate the mess that was now my life.

'I need to get out of this room,' I told her.

'I know,' she said. 'I talked to Mr Gundersen and he said he'd carry you down after lunch.'

'That's great news.' I said. I wheeled the chair back towards the bed and got myself out. I'd become quite adept at manoeuvring myself. I smiled, thinking my left leg was stronger than it had ever been.

Once I got myself sorted, Heather tucked me in, fussed with my pillows and handed me the post.

'I'll leave you to it,' she said, placing my coffee within reach before she left me alone.

I flicked through the envelopes: most of it seemed to be junk mail, circulars, or bills, which were already covered by direct debit. One envelope stood out though. It was made of a heavier weight paper than the flimsy, cheap envelopes from the circulars. I flipped it over and saw it was from a firm of solicitors. Their crest and address were embossed on the back of the envelope. I checked the addressee and, with trembling fingers, I ripped it open.

I'd hoped the assault allegations had been dropped, and

now I was horrified, as I believed that I would be called to account for my actions.

Skim reading the letter I was puzzled to discover it was in relation to damage to a car, so I started at the beginning and read the letter more carefully. Once I'd read it three more times, the confusion began to lift and I picked up my smart phone.

'Stephanie, sweetie,' I said. 'It's me, Lily. I've had a letter about car hire. A Range Rover. Hired on the same day as my accident. Could you come round on Saturday? Maybe take me out for lunch?'

'Yes, of course,' she said.

I let out a long breath, put the phone down, picked up the letter, and read it through once more.

I pushed the bed covers back, eased myself into a sitting position and reached over to my bedside cabinet for my laptop.

Logging on, I tapped in the password for my credit card and paged back through the statements until I came to the one I was looking for. I picked up the letter once more and checked the name of the vendor against the name in the letter. I already knew they would match, but I had to be sure. *What the hell was going on?* I downloaded a PDF of the statement onto my hard drive, put the letter back in its envelope and tucked it under the mattress.

Saturday morning was bright and beautiful. A fantastic autumn day, full of rich colours in the trees. I was able to get myself to the wet room and have a shower, sitting on the fold-down seat which Topher had laughingly installed for our old age. Reluctantly, he helped me dress and supported me hobbling downstairs. I was surprised that he was letting me leave the house without supervision, but I didn't question my good fortune. At least being injured stopped him from inflicting more damage.

In my handbag, now sitting on my knee, I had my smart phone. I was glad I'd taken a photograph of the letter and I had the PDF credit card statement stored on my phone. I'd looked everywhere for the envelope and the letter, which I'd tucked carefully under the mattress. I'd even tried to drag the bed halfway across the bedroom to look underneath it. Anger gave me additional strength and I tugged at the mattress, falling several times before I finally removed it from its platform. I shook the sheets, the duvet, and the pillows. The letter and its envelope were nowhere to be seen. I knew I'd had them; I had the photos as evidence. I knew I wasn't going mad. Where the hell were they? I sat in the middle of the floor and sobbed. Mummy, having heard the noise, rushed into the room. She looked shocked. Topher appeared behind her. He smiled at me and, suddenly, everything fell into place.

Stephanie arrived in a flurry of expensive perfume and a beautifully fitted pair of jeans. They looked tailored and I sighed. I could no longer wear clothes like that. Even if I could, Topher wouldn't approve and would insist I changed. Between them, she and Topher eased me into the taxi. In all honesty, I'd worried how I was going to get from the wheelchair into her low-slung BMW and flashed her a smile of gratitude that she had clearly thought about the logistics of transporting me. We sat back in the taxi and Stephanie buckled me in, whilst she told the driver to take us to The Flask in Highgate. At the end of our journey, I impressed her with how much stronger I'd become, and I got myself out of the car and into the wheelchair. She applauded my efforts and I gave her a huge smile. There were going to be tears soon enough.

When we were shown into the restaurant she refused wine for herself but encouraged me. Then she fixed me with a beady stare and said, 'So, come on Lily. What's all this about?'

I took a deep breath before I answered. 'We've been friends a long time, haven't we?'

'Yes,' she said, 'Lily, tell me, why the secret assignation?'

'After my accident, Topher trapped me in my bedroom,' I began.

'Oh, come on darling, you were hardly trapped.'

'I was trapped. It gave me some thinking time going through everything.' I paused for a moment, wondering whether, when I told her, it would sound as crazy as it did in my head. 'You know when I told you the builders were cancelled?'

She nodded.

'Well, I checked my bank statement at the time. And then I checked mine and our joint credit card statements.'

Stephanie looked at me with a grin. 'So you do check up on him, then?'

'This is serious. A few days ago I had a letter.'

'You're making this all sound very mysterious.' Stephanie paused to sip her sparkling water.

'I am, aren't I?' I said. 'I think I'm going mad. I'm not quite sure what's wrong with me.'

'Oh, don't be silly, Lily. You're the sanest person I know.' Stephanie picked up the menu and started perusing it. 'What's really up?' she asked, as she fixed me with a stare over the top of the menu.

'I'm pretty sure it wasn't an accident.'

Stephanie put the menu down. Her mouth fell slightly open. 'What do you mean it wasn't an accident?'

'I had a letter from a firm of solicitors the other day. When I opened it, I read that they're suing me for a sum of money based on the fact that the vehicle I had hired was returned so badly damaged they had to write it off. The… the waiver or something hadn't been signed. I hid the letter, but now it's not where I left it. When I checked the credit card statements, there was a payment that I couldn't reconcile.' I take a swig from my wine. 'I'm sorry, Stephanie. I know I'm not making sense.'

'Show me the letter.'

'I can't,' I told her. 'It's gone.'

'What do you mean it's gone? Did you throw it away?'

'No, Stephanie. I didn't throw away. I put it back in its envelope and I tucked it under my mattress and now it's gone.'

'So Heather must have it. She must have found it when she changed the sheets or something. Mystery solved,' she announced.

'I don't think so,' I replied. 'I've been in the room when Heather has changed the sheets. Somebody else has got the letter.'

'So who do you think has got it?'

'Topher,' I told her.

Stephanie just looked at me and started to laugh. 'You're kidding me, aren't you?' she said.

I shook my head. 'No, I'm not kidding.' I reached around to where my handbag was hanging on the back of the chair and I retrieved my smart phone.

'You need to look at these,' I said. 'I took a copy of the letter and downloaded a PDF of the credit card statement.' I opened up the phone with my key code and I slid it across the table to her.

Stephanie was silent for several moments while she read the letter and looked at the statement. Finally, she put the phone down and pushed it back across the table to me. 'What's this all about, Lily?' she asked.

'I think Topher's trying to kill me.' There. I'd said it, it was out in the open and there was no going back now.

'Are you kidding me? This is bonkers. What are you going to do?'

'I honestly have no idea,' I muttered.

'Why would he want to kill you?'

'Because I'm trying to leave him. I can't take it anymore.'

'Can't take what?'

I raised my eyebrows at her. 'What do you think?' I said.

'You're trying to tell me he's been abusing you?' she said, her face incredulous, her mouth slack. 'How long has this been going on?'

'Quite some time.'

'But you always seem so happy together.'

'On the surface we are, but Topher doesn't like anything to be outside of his control. He didn't like me working and so I left the orchestra.'

'Yes, but you had to.'

'Did I?'

Stephanie looked at me, realisation dawning across her face. 'What?'

'It wasn't an accident. Topher did that to me.'

CHAPTER SEVENTEEN

Lily

The waitress brought our food. Stephanie hunched over her salad, open-mouthed. 'How long has this been going on? From the start of you dating him or since you married him?' she asked.

'It started not long after we were married.'

'But you never said anything?'

I shrugged. 'What do you say? How do you tell your friends the man you married isn't the man they think he is? Who's going to believe me? Every time I tried to discuss it with my mother, she either told me I was ungrateful, or becoming depressed again, as though I was making it up, looking for attention.'

'You should have told me.'

'I wanted to. I tried to. But I couldn't bring myself to. I was scared. It's like an admission of what a failure I am. You know what I've been like all my life. I've always been untidy. I'm always losing things. Now I think that when I've lost things, they've been hidden instead.'

Stephanie put her fork down. 'How do you mean hidden?'

'Oh come on, Stephanie, I'm five foot three barefoot. Would I really put my sunglasses on top of a six-foot-tall bookcase?'

'It seems unlikely.'

'And my car keys? Why would they be in the freezer?' I stabbed a piece of potato onto my fork.

'The freezer? Why would you leave them in the freezer?' She covered her mouth with her hand and giggled.

'You see, you're laughing at me, but I didn't put them in the freezer. That's where Heather found them. I'd been looking for them on Monday morning and then later when Heather came in, she was making some space in the freezer for the leftovers from the party and that's where she found them. Then there's the milk cartons, the juice cartons.'

'What about them?' Stephanie pierced a chard leaf, raised it to her mouth and put it down again.

I paused before speaking. This seemed ludicrous, even to me. 'Topher is always complaining I put empty cartons back in the fridge. So, I always rinse the cartons out before I put them in the recycling, and lately I've been putting a black mark with a permanent marker on the base of cartons before I put them in the blue bin.'

Stephanie looked at me, an eyebrow half-raised and her head tilted to one side. 'This sounds mad,' she told me.

'It is all mad,' I told her. 'I really have thought I am going around the twist. However, what I'm finding is that, when Topher picks out a carton from the fridge, waves it at me and says I've left an empty one in there, I take it from him, I go to rinse it out, but I always tip a little bit of juice or whatever is in the carton down the sink. And a lot of the time there's just clear water coming out of it from when I rinsed it. And then I look on the base, and I see my black mark. I tried to talk to him just before the party, but we had an argument about it, and he said I was making it up. He said I'm imagining things, but I know I'm not. Then a couple of days after the party I had this accident and now, here I am — housebound, unable to do anything for myself, trapped in my own home. He's got me where he wants me. I took a photograph of the letter before I tucked it under the mattress because... because Stephanie, I feel like he's spying on me in my own home.'

She reached a hand across the table and squeezed mine. 'You think he's gaslighting you?'

I nodded. 'I'll get to that in a minute, but there's another thing. I'm not as clumsy as everybody thinks I am. My hand, my wrist on the day of the party? I hadn't trapped it in a door. Topher twisted it around during our argument about the cartons.'

Stephanie stares at my hand. 'Lily, I'm so sorry. I had no idea. Why do you think he's watching you? How do you think he's watching you?'

'I don't know,' I replied, 'but he always seems to know things that he shouldn't. Things that he couldn't know because he wasn't there when it happened. That's part of the reason I think I'm going out of my mind.'

'What are you going to do about it?'

'That's where you come in,' I told her. 'I need a huge favour from you.'

'Go on,' she said. 'Whatever you need, I'm your woman.'

'I've been to see a solicitor. She suggested I keep a record of everything that's been happening to me, and she recommended a therapist.'

'And this therapist has told you Topher is gaslighting you?' Stephanie asked.

'We've discussed it, yes, and now I know what I'm looking

for, I can see all the signs. She's made me feel as if I can regain some sanity. That's where you come in.'

Stephanie raised an eyebrow but simply sipped her water.

'I need some way of getting closer to him. Someone who can get so close they know what he's doing. Close enough to get evidence of what he's trying to do to me.'

'A spy, you mean?' Stephanie gave me a quizzical look as she dabbed her delicate pale pink lips on a napkin.

'Yes,' I said. 'But it can't be just anyone. It has to be some-body who can get really close to him. Somebody he'll trust. Somebody he thinks he can control. Have you got a female investigator you know who could do it or perhaps a call girl?'

She looked at me. 'That sounds more like an affair. That would be expensive and, in any case, no investigator is going to sleep with a target. That'd be absurd, plus they'd lose their licence.'

'Then what do you suggest? Are you going to do it?'

'He may be easy on the eye, but this—'

'It would make sense.' I tapped my fingers on the table-cloth. Mind racing. It could work. He would trust Stephanie. 'Can you get close to him, find out what's going on?'

Stephanie stopped playing with her salad. All throughout our conversation, she'd been moving pieces of lettuce, tomato, and cucumber around the plate.

'I'm not in the least bit comfortable with this, Lily,' she told me.

'I think I'd be more disturbed if you were comfortable with it,' I told her, with something approaching a smile. 'You're the only person he will trust. If you are having an affair with him, he's hardly likely to believe you're going to tell me anything. Will you do it? Will you help me before I lose my mind?'

Stephanie put down her fork, reached over, grasped both my hands, and squeezed them. 'I'll think about it.'

I returned the smile and called the waitress over to pay for lunch. She brought the machine and I tapped in my PIN. The machine bleeped. The waitress frowned. 'Card declined,' she sniffed at me. 'Got another one?'

Stephanie leaned over. 'Don't worry, use mine,' she said. Her card was accepted with no fuss at all.

'That's something else he does,' I said. 'I checked my bank account a few days ago and I certainly had enough to pay for lunch.'

'Well perhaps there was a bill you forgot about?' Stephanie replied.

'Don't! Don't do that. Don't make excuses. I'm telling you, this is what he does. He moves my money around without my permission or knowledge. I've even contacted the bank and had my passwords changed, but it's still happening.'

'Can't you change them again?' she said.

'That's the point, I complained to the bank, but they told me Topher has Power of Attorney for my bank account.'

'He has what?' She gasped. 'How has he done that?'

I held up my hands and wriggled my mashed fingers in front of her. 'This! He had me committed afterwards on the grounds I was a danger to myself and possibly to the baby as well. That's when he obtained Power of Attorney. I didn't know, so I've not been able to challenge him about it. He's made sure all my money has been used to do up the house. Without a job I have nothing of my own. This is why I need your help.'

Stephanie reached across and held my hands gently in hers. 'I love you,' she said. 'I'll do almost anything I can to help you.'

CHAPTER EIGHTEEN

Stephanie

'To be honest, I'm not entirely thrilled with Lily's suggestion.'

'I'm glad to hear it,' said Denise. She poured the last drops of wine into her glass, giving me a chance to hide my face from her as I grabbed another bottle from the fridge. Was I going to do what Lily wanted or not? I didn't know.

I sat down, putting the fresh bottle in the wine cooler. There was a pool of condensation on the coffee table. Knowing that I should wipe it up, I let it expand across the table. Denise made me jump when she headed into the kitchen for a cloth.

'What does she want you to do?' Denise asked.

'Get close to him and find out what he's up to. Have an affair if that's the only way I can get close.'

'Why would you even do that?' Denise sat again, crossing one foot over her knee, resting her wine glass mid-thigh. 'Has she got something on you?'

'No, not exactly, but I do owe her a favour.'

'Such as?'

I twisted my glass around in my hands. It wasn't an easy question to answer. I'd hidden the story for so long, it seemed as if it had happened to someone else. 'Ibiza,' I said at last.

'She bought you the island?' Denise laughed, but I'd owe Lily less if the favour had just been a property deal.

'Where to begin?' I said. I sucked in a lungful of air and breathed it out slowly. 'We went there for a holiday to get away from university stress. Lots of sun and sangria, letting our hair down, dancing. You know the sort of thing.'

Denise nodded.

'We'd been there a few days, and somebody mentioned a bar near the beach.' I took a sip of my wine and hung my head.

'Go on,' said Denise.

'I met a guy. He seemed nice. We danced. And then he asked me to come back to his flat. So I did. I told Lily where I was going so she wouldn't worry, and I left with him.' I paused, not sure if I could continue the story. Denise came and sat next to me, she put her arm around my shoulders and I rested my head on her chest.

'Fortunately, Lily had watched us leave, and the group of his friends who followed us.'

Denise tensed.

'I don't really remember much of what happened after leaving the bar. I can scarcely remember walking back to his flat. I woke up the next day in hospital, bruised and battered.' I sat up to drink some more wine. 'He'd put something in my drink when I went to talk to Lily, and made me drink up when I got back to him. Lily had followed us outside, and had called the police. She saved me. Possibly even saved my life. The police told me later that their previous victim had not been so lucky. So you see, I really do owe her.'

Denise pulled me into a hug, which I returned. She eased away from me and looked deep into my eyes. She leaned in to kiss me and I leapt from the sofa.

'What the hell are you doing?' I yelled. 'I tell you a story where I'm nearly raped and murdered, and you respond by trying to stick your tongue down my throat!' I raced to the kitchen and splashed water on my face. Drying my face with a tea towel, I looked at Denise. 'You've got to go,' I said.

'I'm sorry,' she said. 'Bad timing.'

'Bad timing?' I retorted. 'Bad judgement more like. I thought we were friends. I don't see you like that. I need you to go, Denise. I feel like you've betrayed me.'

'Okay,' she said, picking up her bag. She gulped down the rest of her wine and left.

I collapsed onto the sofa and wept.

The following morning, I'd decided. I owed Lily, but I also wanted to renew my connection with Topher. At university I'd seen him first. As a law student he was in the same lectures as me. And who could've failed to notice his tall, slim figure with brilliant blond hair cut into short tufts.

Although neither of us had told Lily, Topher and I had had a brief affair before he met her. Once he'd seen her, I was history. Strangely, at the time, it made sense. I could see the connection between them as if it were tangible. Like a silken web, woven between them.

Now I had carte blanche from Lily to smooth down his hair again. Though, of course, I had a mission. She'd made sure of that. But I wondered how much truth there was in her tale. Obviously, the letter from the solicitors seemed genuine, but since she'd lost the original I had no way of checking. And yes, of course, the name of the car company in the credit card statement and the name of the car company in the solicitor's letter matched. I would call the company on Monday to get their side of the story, I decided, but part of me wondered how much of this was Lily's doing. How much was part of her imagination, part of her need to be the centre of attention.

She'd not always been like this, of course. When I first saw her sidling into the bar all those years ago I'd had a pretty good idea of who she was. I'd thought she'd be full of herself, but I'd never met anyone so shy. During Freshers' Week her name was on most people's lips. Lillian Stanton, the wunderkind. She was an amazing violinist, a genuine protégée if ever there was one.

She didn't rest on her laurels, however. She was always a dedicated student and, as our friendship grew, I knew better than to take her away from her studies. Sometimes she would allow me in the music room, and I would sit in a corner, pretending to study, but watching her play. The experience of Lily's playing was as much visual as it was aural.

She had an exquisite touch on the violin. She could make it soothe your soul, she could make it sing, and she could make it squeal. I had often wondered what those hands could do to Topher Gundersen. Now I had a chance to remind him what my hands could do. It did seem very strange, and I struggled with the idea that Topher would do anything to harm Lily. In the first year at university I'd watched the pair of them fall in love. Again, like her mother, I had worried about some of Lily's depressive episodes. None of us believed the accident was simply an accident. Lily's career was begin-ning to wane, and we'd believed it was a convenient way for her to step down from a glittering career, without seeming to give up too much. Now, although I knew about the damage to her hands and how convenient it had been for Topher, I still couldn't believe he was that violent. It didn't reconcile with the man I'd known at university.

I got up from my bed and strolled down the hallway to the second bedroom in my flat, which served as my dressing room. I flicked through the outfits I had hanging there, holding each one up against my body and flinging them down again. Next week, Lily, Topher and I had been invited to dinner at Judge Mayhew's. I wanted to make a good impression on the judge herself, obviously, but I also wanted to make a good impression on Topher. I sighed and slammed the wardrobe door. I had nothing that would sufficiently dazzle the judge or Topher. Grabbing my car keys and handbag, I grinned. There was nothing I loved more than a shopping expedition.

My phone rang as I was heading out the door. It was a private number but I still answered and groaned when I heard John's voice.

'What do you want, John?' I said. 'This has got to stop. We're over.'

'I want to see you.'

'After all you've put me through?' I replied. 'Just accept it, John. I'm done. Leave me alone. I've taken out an injunction against you. I can actually have you arrested for this. Stop stalking me.'

'I miss you,' he said.

'Please, just go away.' I pressed the red icon before he heard my cry and slipped the phone in my bag.

Shopping, I said to myself. *I need some retail therapy.*

CHAPTER NINETEEN

Lily

'Lily, how lovely to see you,' trilled Fran, my therapist. She leapt from her chair and rushed across the room to help me.

I struggled to hobble into the room, trying to manoeuvre my handbag, crutches, and the door without tripping myself over. She took my handbag and my right elbow, helping me into the seat opposite her.

She closed the door behind us and resumed her seat, leaning forward slightly to make sure the tissues were well within my reach. 'How have you been?' she asked. 'Your leg is improving?'

I nodded and sunk into the comfortable chair. Fran looked at me, eyebrows raised, head to one side. This was only our third session, but I already recognised the signs that she was ready to hear me talk. Where do I begin? I sighed. You're safe here. Until *he* finds out, whispered the other voice.

Fran sat patiently, resting her hands in her lap. I knew she was waiting for me to talk, but so much had happened since our last meeting ten weeks ago that I couldn't get everything straight in my head.

'So much has gone on,' I began. 'I don't know where to start. I got fired, I had a car crash — that you know about. Oh, and I'm losing my mind.'

'Okay,' said Fran. 'Let's start at the beginning. When did you lose your job?'

'The day after I saw you,' I said. 'I've been accused of assault on a student.'

'And you deny the accusation?'

'Of course I deny it. I'd never hit a student!' But as I say it, I remember how close I came to slapping Darcy a few days ago. I vowed I'd never turn into my mother and I'd almost broken that vow.

'Tell me?' said Fran.

'I nearly hit Darcy the other day. She was crying, my head was bad. I was struggling to cope.'

'Lily, you've been accused of assaulting a student at the school, haven't you?' Fran's voice went up an octave.

'Yes,' I whispered.

'And now you're telling me that you came close to assaulting a small child. How old is Darcy?'

'Nearly three.'

'You do see how dangerous this is, don't you?'

'I do, but I didn't hit her. I stopped myself in time.'

'Okay, that's good. But, if you are found guilty of the assault on the student, your children could be taken into care,' said Fran. 'If your husband doesn't get full custody of them.'

'I haven't hit anyone, Fran! The charges were dropped.' I folded my arms, my fists clenching and my jaw tightened. No one was going to take my children from me.

'So, what caused the bad head?'

'You mean apart from a three year old howling?'

'Yes, apart from that.' Said Fran. 'Isn't your mother still with you?'

'Yes, that's part of the problem. She makes me feel so tense all the time.'

'I see,' Fran said. She tapped her pen on her teeth. 'And have things improved with your husband?'

'He's been truly kind to me since the accident…'

'I see,' she murmured. 'Is that his normal pattern?'

'I don't know,' I muttered. 'I've been too ill to focus on his behaviour. I'm just grateful he's being nice to me. It's like when we first met. He completely swept my off my feet. I'd never been so happy in all my life.'

'That's a pattern. He does something to hurt you and then apologises, begs forgiveness. Promises he won't do it again. That sort of thing.' Her look was piercing. She saw through me.

I dropped my gaze to my hands, twisting the fingers around and around. The pain was excruciating but it stopped me thinking about anything else.

'Lily?' her soft voice invaded my thoughts. Bringing me back to face problems I wanted to push far away where I didn't have to think about them. 'When we were together last, we talked about options.'

'Yes.'

'You said you didn't feel like you had any?' she said.

'I don't,' I replied. 'Or at least, I didn't.'

'We talked about support from your mother?'

I gave a bitter laugh. I didn't recognise the harsh sound coming from my mouth. 'My mother thinks Topher is God's gift to all women. If I mention leaving him, she says I'm ungrateful. Sometimes I think she's right.'

'Has she changed her mind?'

'No, why would she?'

'You seemed to suggest that you may have an option now?' Fran clasped her hands in her lap.

'I called my father. I've told him everything.'

'And is he supportive?'

'Yes. He's promised to help me.'

'That's good. Tell me more about the feelings of losing your mind.'

I shrugged, raising my palms to the ceiling. 'How long have you got?' I asked. She smiled softly at me and I related everything that had happened since my last appointment, except I couldn't bring myself to tell her what I had asked Stephanie to do.

'You said you hid the letter from your solicitor in the lining of the handbag. Do you have any reason to think he knows about the letter?'

'He knows about the hole in the lining, that's bad enough. He's always subtle. He never says anything that could be overheard and misconstrued as threatening.'

'Are you at risk or physical injury in the home? Are the children?'

'No,' I said. Head down, I studied my hands, unable to look her in the eye.

'You have the numbers of the help line and the refuge?'

I nodded but I couldn't see myself, screaming kids around my ankles, clothes stuffed in an Ikea bag, frantically banging on the door of a domestic violence refuge.

'Yes,' I said, 'I'll be fine.'

CHAPTER TWENTY

Lily

I was always a little intimidated by dinners at Judge Mayhew's home. It was in a fashionable part of London. In the past I'd been unable to understand how she could afford it, but Topher told me she's from old money. Somehow, he seemed thrilled by that.

I was placed at the far end of the table next to Mr Mayhew, although I'd discovered at an earlier visit, his surname was different. He was such a shadow of a man next to his domineering wife. I found it hard to think of him as having anything of his own.

Topher and Stephanie were at the head of the table, either side of the judge. Stephanie was resplendent in red satin, which skimmed her body, resting lightly on her curves but clinging tightly to her breasts, her nipples visible through the sheer material. She raised her glass to Topher — a gesture he returned. Catching my eyes, she winked at me. We'd agreed to act as if we'd had a falling out and not acknowledge each other too much this evening. I couldn't quite see Topher due to the corpulence of the man on my right. A prosecution barrister if I remembered correctly, he hid Topher from my view. However, I couldn't imagine my husband had failed to notice how captivating Stephanie was. I was excited but scared. I needed her to get close to him, yet I knew how dangerous he was. Although I could not imagine Stephanie allowing herself to be subdued by him as I had been. She'd always been stronger than me.

I gulped my wine down to calm my nerves. My neighbour poured me more and Topher leaned forward to glare at me and signal at me to slow down.

Another agreement with Stephanie was for me to wear a taupe silk. It had a nod to the 1950s, with a cinched waist, and it flared slightly over a stiff petticoat, before it fell to the floor. My caterpillar to her stunning butterfly.

'We don't want him distracted by your loveliness, do we?' she'd said. Although I knew she was right, I was rather despondent as I felt like a discarded, stale biscuit — pale, uninteresting.

By the time dessert arrived, Topher was definitely interested. He leaned forward across the table, and a twinge of jealousy made my stomach flutter — he'd used to look at me like that once.

Eventually dinner was over, and we all withdrew to the sitting room. That was the thing with Judge Mayhew, no men stayed around the table with the port in her home. Topher brought me a coffee.

'I hope you're okay,' he said. 'Not too much standing now. In fact, let me get you sat down.'

Obediently I followed him, and he placed the cup and saucer next to an armchair he had secured for me. I was isolated. The only one sitting in a room full of people on their feet. I picked up the coffee and took a sip. Too hot. I placed it back on the table. Occasionally I caught a glimpse of red satin through gaps in the crowd of darkly clothed people. Some more curious people glanced in my direction but immediately looked away as I opened my mouth to speak. I'd never been a party animal. Unlike Stephanie. I heard her laugh. She was in her element.

'Mind if I join you?' I looked up, startled, but nodded at the woman who dropped into an armchair near me.

'Sally Trevena,' she said, holding out her hand. 'You were sat next to my husband at dinner. I hope you weren't too bored?'

'No,' I replied politely. 'He was telling me a very entertaining story about one of his cases.'

'Oh, don't tell me. The one where the burglar tries to pick the lock with his library card, and it breaks off…'

'And leaves the address in the lock.' We finished the story together, laughing.

'Yours is a defence barrister, isn't he?' she asked suddenly, though she must surely have known.

'Yes, he does do the occasional prosecution but he prefers defence work. He says it gives him something to get his teeth into.' I picked up my coffee and nibbled at the petit four nestled in the saucer.

'Does he relate his juicier cases to you?' Sally asked.

'No, he never has. I guess he feels everyone is allowed some privacy, whatever mistakes they've made.'

'I can't shut Ralph up,' she said, a little dolefully. 'Although I have my own interests.' She fanned the skirt of her dress out and brushed imaginary fluff off it.

'You have a job. That must be nice.' I didn't mean to sound patronising. I'd always loved my jobs. Until Topher made me resign.

'Not paid,' she said. 'I'm a charity fundraiser for a women's refuge. It's extremely rewarding.'

'I'm sure it is,' I replied.

'We can always do with more help.' She tilted her head to one side and gave me a little smile.

'It's not for me,' I said, looking at Topher's back. He was chatting animatedly to Stephanie. I turned back to Sally. 'I don't really have the time with my own children being so young,' I said.

'They're not young forever, my dear. Don't forget you have your own life to lead.' She followed my gaze to Topher and Stephanie. He laughed at something she'd just said, and he touched her arm. Running his fingers down to her palm, where he rested his hand just a moment too long.

Sally coughed, breaking my focus on the flirting couple. She passed me a card and I popped it into my handbag.

'Nice talking to you, my dear,' she said. 'Look after yourself. You know where I am if you need me.'

I was left in the armchair, people watching. Occasionally Sally smiled at me, but she didn't return to sit next to me.

Part of me wanted to stand and chat to people, but Topher's words came back to haunt me.

'No one wants to hear your concert stories anymore, Lily. Everyone's bored of them. If they try to encourage you it's because they're being polite. Don't embarrass yourself. Don't embarrass me.'

The room was warm and I was pleasantly full. My eyelids were heavy. *I'll just close them for a moment.* The voices faded away into the distance.

CHAPTER TWENTY-ONE

Topher

Topher was surprised but not displeased at the sudden change in Stephanie Silcott's reaction to him. He had always found her pleasant enough, a good brain but too spiky to interest him long-term. He preferred demure women; biddable, like Lily. He was sure he could not have coped with Stephanie's insistence on independence. But a resumption of their university affair? Now that was another matter entirely.

Mentally, he ran his forthcoming cases through his head, trying to work out when he could tell Lily he needed to be away overnight. Yes, it could work. He could make it work. And if Lily found out, well it was the perfect way to be rid of her last friend. They had grown tiresome, those university friends. Always tempting Lily away for lunches and outings with the children. He wanted her at home where he could keep her safe. Who knew what could happen when she was out of the house?

He had no concerns she would start an affair herself. At least not anymore. He'd scared that idea out of her head. And why would she? He'd made sure she had everything she wanted. Although she could be tiresome about money, frequently insisting on earning her own. Of course, he was generous and allowed her to get the occasional job, but when she started to neglect her duties at home, he'd always made sure the job came to an end. After this latest accident she was unlikely to look for a job for a long time. Even if she did, being accused of assaulting a student was something that could be whispered in several ears. No, he was safe from her job-hunting for a while. Perhaps she needed something to keep her occupied?

Another child perhaps? But her figure was a little slack after the last one. He didn't want her to get fat or have her tits droop any further. As it was, he was going to have to suggest implants or something to stop them sagging.

He missed what the Silcott woman had just said, but she was smiling broadly and so he laughed as if she had just told him a joke. Perhaps she had. He touched her upper arm and ran his fingers lightly down her arm until they were hand in hand. He allowed his hand to linger, just a fraction too long. Yes, that was it. He was sure he'd got her hooked once more. He just hoped her lithe body would be as good in the sack as he remembered.

He hated being disappointed.

But it seemed he was destined for disappointment. Getting ready to leave, he looked around for Lily. Damn that woman, where was she? He collected her coat from the judge's husband, but there was no sign of her. Hearing titters of supressed laughter, he strode to the corner of the room. There she was. Drunk. Asleep on the judge's sofa.

'Lily!' He shook her violently. Her eyes opened wide

when she saw him. Round with fear. 'How dare you get drunk and fall asleep!'

'I'm not drunk,' she slurred.

'Of course you are. You're such an embarrassment. I should send you away to dry out.'

'No, don't send me away, Topher. I'm not drunk, I promise.' Her voice rose, drawing the attention of the stragglers.

'Stop shouting,' he said. 'You're a disgrace.'

He dragged her to her feet and placed her coat around her shoulders. 'I'm so sorry for my wife's behaviour,' he said to Judge Mayhew. 'Too much to drink.'

Judge Mayhew nodded, clutching her husband's arm. Her knuckles white. Her face wooden.

He propelled Lily down the steps and into the waiting taxi. After giving the driver directions, he sat back in his seat.

Next to him, Lily shifted her position, moving away from him and pulling her coat around her. 'I'm not drunk, Topher. What did you put in my coffee?'

He stared at her. 'What are you talking about? You had too much to drink. You made a fool of yourself. You humiliated me, Lily. I love you so much. I take care of you and this is how you repay me?'

Seeing the sympathetic glance from the taxi driver, he placed his arms around her, pulling her close. As expected, she pulled away, falling onto the floor of the taxi.

Gently he lifted her back into place and put the seat belt around her. 'Let's get you home. You can sleep it off.'

Up front, the taxi driver nodded. Topher knew the man had seen it all.

CHAPTER TWENTY-TWO

Stephanie

For the next couple of weeks, John continued to bombard me with calls and hang ups. I stopped answering calls from private numbers on my mobile and installed a nuisance call blocker on my landline. The injunction made no difference. He was arrested when he turned up at my office. It seemed that nothing could stop him.

I returned from work late one night and parked in the underground car park. I got out the car, collecting my suit jacket, briefcase, and handbag from the back seat. I held my breath as hairs on the back of my neck prickled and rose. There was no sound other than the beating of my heart, yet I was convinced someone was there, watching. Stop overreacting, I told myself.

I shivered despite the warm summer night. Looking over my shoulder I saw nothing. Gripping the handles of my handbag and case, I staggered to the lift. My knees were ready to fold, dashing me to the ground. I licked my lips but my mouth was dry. My head spun and I leaned one hand on the back of a car to steady myself. As I stood stock still, senses primed like an anxious antelope, the movement sensor lights went off, plunging me into darkness. Biting back a whimper, I panicked, whirling around. Was I alone? The lights came back on, bathing me in bright light.

I tried to swallow, and with renewed confidence I strode to the lift, my heels click-clacking on the concrete floor. I would never hear anyone over the noise I was making. But, as I moved towards the lift, in the furthest corner of the car park the lights flickered into life. Out of the corner of my eye I saw movement and I whirled around. Nothing. Just a crisp packet moving in the wind. Except I was sure there was no wind.

I grasped my keys, ensuring the front door key was gripped between my index and second finger, the jagged edge of the Yale pointed outward. At the lift I pressed the button for my floor. As I stepped in, I heard a man's voice asking me to hold the lift. I jabbed at the button for the third floor again and again. I glimpsed my neighbour's face just as the lift doors began to close.

Oh. come on girl, I told myself. You're getting too jumpy. It's not like the Mehic case. John is annoyed but he's not going to start anything like that. Is he?

I thought back to the Shubhendu Mehic case. He had been a client when I first qualified. He was guilty of trafficking drugs and girls, but the police had charged him with handling stolen goods. It was a ridiculous charge and one of which he was innocent. I got him the best barrister I could, and he was found not guilty.

All throughout the case I was openly followed and threatened. I moved three times in eighteen months, but they, whoever they were, kept finding me. One night my car was set alight. After that, I'd gone to visit Mehic.

'Thank you for seeing me,' I'd said as I sat down. I was shaking, terrified at what he could do to me if I upset him. 'I'm still being threatened. Do you know who it is? Is it your guys? Please, you must call them off. Get your guys to leave me alone.'

He'd sat back in his chair and glared at me. For several moments he'd said nothing. Just cleaned out his fingernails with the index fingernail of the opposite hand.

Then he'd looked me in the eye. 'I am sorry,' he said. 'It is not my people and it has not been on my orders. My nephew set me up. He wanted to take over my *Brigăzi* and to distract you from your job, which you did well. I will see what I can do. Let me know if you ever need anything.'

The stalking stopped immediately, but ever since then I'd been on high alert.

When the lift reached my floor and the doors slid open, I was still shallow breathing and close to panic. At my front door, there was a bunch of flowers. I hesitated. Was this something sinister?

I crept towards the door, crouched down, and plucked the card, which was pinned to the bouquet. I ripped open the envelope. They were from Topher, and I began to wonder how much of what Lily had told me about him was true. With relief, I opened my front door; my keys, which I had been gripping so tightly, had left an imprint on my palm. I nudged the flowers over the threshold with my foot whilst manhandling my handbag and briefcase. I pushed the door closed and leaned against it, breathing heavily.

· · ·

I felt much happier and more confident the following day when I left my flat. I went down to the car park; it was less intimidating as the weak morning sun filtered through the wrought iron railings. However, as I reached my car, I stopped in my tracks. All of the lights on my car had been smashed. A hammer — I guessed it was a hammer — had been taken to my windscreen and some sort of paint stripper had been flung across the bonnet. The special blue metallic paint I'd ordered as an extra was pockmarked with bubbles and rivulets. I phoned work to let them know I'd be late, I called the police for a crime number, I called for a taxi, and finally I called Lily.

'You will not believe what has just happened,' I said.

'Tell me,' she said, sleepily.

Irritated, I looked at my watch. It was nearly half past seven. 'Wake up Lily, this is serious.'

She yawned. 'Go on.'

'My car has been damaged,' I said. 'Is it the sort of thing Topher does?'

'Damage?' She said. 'No. No, not normally, although…'

'What do you mean, "not normally"?' I growled down the phone.

'Well…' she sighed.

I sighed back at her so she'd know I was annoyed and waiting for her to speak.

'Do you remember I did that cake decorating class?'

'Yes-s,' I replied, emphasising the sibilant. I saw absolutely no connection between the damage done to my car and a bit of icing sugar.

'Well, I booked in for some extra classes. I really wanted to get the hang of sugar crafting. You know, making little flowers out of moulded icing sugar paste.'

'Lily, is there any danger of you coming to the point any time soon?' I was breathing so heavily I could feel my nostrils flaring.

'Yes, sorry. Just hear me out,' she said. 'I was really enjoying the classes, and then coming home and telling Topher how much fun I was having. I hadn't really appreciated how much my enjoyment was annoying him. Then one day he turned up at the class...'

'Go on.'

'He burst into the classroom, swept everything off the workbench where I was working — absolutely everything. Then he grabbed my hand, twisted it around and up my back, and marched me out of the classroom. I was too ashamed to go back. I wrote to the school and offered to pay for the damage, which they were happy about.'

'Why did he do it?' I said.

'He thought I was having an affair with the teacher.' She gave a hollow laugh. 'It didn't matter that the teacher was a woman. He said, "it wasn't impossible to have an affair with another woman".'

Lily fell silent. I was speechless too. This was a side of the gentle and affable Topher I had never seen.

'Was that the only time he's been violent?' She didn't answer for a while, and I wondered if we'd been cut off.

'Lily?' I said.

'Still here,' she replied. 'No, there have been other times. Perhaps I shouldn't have got you into this. He's only ever been violent to me. No one else. Not even the children. I'm so sorry, Stephanie.'

Then the line went dead, and after a moment all I heard was the hum of the dialling tone. I didn't know what to make of the conversation. I was genuinely concerned about my safety, but I could not imagine either John or Topher taking a hammer to my car. I wandered out of the car park to the front of the block where my taxi was waiting. Going through recent releases of disgruntled clients seemed to be the best place to start.

CHAPTER TWENTY-THREE

Lily

Naturally, I was concerned that Stephanie seemed to be being singled out again, but I assumed that it was the ex, John, at the bottom of it. I couldn't believe Topher would put himself at risk with undertaking criminal damage. He'd be cleverer than that.

'I can't believe you just did that,' my mother said.

'Did what?' I said, whirling around to face her. I hadn't realised she'd crept up on me. For a moment I thought about getting her a collar and bell.

'Lied about Topher like that.' She folded her arms across her chest, but I still kept my distance, wary of the speed of her slaps.

'I beg your pardon?' Even though I was still afraid of her, she had begun to outstay her welcome. Although, I reflected, it wasn't at my invitation she was here. 'It wasn't a lie, mother,' I said, skirting around her to get to the sink and a clean dishcloth.

'Oh yes, that's right, just push past me,' she said.

'I didn't push past you, Mummy,' I said. 'I did nothing of the sort.'

'Next you'll be telling me Topher beats you.' She stood, hands on hips, defying me to argue with her.

'He does much worse than that,' I replied, hanging my head, staring at the floor. Why couldn't I look her in the face and tell her what I really felt? That I'd lived a lie for so long. That I was fed up with her bullying me, making me feel inadequate. That a mother's love should be unconditional.

I thought of Darcy and James and I shuddered, recalling how close I'd come to losing it. The incident I'd told Fran about was the worst, but the stress of the court case in a few weeks' time had put me completely on edge. *I won't let her do to them what she has done to me. I won't let her damage them in the way she did me*. Yet I was too ashamed to look her in the face and have this conversation. I'd lived a lie for so long.

'You always told lies as a child. That's why we called you Lily liar,' she sneered.

Heat crept across my cheeks. 'I've never lied, Mother. You are a liar, not me. That's why Dad left.' I clenched the dishcloth in my fist, willing myself to be brave. My mouth was dry and I tried to calm myself with my old breathing exercises.

'That's not what happened at all,' she retorted.

'Then you tell me why he left.' I finished wiping down the breakfast bar. The breathing meditation had helped and I felt calmer. I wanted to go back to the sink but I remained wary of how quick she'd been with a slap when I was a child and, even now I was a grown woman, I could still feel the sting. 'I've heard his side of the story, now let's hear yours.'

'There's no story,' she said. 'There's the truth and then there's what he'll have told you. Leaving me on my own with a child. He never bothered with us after that. Not a word. No money. Nothing.'

'That's not quite true either, is it?' I said. 'Where are the letters he sent me after he left? What have you done with them?'

'There were no letters, Lillian. He wanted nothing more to do with us,' Her eyes glittered, the bright sheen of unshed tears.

'Where are the sodding letters, Mother?'

'You need a cup of tea,' she said. 'You're getting over-wrought. You always got overexcited as a child. I did hope you'd grow out of it.'

'I'm not overwrought, Mummy,' I said. 'I'm perfectly well, but I do think it's time you returned to your own home.'

'Fine. I won't stay where I'm not welcome,' she said, flouncing out of the room to go upstairs.

I continued wiping down worktop counters, which were already clean. I tried to bite back the tears but eventually I let them fall.

It was the first time I'd stood up to my mother and I was still shaking. It didn't feel as good as I'd hoped it would. All I felt was that I'd lost another friend.

However, now I had set this action in motion I was not going to step down. I picked up the landline and called a taxi for my mother, asking if the driver could come in the house and bring the suitcase downstairs. There was a deep sigh from the taxi company bod, but I promised a large tip in return.

Mummy eventually came downstairs, her eyes red, her mascara smeared on her cheeks. She looked at me, her chin jutting out. There was going to be no kissing and making up today. Even if it had been something I wanted to do.

'I've called a taxi for you. He'll be here in a moment. I've also asked for him to bring your case downstairs.'

She sniffed, rolling her eyes at the ceiling and pouting. She stalked out of the kitchen and went to sit and wait on the boot bench in the hallway.

I pottered around in the kitchen, trying to fill the time before the taxi arrived. I opened a cupboard to tidy the tins, but they were as straight as a platoon of soldiers. I flicked the cloth over the tops pretending I was dusting.

Each time I moved towards the kitchen door, I stopped myself, clenching my jaw and fists. *No, you are not going to give in this time. It's always worse when you do.* I heard the buzz of the comms panel and my mother speaking to someone. A man's footsteps going upstairs then panting as the suitcase thudded on the stairs. The front door slammed. Silence.

I shrugged, although I was still trembling. I refused to play her games any longer.

CHAPTER TWENTY-FOUR

Lily

It was very quiet in the house after my mother had gone. I made myself a coffee and sat in the kitchen, looking out the window, enjoying the September sunshine. Darcy's third birthday was in a few days and to my surprise, Topher had said we would be hosting a party. This time, though, I wouldn't have my mother here to help. I considered asking Stephanie, but she was more help at downing wasted drinks than preparing them. I grinned. I'd simply leave her to do that. I got a notepad and started preparing a list of all of the things I was going to need to pick up from Waitrose.

When Heather returned later with the children, I had a long list and a menu. I was sitting at the table, having drunk yet another coffee, and I was humming to myself.

'You're in a good mood,' Heather said.

'I am,' I replied. 'I really am.'

'Have you thought about what you want for lunch?' she asked.

'I think just a sandwich,' I said.

'Okay, and what about some soup? It's a bit cold out there.'

'I was just thinking how lovely the sunshine was.'

'Yes, but it's getting a bit nippy now,' said Heather. 'What about your mother? Will she want anything?'

'My mother's not here. She left while you were out.'

'That was a bit sudden,' said Heather. 'But probably for the best.'

'Yes, I think so too. The kids were getting a bit fed up with her as well. I know I was.'

'I can't say I blame you,' Heather smiled. 'Right, lunch for four then.'

While she began to prepare food, I helped the children remove their coats and scarves and I blew on cold little hands to warm them up. Although they were upset Granny hadn't bothered to say goodbye to them, I think they were quite pleased we had the house to ourselves again.

When Heather left at four o'clock, I gave the children their afternoon snack and we sat and played for a while, doing some drawings. At five p.m., I wondered whether to start preparing a meal for Topher. I checked my phone. There was no text, so I decided to text him instead.

What time would you like to eat?

A text came back around ten minutes later.

Don't bother about me. I've got to work late. Will grab something from a takeaway. Don't wait up. T x.

Dinner for one, I thought to myself. I pottered around the kitchen, clearing up after the children's snacks and games and, at six, we all strolled upstairs for bath time and extra-long story time. I had plenty of time since I didn't have to cook for Topher. Peace descended over the house. A calm it didn't normally have. I thought it was because Topher wasn't here to frighten me or the children. He wasn't here to belittle me. After the bath, we sat in James' room. He got into bed and Darcy and I snuggled up together on the rocking chair and we had lots of stories — *The Hungry Caterpillar* was still a favourite and, as Darcy fell asleep in my arms, I realised that, like the caterpillar, I was quite hungry myself. I took Darcy into her room and tucked her in. I snuggled the duvet around her shoulders and kissed her, stroking her straight mousy hair and little head, smiling as her thumb made its way to her mouth. I left the hall light on, the door slightly ajar so that if she woke she wouldn't be scared. Going back to James' room, I found he was asleep and had already kicked the duvet off. I gave him a kiss, put his feet under the duvet and pulled it up to his chin, leaving his arms out, because he would fight it later. I would check on him again before I went to bed myself, I told myself.

I wandered downstairs, hesitated, but went into the music room. I ran my fingers over the case, rubbing my thumb against the catch. It sprang open and I gazed at my violin. I breathed in the pine smell of the rosin block, and before I knew it, the violin was in my hands. I stroked the bow over the strings. Hardly a sound. I placed the violin on a chair and dug around in the case for the block of rosin. Without the rosin on the horsehair bow there was no resonance. I brought the block to my nose and breathed in the smell. I moved to another time. Another place. A place where I was admired. Respected, and perhaps even loved. I sat on the floor and, holding the frog in one hand and the tip digging into the carpet, I stroked the block of rosin up and down the bow, coating the horsehair. I used to do this before every concert. It was akin to meditation — the smell, and the rhythm. I struggled to my feet. My fingers reached out, curling around the violin's neck, caressing the smooth wood. I cupped my chin into the plate, feeling the long-forgotten rub of boxwood against my neck. My fingers found the chords and I quickly tuned the instrument, swaying as I played a doleful waltz I'd not thought of in years.

With my eyes closed, it was as if I was back in New York, playing in the Lincoln Center. I opened my eyes to see Topher in the audience. He wasn't smiling. He was angry with me, but as for why I had no idea. I closed my eyes again and carried on playing as if he wasn't there in the front row. I shivered as a drop of water fell onto my chest. I placed the bow on the music stand and searched my pockets for a tissue. The chin rest was soaked, my face wet with my tears, and I tried to dry both with my tissue. I wasn't in New York; I was back in my home in Muswell Hill. There was no audience. I was no longer that woman.

I stood and replaced the violin in its case. My finger movements were not as good as they once had been, not as deft. It sounded clumsy and inept. I headed to the kitchen to forage in the freezer and finding some leftovers from an earlier party I microwaved those for my dinner. I sat at the breakfast bar, put a CD on, one I'd recorded many years before, the soulful strains reaching every corner of the kitchen.

I thought back to that night after the Lincoln Center concert.

Topher drove us back to the old house we were renting in Arlington. His anger filled the car — a black cloud waiting to burst. Was he angry about the baby? No, we'd talked about having children. He wanted babies too. I was sure of it.

'You okay?' I asked. We were nearly home and I didn't want to go to bed on an argument.

'Fine,' he said, but his hands tensed on the steering wheel.

'Are you angry about the baby?' I ventured.

'Is it mine?' He stared straight ahead, never taking his eyes off the road.

'Of course it's yours! Who else's would it be?'

'Not your conductor friend's?'

'Philip? Why on earth would you think that?'

'I saw the pair of you on stage. You were flirting with him like a whore. Making doe eyes at him. I saw it all. I've been such a fool.'

'You're wrong,' I said. 'We're just colleagues. That's all.'

He turned into our driveway, skidding slightly on the wet gravel. He jumped out of the car, slamming the door shut behind him and striding into the house.

I remained in the car. Lights from the house glinted on the driveway. Was he going to turn on every single light in the place?

I opened the door, shut it quietly, and tiptoed to the house. Behind me the car's locks clicked. So he is watching me, I thought.

The front door was unlocked. Topher was in the kitchen, gulping down a glass of clear liquid. He emptied the glass, wiped his mouth with the back of his hand and poured more vodka into the glass.

'The baby is yours,' I whispered.

He whirled around. His face twisted with hatred. The glass sailed past my head, shattering against the wall, showering me with tiny shards.

I screamed in fright and dashed out the door into the garden. The storm was beginning, lifting leaves and twigs into the air. I saw Topher silhouetted in the doorway. He called my name. I ran.

CHAPTER TWENTY-FIVE

Lily

On the Wednesday before Darcy's party, Heather and I struggled with the bags from the Ocado delivery, dragging them down the hallway into the kitchen and checking each item off against the list I'd prepared. In the conservatory, there was an extra fridge freezer, hired especially for the occasion, so food could be prepared in advance and kept at the right temperature. As we worked, preparing the food, I found myself humming and relaxed in a way I had never been before. Especially not when preparing for a party.

'Nice to see you so happy,' Heather said, taking a tray of vol-au-vents out of the oven. She placed them on the cooling rack and stood watching me swaying in time to the music, which could only be heard in my head.

I held my hands out so she could dance with me, but she waved me away with the tea towel.

'Yes, I don't know what's come over me,' I replied, laughing. 'I usually panic so much about parties. I mean, obviously I'm nervous about this one. It's a shame that so many people have declined, but I hope everything goes well.' I turned back to the tiny sandwiches I was slicing. I *was* nervous about this party. My father had agreed to come so he could see his grandchildren for the first time. Truth be told, I was quaking.

Heather nodded, but said nothing. For Darcy's second birthday party, the garden had been overflowing with guests. More than we could cope with, but the list would be smaller this year. Last year I'd not been accused of assault on a student, nor was I due to appear in court on a charge of death by dangerous driving.

My solicitor assured me that I'd get bail ahead of the formal hearing, and although technically I was still allowed to drive, I'd elected not to. I was terrified of putting myself behind the wheel of a car; petrified of what could happen if I put myself at risk.

I continued chatting to fill the chasm of silence in the kitchen. 'I usually panic so much. Parties really stress me out. I feel oddly organised this time. I'm glad you're here to help me though. It's much more fun with two.'

'I thought your mother usually helped you?' Heather said.

'Yes, only...' I said, 'but...' I thought back to the weekend of our wedding anniversary. Mummy had been there to "help" as usual.

'Lillian, why are you chopping the parsley like that? Here, give the knife to me. I'll show you how to do it properly.'

She wrenched the knife from my hands and with the tip of the knife on the board, she maintained a rapid chopping motion, which reduced the herbs to fine shreds of green. I wandered away to fill vol-au-vents with mixes of creamy chicken and mushrooms. She elbowed me to one side.

'Do I have to do everything for you?' she snapped. 'I thought I'd brought you up better than this?'

'Stop telling me off, Mummy,' I replied. 'I'm a grown woman

now, with a house and children of my own. I do know what I'm doing.'

'Oh, here were go again. Why are you snivelling?' she said. 'You're so sensitive. You take everything to heart. I'm only here to help.'

The image faded as I suddenly realised Heather was waiting for me to speak. I smiled and shook my head. 'My mother wasn't really much help,' I said. 'She was much better at telling me how I should be doing things.'

Heather nodded. 'Sorry if I spoke out of turn.'

'No, no, not in the slightest. Not at all. You said it like it is. It's just that I didn't have many parties when I was younger. I think I had some when I was really little, but then after my parents…' I stopped, not sure what to say next. 'I think it was just too much work for Mum.'

I wasn't entirely telling the truth, but I didn't want to burden Heather with that part of my past. My last party had coincided with a dreadful shooting at a primary school in Scotland. The shooting had taken place on my birthday and the party was at the weekend. I'd been so excited, really looking forward to the bouncy castle, balloons, and pony rides. But then, one by one, my friends had cancelled. Their parents had been too scared to have the children gathering together after what had happened. On the afternoon of the party, I went to the zoo with my dad. It was an incredibly quiet day. Mum had decided not to come. While we were there, Dad had taken me to one side. We'd sat by the elephants and he'd told me he was leaving; he'd told me he loved me, that it wasn't my fault, but he didn't want to be with my Mum anymore. We'd sat there, staring at the elephants. I'd watched a baby elephant holding the end of his mother's tail, afraid of being left behind. I've always hated elephants ever since. That was the last time I'd had a party.

Until I met Topher. Topher had swept me off my feet. He'd been incredibly romantic in the beginning and was ecstatic about parties. He knew about my past and my anxiety, but assured me that more parties would help overcome my problems. I was swayed by his promises of helping me, working side by side for our guests as he assured me it would be fun. After we were married, he insisted on regular celebrations, but never did any of the work for them, knowing how it would impact my mental health. My mother had stood over me, criticising everything I did.

And yet, that day and in fact for the previous few weeks, without either of them there, I couldn't believe how much better life was. How much happier I was. And over the last few days, I'd stopped losing things. My possessions were where I'd left them. My glasses were where I'd seen them last. My keys were on the hook by the front door. There had been no Topher constantly berating me about what I'd said or done, or how I was dressed. I was looking forward to life.

I looked around my beautiful house, a feeling of dread snuffing out my optimism. I would have to give it up. There was no way Topher would let me and the children live here without him. You can downsize, I told myself. *If he lets you take the children*, doubting voice said, but I brushed it away along with the tears pricking my eyes.

You'll manage, I told myself. You'll be fine. Leaving him is the only option. I'll keep my children. I'll keep my sanity. I'll lose my fear.

It was all I'd ever wanted.

CHAPTER TWENTY-SIX

Topher

Topher watched Stephanie as she moved around the sitting room, handing out canapés. He had to admit, she looked sexy, dressed completely in black with black high heels, kitten ears and whiskers protruding from a mask, the epitome of Catwoman. How the hell was he going to keep his hands off her all evening?

Lily, on the other hand, had chosen to dress as Alice in Wonderland. She was a pale replica next to the glamorous Stephanie. And he began to wonder how he'd chosen her over her friend.

Still, as he looked around and saw his guests enjoying their food, he knew, for all her shortcomings, Lily made the better wife. Now that he'd managed to get her to stay at home. She was an excellent mother and an adequate cook. Stephanie may be mistress material, able to showboat and entertain, but he would never want children with her.

'We have to go.'

Topher stared at the man, unable to place the face. A

neighbour, perhaps; there were so many with their howling brats, he lost count. 'Of course,' he said. He gave a wide smile and chucked the sleepy toddler under the chin. The child batted Topher's hand away, snuggling into her father's neck.

Topher grabbed James and Darcy, dressed as a diminutive Batman and Robin. 'Time to say goodbye to your guests,' he said, shepherding them into the hallway. He opened the door to allow Darcy's guests to leave. Lily was on hand to make sure that every child had a party bag with toys and cake. God, how much was this costing? He slammed the door shut. It was nearly nine o'clock. When would this hell be over so it could be adults only? He looked down at James and Darcy, bright-eyed from too much sugar. It would be hours before they'd go to sleep. He grasped James and Darcy by the wrists and marched them into the kitchen.

'Lily,' he said. 'It's nine p.m. These two should have been in bed ages ago. What on earth were you thinking?'

She turned around quickly, the skirt of her Alice frock flaring slightly. 'I was thinking, Topher darling,' she said, 'that you could take them up and give them their baths and read the story as you can see I'm still preparing food and canapés for people. I'm sure you won't mind just this once, will you? The kids will be delighted.'

Topher drew in a sharp breath. For once he was speechless. She had not spoken back to him like that in a long time. Not since New York. The fact that she felt it reasonable to do so now demonstrated how he'd let things slide. He needed to get back on top of matters at home.

And soon.

Topher stamped into the hallway and, picking Darcy up, he pushed a reluctant James up the stairs.

'Come on, it's time to go to bed.'

'I'm not tired, Daddy,' grumbled James.

'Tough,' said Topher. 'I'm sick of you two getting your own way all the time.'

Stephanie appeared at the sitting room door. He smiled at her, but she didn't return the smile. What was her problem? Never mind, he thought. He'd wipe that sour expression off her face later.

CHAPTER TWENTY-SEVEN

Lily

Stephanie wandered into the kitchen the morning after the party. Despite the amount of wine she'd drunk last night, she looked fresh, with no sign of a hangover. Her hair was loose and, unlike mine, her skin was scrupulously clean with no signs of yesterday's make-up. I raised a hand to my hair and smoothed down a couple of spiky bits that always poked up until I'd washed it.

'Great party, Lils,' she said. 'Again.'

'Thanks,' I replied and passed her a mug of black coffee. I watched her pop two lumps of sugar in it. How did she stay so slim? I ran my hand over the curve of my stomach, telling myself that it was okay. I'd had two children.

Topher came into the kitchen and I made coffee for him too. He and Stephanie strolled out into the conservatory and reclined in the sun loungers. I stood by the back door so I could hear their conversation.

'Sleep well?' he asked.

'I slept better after your visit,' she giggled.

'Good, me too,' he said.

I didn't remember Topher coming to bed last night. But I did recall he smelt freshly showered when I woke. Had I slept so deeply he'd managed to shower before he came to bed without waking me? Unlikely, but he could have showered in the first floor bathroom. I clenched my fists, my fingers closing on the metal knife I was carrying. How dare they sleep together, making a fool of me under my own roof?

I was about to walk away when I heard her call him Tofu, and I winced. I knew how he hated being called that.

But I heard him chuckle. 'You know, I always hated it when Lily called me Tofu. Somehow it sounds so much better coming from you.'

'Good,' she whispered.

My stomach churned. How I hated them both in that moment. I heard a creak as one of them rose and I headed back towards the breakfast bar and made sure the children were eating their breakfast.

I cringed as Topher kissed the top of my head. 'How are you this morning, my lovely wife?'

'Fine,' I replied, moving away to take Darcy's plate. Today she'd decided she didn't like scrambled eggs and the eggs were scattered all over the bar.

'Yogurt?' I asked, and she nodded enthusiastically.

'Don't spoil them,' he said suddenly. 'She should eat what she chose first time round.'

Darcy looked up at him. Tears forming in her baby blue eyes, her bottom lip starting to quiver. Topher glared at her and she put her head down.

'It doesn't matter Topher,' I said. 'It's just one time. It's not like she does it every day.'

I put yogurt and berries in a dish, squirted some raspberry sauce on top and placed it in front of her.

She pushed it away, sobbing uncontrollably.

'See, spoilt brat!' Topher bent down and pulled Darcy's head up. 'Eat. It. Up. Now.' Silently, Darcy picked up her spoon and began to push berries into her mouth, tears streaming down her face.

CHAPTER TWENTY-EIGHT

Lily

Topher glared at me. 'This is your fault, Lily. You need to set a better example and stop behaving like a spoilt brat yourself.'

I returned his glare, furious that he should pick on Darcy yet again. I clenched my fists by my side, wanting to scream at him, but stopped when Stephanie wandered into the kitchen.

'You okay?' she said.

I shrugged.

'Lily?' She came towards me to give me a hug. I wasn't sure I could cope with the smell of my husband on her skin, but she hugged me anyway.

I couldn't help myself. I burst into tears.

'Oh come on,' she said. 'What's this all about?'

'You two,' I replied. 'You weren't supposed to fall in love with him. Or him with you. I told you he was dangerous. Don't you believe me?'

'Love?' She sounded incredulous. 'Is that what you think

is going on here? Don't be so stupid. You asked me to get close to him and that's exactly what I'm doing. Look, come outside and we can talk properly.'

She dragged me out to the sun loungers and plonked me down. 'Here,' she said, and passed me a small tin.

'What's this?'

'Open it,' she said.

When I did I saw a lump of something like plasticine and a key shape pressed into it.

I shrugged and looked at her. 'What's that?'

'I've got an impression of the key to his office,' she whispered.

I looked in the direction of Topher's garden office and she nodded excitedly. 'Exactly. One of my less salubrious acquaintances is going to get me a key cut and then you can break in and see what he's been up to.'

'I have a key already,' I said, irritation building inside me at Stephanie's amateur attempt at detective work. 'The builder gave me a spare.'

'What about filing cabinets?' Stephanie sniggered and tipped the plasticine into her hand. On the other side there were two smaller key imprints. She held them out.

'I'm sorry,' I said. 'I'm just uncomfortable with all of this.'

'And you don't think I'm not? This was your idea, Lily. You seem to have forgotten what I've given up to do this for you.' She leaned back on the sun lounger, blinking rapidly.

'I'm sorry,' I repeated. It's all I could think of to say. I was so conflicted. If she wasn't in love with Topher, she was giving a convincing performance.

'I hate what's happening here,' she hissed at me. 'I wish you hadn't got me caught up in it. I'd like a chance to be with someone. Maybe even have sprogs of my own, but I've put that aside to help you, because I love you and I'd do anything for you.'

I shivered. Her words made me cold. I was ashamed of myself and what I was putting her through.

'What are you two whispering about?'

Topher had crept up without us being aware of him. I glared at Stephanie and she gave me a small shake of her head. I hoped she was right, and he hadn't heard what we were saying, but I was never sure. He always knew things he shouldn't have a clue about. I didn't know how he did it. In my more paranoid moments, as I had already told Stephanie, I really wondered if he was spying on me.

Stephanie smiled at him. A sexy curve to her lips. 'Nothing much, Tofu darling,' she said. 'Just girl talk.'

He laughed but his eyes flickered, the merest flash of annoyance that I was so familiar with. He was trying to keep a jocular note to the laugh, but underneath I saw he was angry with her. I hoped he wouldn't direct his anger at me once Stephanie had left.

'Well, if you'll both excuse me, I must start the clean-up after last night's party,' I said, and pushed myself to my feet.

I was shocked when Topher offered to help and showed me the black bin bag of bottles and cans. 'I collected these up last night before I came to bed,' he said. 'I'll take them to the recycling centre. Want me to take the kids to the park?'

Ah, that kind of help, now it all made sense. He'd play with the children and I'd clean. But I smiled and nodded at him, trying to ensure he knew I thought it was a great idea. But he did put clean clothes on the children before they headed out for their promised ice creams.

CHAPTER TWENTY-NINE

Lily

Stephanie and Topher left the house at the same time, and I resisted the urge to watch and see if they went in the same direction. Surely even Topher wouldn't let the children see he was interested in her. I set about cleaning the house. It was a Sunday, hence Heather's day off, but since Topher had taken the children out for a while I concentrated on clearing up the party mess. It didn't take as long as I thought it would and I went to the fridge thinking I'd enjoy a light lunch of the leftovers. I ran my eyes over the platefuls of brown buffet. *Why, Lily?* I muttered. *Why are you the only one who'll eat the leftovers?* I pulled the kitchen bin over to the fridge and tipped every single hors d'oeuvre, vol-au-vent, sandwich, mini sausage, and cheese on a stick in the bin. I hauled the bag out of the kitchen bin and threw it into the wheelie bin outside.

Feeling better, I washed my hands and prepared myself an omelette. Tempted as I was to have a decadent glass of lunchtime wine, I stopped myself, knowing Topher would not approve. Sod him. I gritted my teeth and poured myself one anyway.

I emptied the dishwasher again and popped in the crockery from my lunch. Time to tackle upstairs. I restored order in the bathroom where Stephanie had left bath towels on the floor. I polished the mirror and the basin until they sparkled. I knew I was procrastinating. I was avoiding going into the guest room, where Topher and Stephanie had probably made love last night. How could she do this to me? I'd asked her to get close to him, not make a fool of me under my own roof.

At the doorway to the guest room I stood for a while with laundry basket in hand. I could smell the mix of her perfume and his aftershave. At that moment I hated them both. I rushed to the bed, pulled back the duvet and saw the unmistakable patch of semen stains. I doubled over as if in pain. My stomach turned to liquid and I rushed to the bathroom, destroying the order I'd created. Each time I thought I was ready to stand and return to the bedroom, another bout of diarrhoea hit me, and I flopped down onto the toilet again. When at last my stomach felt well enough for me to stand, I made my way to the master suite, showered and collapsed, exhausted, into bed.

The sun was setting when I woke, the last rays streaming through the light-coloured curtains. It was nearly eight p.m. and the house was silent. Perhaps Topher was keeping the children quiet and entertained downstairs, but as hard as I tried I was unable to hear even the muted sounds of the television. Pushing the duvet back, I swung my legs to the floor and tried to stand. I was a bit wobbly, never having been the sort of person who was better for an afternoon nap. I grabbed my kimono and wandered downstairs.

The house was in darkness. No Topher. No James and

Darcy. Where could they be? I scrabbled in my handbag and found my mobile. No messages. No missed calls. I called Topher, but my call went straight to voicemail. I tried Stephanie's number. The same. Voicemail. Where were they? Where were my children?

I Googled the numbers for local hospitals and started dialling round accident and emergency units. I did an Internet search for accidents in and around London, but there were none. I called Topher again. Still no answer. The same with Stephanie. Then the thought occurred... they'd gone away together and taken my children! I threw my phone across the kitchen and it came to rest against the table leg. For a moment there was nothing, and then it began to ring. I skidded across the floor to snatch the phone up. It was my mother. Was she calling to apologise? She'd picked a fine time to call. I wanted to reject the call, but my index finger hovered over the green icon.

'Yes?' I snapped.

'Well, that's no way to answer the phone to your mother!' she said.

'You've called at a bad time, Mum.'

'Topher asked me to call and let you know he and the children are heading back now. He's been having some problems with his phone. He said to say they'll be home in an hour and a half.' She gave one final sniff and ended the call.

I sat on the floor, staring at my phone. I gasped. My babies were safe. Clenching my jaw, hot angry tears fell onto the floor in front of me. How dare he do this? How dare he take my children to see her without mentioning it to me? My breath came in short pants. My body tense, I squeezed my phone in my hands until they ached. I don't know how long I sat there but I only got to my feet when I heard his key in the front door. I went to the sink and washed my face.

He smirked at me, and it was all I could do to keep my cool. I spent time preparing a snack for the children and listening to their stories of the day out with Daddy and Granny.

Topher fetched himself a beer from the fridge and, as he walked past me to get himself a glass, he whispered in my ear. 'If you ever, ever behave again the way you did last night, I will make sure you never see your children again. Don't forget, if you go to prison for death by dangerous driving, I'll need your mother to look after the kids long-term. So, I for one need to keep the old bat sweet.' He toasted me with his beer and James smiled at us, contented to see we were happy together. He leaned over to help Darcy with her cheese and my heart melted a little.

A tear escaped from the corner of my eye. James came to give me a kiss. 'Silly Mummy, we were with Daddy. Don't cry. We were safe. We're always safe with Daddy.'

'I know, sweetheart. Mummy just got a bit scared, that's all.' I hugged him close and Topher smiled sweetly at him.

I excused myself and went to the toilet. I sat on the lid and took my mobile out of my pocket.

Daddy, he's threatening to take the children away from me. I texted. *He says Mummy will have to look after them if I get sent to prison.*

You're not going to prison. But if you really think he was trying to kill you in the car accident, you need proof. Can you get in his office?

Yes, I have a key. I just need him out of the way for a while so I can have a good look. I replied.

You need that so-called friend of yours to take him away for a weekend, he typed.

I'll see what she can do.

I texted Stephanie and outlined my plan.

Fine, she replied. *But just as soon as you've seen what he's up to, let me know immediately and I can break it off with him. Tell him how guilty I feel about betraying you.*

Okay, thanks. I replied. I was grateful for what she'd done, but I felt she had betrayed me and put a strain on our friendship — could that be repaired? I wasn't sure it could.

CHAPTER THIRTY

Lily

Peter Robinson rose to greet me with a doleful expression, and my heart sank. He pushed his glasses up his nose, making his large eyes look even bigger. Was he going to cry? I really needed to get my own lawyer. One that I could trust.

'How are the investigations into the accident going, Peter?' I asked. I tried to keep my voice optimistic. His grey, lined face told its own story.

'Not well, Mrs Gundersen.' He shifted legal pads around on his desk. 'The lorry driver is still unconscious. He could die, which doesn't help your case at all.'

This was the first time he'd told me that Vinnie Craycroft was so ill he might not live. I jumped as the cold water in my plastic cup dribbled onto my trousers. I put the cup down and mopped at the water but the tissue simply left white bobbles on the black material. I was making everything worse.

'I didn't realise he was still in a coma,' I said. My chest tightened. A crippling pain gripped my heart. I clutched my ribs under my breast and leaned forward, trying to make the agony subside.

'Are you alright, Mrs Gundersen?' Peter stood behind his desk, wringing his hands.

I took a deep breath. 'I'm fine. Have you got hold of a copy of the CCTV yet?'

'Er, no, there seems to be something of a hold-up there. The Highways Agency are saying the footage has gone missing.'

'Missing? How the hell can CCTV from the Highways Agency go missing?' I spat the words out, furious with this incompetent, pompous little man.

'I, er, I don't know,' he said.

At least he had the grace to look embarrassed.

'Have you been able to find any other witnesses?'

'No,' he said. 'No one has come forward.'

'So, you're telling me that we have no CCTV and we have no witnesses.' I folded my arms and glared at him. 'Please explain to me, Mr Robinson, exactly how you're planning my defence?'

He flushed. The colour flowed across his face, even as far as his receding hairline, and with a sense of dread, I realised I was on my own. I rose and placed my knuckles on the edge of his desk. 'Mr Robinson. You're fired.'

I stalked out of the building and into the busy London street below. The noise was deafening, and I needed somewhere quiet to make a call. On the other side of the road with a grinding of gears, a red bus pulled away, belching out black smoke behind it. As the smoke cleared, I saw a small café, the owner on the pavement trying to waft away the diesel fumes with a tea towel. It wasn't the Ritz, but it would do. Checking the road was clear, I dashed to the central island and made it to the other side of the road.

Despite the stench outside, inside the café was cool and dark. I ordered a coffee and went to sit at the back, away from the street noise. I pulled my mobile out of my handbag and stared at my contacts list. Who are you gonna call, Lily? I flicked back and forth between Stephanie's number and my father's. When the coffee was placed on the table in front of me, I'd decided.

'Dad,' I said. 'Thanks for your email. I've missed you too. And now, I really need your help.'

I related to him everything that had been said in Peter Robinson's office.

'I'm with you,' he said. 'Seems a bit convenient that the CCTV has gone missing'

'I don't even understand how that could have happened.' I sipped some coffee; it was surprisingly good.

'And you're sure footage has really gone missing? It's not just the case that your solicitor has failed to get hold of it?'

'I don't know, Dad,' I said. 'He is incompetent, I'll give you that.'

'Right, here's what you're going to do. You need to find a new solicitor and you need them to organise a private investigator to find out what's happened to the CCTV stuff,' he said.

'Okay,' I said. 'But how am I going to pay for it? Topher controls all my money.'

'Oh Lily,' he sighed down the phone. 'I should have tried harder to keep in touch with you. Look, don't worry, once you've found someone, let me know and I'll pay for them. It's the least I can do.'

'Thanks, Dad,' I said. 'I'll find a new solicitor straightaway.

I just needed someone to hear me out and tell me I'm not going completely mad.'

'And when you've done that,' he continued in a brisk tone, 'you need to go home and pack some things for you and the kids and come here.'

'The police have told me I need to stay in London.'

'Nonsense. You're not leaving the country and you'll be there for the court appearance. They can't stop you.' He sounded annoyed.

'I'll ask them, Dad. But DI Blaine told me I couldn't go anywhere.'

CHAPTER THIRTY-ONE

Stephanie

Returning once more to the car park underneath my flat, goosebumps rose on my skin. I rubbed my arms, trying to soothe the tingling flesh. I knew I was being watched. The police had spoken to John, but he'd denied damaging my car. He was lying. I knew it was him. The injunction appeared to be useless, he'd just ignored it. All the same, the sense of being spied on was becoming the new normal and I hated it. I walked to the lift with my keys protruding from my clenched fist. I was hyper-alert, swivelling my head constantly so that I could maintain all-round vision. In truth, all it did was give me a headache and blurred eyesight.

A car alarm went off, making me jump. Damn. It was my hire car. I trotted back to it, wishing I'd changed out of heels, and clicked the remote. The alarm stopped and the hazard lights ceased flashing. My heart pounded. Hairs on my arms and the nape of my neck prickled. I turned back to the lift, telling myself to walk, but I couldn't help it. I lost it and sprinted for the lift, stabbing the button for my floor. I stood with my back to the lift door, keys still clasped in my fist, staring around the car park for movement. I was met with nothing but darkness. Only the spot where I stood was illuminated. I heard the lift, the creak of the cables and the shudder as it made its way towards me. I let go of a breath I was unaware I was holding. Sobbing with relief, I stepped into the lift and squashed myself against its reassuring solid wall as the lift doors began to close. Happy at my reprieve, I exhaled contentedly until a light in the far corner of the car park flickered into life.

I gasped. Who moved and tripped the sensor? Was it John again? A tiny drop of urine trickled into my pants and I clenched again to make sure I got home before I wet myself. I wanted to vomit too. I knew it was just coming down from the adrenaline rush but the knowledge did nothing to reassure me.

The doors slid open and I saw my front door. Outside were more flowers from Topher. He'd started using a company that delivered the flowers in a box, but he'd brought me a beautiful Waterford crystal vase to display them. I smiled. The horrors of the car park were behind me. Opening the front door, I pushed the box of flowers over the threshold with my toe, slammed the front door and rushed to the toilet.

Recovering and back in the living area, I picked up the box and placed it on the kitchen counter. I removed the recent flowers and put them in the bin. The vase I rinsed out and filled with fresh water. Before I opened the box I poured myself some wine. I needed it after the shock in the car park. Briefly I wondered if I should consider moving again, but it was such a hassle.

I sniffed the air. Something must have died in the back of the fridge. I noted *clean fridge* on my list of things to do this weekend. Gulping my wine, I opened the box. The smell was overwhelming, but so was curiosity. I raised the lid, gagged, dropped my wine and staggered away from the box.

It was full of rotting vegetation and rancid meat. Maggots crawled over everything, wriggling out of the box, onto my work surface and the floor. I clasped my hands over my nose and mouth to suppress the smell. Shaking and gagging, I stood over the sink until I saw one wriggle close to my foot and I stamped on it. That was all I needed to spur me into action. I put on rubber gloves, grabbed a bin bag, and shoved the box into the bag. Snatching kitchen cleaner from under the sink I sprayed the work surface and the floor to kill the maggots, but they simply wriggled away from the liquid. *Does nothing kill them?* I thought. Bleach! I covered the kitchen work surface with bleach and wiped them into the kitchen bin, stamping on the ones that had fallen on the floor. I went out into the hallway and placed everything into the chute, which fell into bins in the car park. I left my kitchen bin in the hallway but brought a kettleful of boiling water to the bin and drowned the little monsters in scorching water.

Back in my flat, I repeated the process of bleach and boiling water until I was sure that every last one of the wriggling miscreants had died. I took a black bin bag and stripped off my clothes; I was never going to wear any of those again. Once in the bathroom, I stepped in the shower and scrubbed myself until my skin was sore. I wrapped myself in a towel and my dressing gown.

I couldn't face the kitchen but poured a large whisky and brought the glass to my lips. My hands still stank of bleach and I began to retch again. I made myself take a swig of whisky and, as the liquid slid down my throat and warmed my stomach, I felt more in control.

I took another swig. Who could have done this? The box

was from the same company Topher had been using, but I couldn't believe he would do something so cruel, despite the stories Lily had told me.

It must have been John. He's still watching me. He knows the flower company Topher's been using. Should I call the police again? But what could they do? They'd not helped so far.

Then I decided to call in a favour.

In my briefcase I kept a black book of contact numbers I didn't want on my phone. I turned to M and ran my finger down the list. I dialled the number.

'I'd like to speak to Mr Mehic,' I said. 'Mr Shubhendu Mehic?'

'He's not available,' came the reply. 'Who is this?'

'Steph... Stephanie Silcott,' I finally managed to stutter.

'Hmm,' growled the voice. 'I'll tell him you called. Await instructions.'

The line went dead and I staggered to the sofa, sinking into the cushions, wrapping myself in a cashmere blanket, my mind racing. Finishing the whisky, I poured another.

In the early hours of the following morning, my phoned skittered across the coffee table. A text. Instructions.

Mr Mehic will meet you tomorrow. At 7pm. Location will be sent to you in morning. Come alone.

I poured some more whisky and sipped it slowly, thinking about what I wanted to ask of Mehic. Eventually exhausted, my head swimming from the booze, I laid back on the cushions and fell asleep on the sofa.

CHAPTER THIRTY-TWO

Lily

I was surprised to hear from Stephanie so early the next morning, because she usually headed into her office early, arriving long before her colleagues. She was still hoping to make partner in the next few years.

'What's up?' I asked.

'Something awful happened last night,' she said. 'Can I come over?'

'Of course, but aren't you going to work?'

'No, I can't face anyone today. But I need to get out of my flat. Has Topher left?'

'Yes. He was out the door about six a.m. and won't be back until after six this evening.'

'Good,' said Stephanie. 'I'll be with you shortly.'

Within half an hour there was a ring at the doorbell. Stephanie was on the doorstep, and was halfway through the front door before it was even fully open. I was shocked at the change in her. Far from her usual groomed perfection, her hair needed washing and was stuck out at all angles, as if she'd gone to bed with wet hair and had had a very sleepless night.

I peered past her, the whiff of stale alcohol overwhelming. Her sports car was parked haphazardly on the driveway. 'Stephanie, are you crazy driving over here? How much have you drunk?'

Following her into the kitchen, I motioned for Heather to take the children upstairs to the playroom.

I put the kettle on. 'I think you need coffee,' I said.

'I need something stronger.'

'Stephanie, it's half past nine in the morning.'

'Please, Lily. I'm in shock.'

Sighing I went across to the drinks cabinet and poured her a brandy. She snatched it from me and gulped half of it down in one mouthful. 'What on earth has happened?' I asked.

'I got home last night to discover a box at my front door. I thought it was flowers, so I kicked it over the doorstep and into the flat.' She sat for a moment, playing with the glass, and then gulped the rest of the brandy that was in there. She reached for the bottle, poured herself another drink and cradled the glass in stiff hands.

'I put my bags down, shut the door, put the box on the work surface, got a vase and I opened it.' She screwed her eyes shut and took another slug of brandy. 'It was disgusting,' she said. 'It was full of maggots. I've never seen anything so horrible in all my life. Who would do that to me? Is that the sort of thing Topher has done, would do?'

I shook my head. 'Topher would never do anything like that. That's horrible! He's done some things I hate him for. But that sounds truly spiteful.'

'Sure he's never done anything like that to you?' she asked, taking another sip of brandy.

I shook my head. 'Never.'

'Thank God,' she said.

'No, Topher is more of a "flowers the day after" kind of a guy,' I replied. 'He did it when the children were born. James was dark-haired at first. You remember? Just a little sprinkling of dark brown hair. Topher didn't speak to me for days. And then he changed. It was if the sunshine been switched back on. He sent me flowers with an apology. It wasn't until a few months later that I found the letter from a company confirming his paternity. He did the same with Darcy as a matter of course. He always apologises afterwards. But he's always convinced I'm doing something to hurt him.'

'Why don't you just leave him?' Stephanie asked.

'Don't you think I've tried? He's always several steps ahead,' I said. 'That's why I need you. I need you to help me prove that he is trying to make me go mad. The solicitor said I need proof.'

'I don't get it,' said Stephanie.

'He has told me if I try to leave him, he will use every single one of those instances — losing things, forgetting things, all of those — as examples of why I've been an unfit mother. And unsuitable to be left in sole charge of my children. So you see, Steph, if I leave him and I can't prove he's gaslighting me, I lose my children. And I am not...' I said, grabbing her glass and taking a slug of the brandy for myself, 'I am not going to lose my children.'

CHAPTER THIRTY-THREE

Stephanie

Lily made me take a taxi home. I didn't blame her, but I had to take a taxi again to get to the meeting with Mehic. It was only a ten-mile journey, but it took nearly an hour, even in evening traffic. It gave me time to think things over. So far, John had paid no attention to the injunction I'd raised. If the rotten flowers hadn't been from Topher, they had to have been from him. Who else could it have been? I'd gone through ex-clients, but none seemed disgruntled enough to wage such a terror campaign. The only person who had been was Mehic's nephew, Nicolae. I knew Nicolae had wanted to take over the running of the organisation but was unable to as I'd kept his uncle out of prison. Nicolae was not a man to annoy. If possible, he was even more disagreeable than his uncle. And here was I, about to ask for their help.

I parked my car in the club's car park and strolled across to the main entrance. A security guard who looked like a cross between a heavyweight boxer and a golem stared at me with a mixture of loathing and contempt.

'You can't take anything in with you,' he said. 'Mr Mehic's orders.'

'Okay,' I said, placing everything in a plastic box. I even submitted to a perfunctory search, glaring at the meathead who lingered too long at my breasts.

I followed another man stuffed into a dinner jacket upstairs and past closed doors until we reached one marked *Private*. The gorilla knocked on it and waited for a reply.

I stepped over the threshold, jumping when the door was pulled shut behind me. Mehic waved me to a chair. I sat, placing my hands in my lap. He was unrecognisable. I would have passed him in the street. I wondered what had caused the damage to his physique. Perhaps it was the battle with his nephew.

'Hello,' I said. 'You're looking well.'

'Liar,' he said. 'I look like shit and you know it. Stage four lung cancer.'

'I'm sorry to hear that.'

'So, what do you want?' he said, sweeping my apology aside.

'I'm being followed again.'

'Nothing to do with me or my family.'

'I think it's an ex-boyfriend.'

'How is this my problem?' he leaned forward, resting his forearms on the empty desk. They'd shrivelled compared to the man I remembered. Pale replicas of the muscled arms I recalled.

'He's damaged my car. He's left a box filled with maggots on my doorstep. I just want him to stop,' I begged. 'You promised me a favour when I needed one. Now I'm asking. Please!'

'Take out an injunction against him.' Mehic glared at me. No sympathy in his deep-set dark eyes.

Tears pricked my eyes. 'I've already done that, but it's made no difference.'

Mehic merely raised his eyebrows. 'You have friends in the Met,' he said. 'Why aren't you asking them for help?'

Briefly I wondered how he knew about my friendship with Denise Jones. *Was he still having me watched? Was this all his doing?*

'I can't ask her and you know it,' I said. 'I need someone to have a quiet word with him.'

'I will think about it,' Mehic said. He rose. The conversation was over. Mehic called out and his bodyguard came back into the room.

I was escorted away to collect my handbag and briefcase. I wasn't sure if I had wasted my time coming to see him or not.

CHAPTER THIRTY-FOUR

Lily

When I ran the conversation with Stephanie over again in my mind, I began to feel I might have exaggerated Topher's shortcomings. However, since he was spending less time at home and was focussed on other matters when he was here, I'd finally begun to enjoy life. Without Topher creating the constant need to tiptoe over eggshells, the children were happier and better behaved. They were sleeping and eating better. Even the nursery school had told me that Darcy was chattier and starting to make friends. This is what life could be like without my husband in it and, for the first time in many years, I was looking forward to the future.

I skipped down the stairs and, once again, was drawn to the music room. I'd wanted to make so much of this room. I'd imagined it filled with life, tutoring students, but since the car crash and the assault allegations I hadn't felt inclined to advertise. Even private students I'd seen in the past had stopped attending my classes.

Whilst I was angry that people had chosen to believe the

allegations, allegations I knew to be lies, I had lost the trust of the parents. I paused at the door, then pressed the handle down and marched into the room. I'd left the violin in its case on a chair when I was last in here, disgusted at my lost skills. I picked it up, blew some the particles of dust away and practised scales. Something I hadn't done since living in Arlington. The sound was terrible. Tentative and stiff. I practised again and again.

My fingertips were becoming sore, softened through a lack of rigorous practice. How had I allowed myself to be so lost?

Gritting my teeth, I began again until my hands blistered. I put the violin back on the chair and rubbed my hands, forcing blood back into them as I used to do.

The sheet music from my last visit to this room sat on the music stand in front of me. Tentatively, I raised the violin to my neck, rested my chin and drew the bow across the strings. Here goes nothing, I told myself, taking in a deep breath.

Eyes closed, I released the breath and began to play. I swayed in time to the notes, and, as my body relaxed into the rhythm, I gasped. I played more. Tears came, but this time they were tears of joy.

All I needed was practice. But since the accident and the incarceration at the psychiatric hospital, my confidence had been eroded. I needed it back.

I vowed to practise each day. This was something I wouldn't let Topher take away from me.

I headed to the kitchen to make lunch. It wasn't one of the days Heather came to help me and I was grateful, as she'd be horrified at the state of my fingertips. I rinsed them under the tap and wrapped them in a tea towel whilst I struggled to get the first aid tin out of a cupboard and onto the work surface. At last, I managed to stop the bleeding and bandaged them up. I cleared up the trail of blood splatters I'd left around the kitchen, remembering to put the tea towel in cold water to soak.

Proud of my domestic achievements, I pulled ham and salad from the fridge and bread from the pantry and built myself a sandwich. It was always surprising how hungry practice made me. Yet in those days I could eat what I liked and never put weight on. Two children had certainly put paid to my efficient metabolism.

I glanced out the window and saw Topher's garden office in darkness as it had been ever since Stephanie took him out of my life. Her words came back to me and I began to wonder what secrets he kept in there. I couldn't dwell on it until Topher was guaranteed not to return. It would be catastrophic if he were to find me in there.

Stephanie had given me the two tiny filing cabinet keys and agreed to take him away for a weekend. He'd told me he would be away at a conference. Gosh, Friday seemed such a long time to wait to get into his office. I breathed out. I just hoped I'd find what I was looking for. Something that would free me from this mad excuse for a marriage.

The divorce lawyer I'd met with before the car crash had told me I needed to get evidence of his income, and if I could find any evidence of how he was trying to manipulate me I should get copies of that too. Like any child excited about a party, I had decided what I was going to wear to break into Topher's office. I couldn't wait to see what I was going to find in there.

I thought about my therapist, Fran. She'd made me see the truth of what was happening to me. I knew I had a huge fight ahead of me, but at least I was preparing for battle.

CHAPTER THIRTY-FIVE

Lily

Going in to meet Fran still felt like a visit to the head-mistress's office.

Had I got my story straight? It was stupid really; she had convinced me time and time again that she was there to help me. Had I lost trust in everyone around me? Everyone close to me seemed to have turned their back on me. I knocked on the door and twisted the doorknob when I heard Fran call "come in".

'Hello,' she said. 'How have you been since we last met?'

I panicked. How had I been? I began shaking.

'Have you been keeping your journal?' Fran prompted.

Of course, the journal. I retrieved it from my handbag. Learning my lesson over the letter about the hire car, I'd hidden the journal under my side of the mattress when I was in bed, but kept it near me during the day. 'I played my violin,' I said.

'That's marvellous!' Fran squeaked. 'How was it?'

'Awful,' I said, 'at first. Then I went back to it again and it was better.'

'How did it make you feel, holding it in your hands again?' She slid the box of tissues closer to me. I grabbed one. Twisting it around in my fingers, holding it at the ready.

'Scared, happy, annoyed.'

'How come?'

'I was scared I wouldn't be able to play anymore, then I could and I was happy.'

'That's good,' she said. 'But what annoyed you?'

'I was annoyed with myself for leaving it so long. For allowing myself to get so out of practice. However, I've been practising every day.'

'That's terrific news. Very empowering.'

I smiled and sat up straight in my chair, reminded again of being at school and receiving praise for my playing and dedication.

'How are things with your husband?'

My blood ran cold, sweat beads formed on my top lip. I looked down, said nothing.

'You said before that he blamed you for the car crash,' Fran continued. 'How about you tell me about that?'

'His parents were killed in a crash when he was very young. He asked me if I'd crashed on purpose to hurt him.'

'And had you?'

'No of course not. That's a terrible thing to say. I'd never do something like that.'

'Why would he think that you would?'

'We had an argument at the weekend. On our anniversary. And he hurt me. He grabbed my arm and twisted my wrist around.'

'Is he often physically violent?'

'No, you don't understand. He lost his parents. Mine

divorced when I was young. We both had intimacy issues when we met. We kind of cured each other.'

'Cured?'

'That's how he's always described it. He tells me that I'm the first woman he's ever really trusted.'

'And yet he hurts you? Does he hurt the children?'

I was too shocked to answer. Blood pounded in my ears, and my face grew hot.

'Lily?'

I scowled at her. 'The children are fine.'

'No bed wetting? No nightmares?'

'Darcy still wears a nappy at night-time. James is fine.'

'How old is Darcy now?'

'Three.'

'I see. How is Topher with the children?'

'They adore him,' I replied, hanging my head.

'Lily?' Fran leaned forward. 'It is okay to talk here. This is a safe place.'

'James adores him. Darcy is terrified.'

'When was Topher first violent towards you? Was it before the children were born or afterwards?'

'Not before.' I shook my head. 'It first happened when I was pregnant with James. He was sorry afterwards. He says he just lashes out when he feels powerless. After his parents died he lived with his aunt. Her boyfriend was abusive. Topher wasn't able to stand up to him and said he felt unable to stop the guy hitting his aunt.'

'And now does hitting you make him feel powerful?'

'I don't know. It's not something I've asked him.'

'That's something I want you to think about before next time, Lily.'

CHAPTER THIRTY-SIX

Lily

For the next few days, Fran's words rang in my ears. I wanted to be free of Topher, but I didn't want to give in without a fight. That meant getting into his office. Having a plan gave me more confidence.

With the keys safely in my pocket I felt them burning away at me all Friday afternoon. I didn't know where else I could put them to keep them safe. Topher's usual hiding places for my things might have seemed like a good idea but, if he were trying to trick me again, wouldn't he find this betrayal?

I'd thought of little else except when I was going to try and break into his study. Earlier in the week when he'd told me he was going away for a conference over the weekend, I knew it was a lie. Stephanie had already warned me, but I wished she hadn't. I wasn't sure if my acting was good enough to fool him. I packed his case for him but came upstairs to find him repacking it. The expression on his face was enough to let me know I'd not done a good enough job.

I patted the key in my dressing gown pocket where it was safe. I'd kept it with me. Even taking it into the shower with me.

On Friday morning Topher bade me goodbye, with a promise to call me in the evening when he got to his hotel. I tried to remember what it had been like when we were parted in the early days and I told him how much the children and I would miss him. The day passed interminably slowly. I couldn't focus on anything but I knew I should leave it until after the children were in bed. I patted the keys all day through. At seven o'clock in the evening, the children were ready for their baths before bed and Topher called them on FaceTime. James, naturally, was so excited to see him that I scarcely had to act my part of doting wife at all, apart from coaxing Darcy to wave at him. Afterwards, I put the children to bed, read them a story, and then took James through to his room. I chatted with him for a while until he fell asleep. Darcy had become better at self-soothing than James. I cursed myself for the damage my marriage was doing to my babies.

At nine p.m. I decided to take myself into the garden. I'd dispensed with my plan to wear dark clothes. The neighbours were more likely to think I was a burglar and call the police, but I did pop a Buff headband over my hair in case the mousy brown glinted in the security light from their garden. I crept across to the office, heart pounding so loudly that the neighbours must have been able to hear it. My trainers were soaked in the damp from the grass and I shivered, though whether that was from the cold or the fear, I didn't know. I took the key out of my jeans pocket and put it in the lock. I turned. It was stiff at first, but I tried to force it around. Then it clicked and... it turned.

I was in.

I stepped over the threshold and pulled the door shut behind me.

Once the door clicked shut, I was plunged into darkness. I scrabbled around for the light switch, but before I turned it on I panicked in case the lights from the office, flooding across the grass, might alert my neighbours.

Get a grip, Lily. Why would they care if you're in here? All the same, I was afraid of some idle mention of it to Topher. I edged further into the room, hands out in front of me, trying to find a clear path to the window without knocking anything over. I finally made my way to the window, pulled down the blind and switched on my torch.

I was breathless. Even though I was on my own property, this room wasn't my property. I felt like a thief, as if should I have worn gloves. Whilst I regained my composure and calmed my breathing, I switched on the main light and looked around the room. Everything was quite clearly in its place and I knew I would have to return everything exactly as it was, or Topher would know I had been in his office. I walked to his desk and moved behind it, pulling out his desk chair and plonking myself down. Either side of the gap for his knees, Topher had a series of drawers. I leaned to my right and pulled each drawer, but they were all locked.

I tried on my left-hand side with the same outcome. I pushed myself away from the desk and headed to the filing cabinets. These were locked too. I pulled the keys Stephanie had acquired for me, put one in the lock, turned and the cabinet opened. I rifled through the files; they were all related to his professional work: court cases that had absolutely no interest for me.

Unusually, for someone as tidy as Topher, one file seemed

out of alignment. It was only half a centimetre, but it was sufficient to arouse my curiosity. I pulled out the file, making a note of where I should return it. Going back to the desk, I sat down to read.

Mark Brown, I discovered, was a small-time thief and he'd been represented by Topher several times in the past. What was more interesting about Mr Brown though was his ability with cyber-security. As I read, I found I was puzzled as to why Mark Brown continued thieving rather than developing this obvious skill. Was that what drew Topher to him?

There was a dirty scrap of folded paper. Definitely not something I imagined Topher keeping. I unfolded it and laid it on the desk. Several names and mobile numbers. I took some photos of the paper and some other file contents with my smart phone, and returned the file to the cabinet.

The room was lined with bookcases as Topher had requested. Each of the books was related to the study of law and past cases. I ran my fingers along the shelves and was surprised there was no dust as Heather wasn't allowed in here either, but I couldn't see that any of the books appeared to have been used more than any other.

I reached down for Topher's laptop bag that was sitting by the side of his desk. It was disappointingly light when I picked it up and I was unsurprised to find it was empty. Of course, he would've taken his laptop with him for the weekend.

That left his desktop, which I knew would be password protected. The tower unit was under his desk and I bent down to switch it on. Pulling the keyboard towards me, my fingers hovered over the keys, wondering what password he might have used. The monitor burst into life and I saw the permanent background photo was one of him and James. They were in a boat together, laughing and holding up a miniscule fish. I remembered taking the photo, and how proud James was of his first fish caught on that expedition. It had been Topher's birthday that day. I typed in his birthday in numerals, and then using the shortened version of the month and then the long version.

I swore softly under my breath. I did the same with our wedding day, and tried the same with James's birthday, with Darcy's. Nothing worked. I leaned back in the chair, sick with frustration. I just needed to find some evidence. Any evidence. My eyes scanned the room looking for clues. They finally rested on the desk calendar. It was the one I'd bought him for Christmas. Beautiful photos of Danish mountains and coastlines. Then it occurred to me. Of course. Why didn't I think of that before? With renewed energy I typed in James' birthday using the Danish word Marts for March. It worked.

I was in.

I opened the File Explorer so I could see the most recent files he'd accessed, but they were all related to cases that he'd been working on: notes, pleas, opening arguments, proposed closing arguments. Nothing that looked as if it would tell me what he'd been up to. I checked his browser history too. Clear. Damn him.

As I was about to give up, I took one last look at the file explorer. There was a word file called *dagbog*. I knew it was likely to be Danish but I had no idea what it meant. I switched back to the browser to use Google Translate. I stopped myself in time. Topher would know someone else had been here. I must leave no trace that I had used his computer. I pulled out my smart phone and used the translation app on there.

Diary.

I nearly punched the air with excitement, but double-clicked on the folder and had to remind myself to breathe as it opened.

I didn't know what I'd expected but, of course, it was all in Danish. The title and the paragraphs were frequently headed by what I recognised as a date, leading me to believe this was his journal. His record of what he'd been doing to me.

I knew better than to email a copy to myself. I looked around frantically for the printer, but couldn't see it anywhere. In desperation I opened the stationery cupboard he'd insisted upon, and the printer was perched on a shelf in there. I switched it on and it bleeped at me. No paper. My hands were shaking as I took a few sheets of paper and loaded them into the tray. I returned to the desktop and pressed print.

The printer churned out sheets of paper. My heart was in my mouth, hoping that nothing else would go wrong. When it finished the job, I switched it off and remembered to return the paper to the packet. As I closed the door, I saw a few familiar looking envelopes. I picked one up and found it was the same heavy paper that I had held before. I turned it over and saw the crest and the address. I wasn't mistaken, but why had he done this? Did he honestly believe that I was too stupid to work this out for myself? I gritted my teeth, breathing noisily through my nose. My heart was pounding again. Anger caused my blood to race through my veins. I was no longer scared.

I returned to the computer to switch it off, when I saw an icon I'd never seen before. Wondering what the app was, I double-clicked on it. The application burst into life but it didn't seem to be working. On the left-hand side, however, there were some numbered buttons and I clicked on each one in turn. Then I saw it. My kitchen. Brilliantly lit. I scrolled through the other images. Most were in darkness except where I could see the child light on the children's landing. So, that's how he knew everything I'd been doing? Sickened, I didn't look to see if he spied on me in the bathroom too. I logged off and tried to return everything to as it was. I turned off the light, raised the blind and locked the door behind me.

When I got back to the house I felt my phone vibrate in my pocket. It was Stephanie. Her message chilled me more than my excursion into the garden office had.

Cameras everywhere.

I sank to the tiled floor, heart pounding.

I replied to her text. *I know, just found out myself.* It became clear why Topher was so interested in Mark Brown. Leaning back against a kitchen cabinet, I sat, elbows on my knees, head in hands. Under my warm clothing, my skin prickled as hairs on my forearms rose. What if he had cameras in his own office? But no. Surely not. As far as he knew there was only one key to his office. Unless he knew about the spare? Could he know? I wasn't sure but Topher was a very prudent person and I wondered if he could have filmed what I had just been careful to do so discretely?

I sent Stephanie another text. *Please be careful.*

CHAPTER THIRTY-SEVEN

'Just in time,' she said, flinging the door wide open. 'Dinner's nearly ready. Though it's not looking quite how it does in the recipe book.'

I shrugged. 'Cooking never was your strong point, Stephanie. I don't know why you don't just get a takeaway instead. At least that would be edible.'

She pouted and, for a moment, I thought she was going to shut the door in my face.

'Are you going to let me in?' I said. 'It's gloomy out here. I see the lights aren't working again.'

She stepped back to allow me to cross the threshold. 'The CCTV isn't working either. I keep complaining to the landlord. I think he's screening my calls now.'

I kissed her on the cheek, thinking that I'd do the same if she were constantly nagging me. I followed her to the kitchenette and placed the wine and flowers on the work surface.

'Thank you.' She took a bottle of champagne from the fridge, opened the bottle, and took a glass off the draining board and poured the wine into the damp glass.

I shuddered, hoping she wouldn't do the same to the red I'd brought over. Then I chastised myself. Don't be such a wine snob!

'What are you cooking?'

'Beef,' she said. 'It's called *culottesteg*, a top sirloin roast. I thought you'd be pleased.' Her brow furrowed as she arranged the flowers in an old vase. I had much nicer ones at home. Perhaps I should buy her a new one? But then it wouldn't make her any better at flower arranging. *Why am I here?* I thought to myself. I wandered over to the sofa and opened up my Dell.

'Here's your drink,' she said, raising her glass to me. 'I've got some smoked oysters for you too.'

I slammed the lid of my laptop shut as she walked towards me with a glass of champagne in her hand. She stumbled on the edge of the rug, spilling some of the wine on my jeans.

'Look what you've done!' I shouted, holding the laptop up and shaking wine off it. 'I'll have to change now.'

Stephanie shrugged her apology and sipped from the glass she had brought over for me. 'You brought spare clothes, didn't you?' she asked.

I nodded. 'Of course.'

'Then go change. Problem solved.'

I glared at her, picked up my overnight bag and stomped across the room to where the bedroom and bathroom were located. I left the door slightly ajar and watched as she lifted the lid of my Dell. Damn, the application was still running. It should have shut down when I closed the lid.

I saw she was puzzled by what she saw. I knew it was a series of cameras placed carefully around someone's home, but would she realise whose home it was? I crept towards her, but I'd forgotten the loose floorboard in the bedroom. It creaked and she slammed the laptop shut, placing it back on the sofa where I'd left it.

She raced to the kitchen area and opened her handbag. She sent a text to someone. Who was she texting? She slipped the phone back in the bag just as I strolled back into the room. I'd changed into fresh jeans and, wandering towards her, I took the half empty glass and refilled it. I sipped the wine as I prowled towards her.

'Did you see everything you wanted to?' I purred.

'What you talking about?' she said.

'My laptop,' I said, pacing towards her.

'What about it?'

'You were looking at my laptop,' I whispered, stroking her upper arm.

'I was just mopping around, making sure that there was no wine on it. That was all,'

I gripped her arm tightly, making her squeal. 'Liar!'

Stephanie stepped backwards, trying to release my grasp on her arm. She was wedged against the kitchen counter-top, unable to back away any further. Reaching behind her with her free hand, she was feeling for something, anything. She grabbed something and pulled it around in front of her. It was the vegetable knife — a simple three-inch blade.

I looked at the knife in her hand. Stepping closer, I released her arm and pressed the knife into my stomach. 'Go on then! Kill me.'

'You bastard!' Stephanie hissed.

I dropped the knife and pressed my mouth roughly on hers, parting her lips with my tongue and probing her mouth. She relaxed, and I ran my hands up her arms until I was holding either side of her head, and kissed her deeply. As she started to return the kiss, I slid my hands down to her neck, beginning to squeeze. I felt her body freeze as she realised what was happening, and I pressed harder.

'I always knew you were a plant,' I whispered. 'You and Lily thought you could trick me. I knew your plan from the start, but I remembered what you were like in bed. I wondered if you'd learnt any new tricks and it seemed a shame to pass up the opportunity.'

She struggled, long red fingernails scratching at my hands. I increased the pressure. Feeling her wriggling around, her hands patting the counter-top behind her. Going for the knife again? With a strong grip around her neck I simply edged her away from the worktop. As her body started to go limp, I eased myself back and stared at her.

Her beautiful face was transformed. Ugly. Her eyes bulged. Her purple tongue protruded from her mouth. It was obvious she was dead. I released her and let her fall to the floor. I stepped away, went to the bedroom, packed my overnight bag. I flung my laptop on top of the clothes inside the case. I put these beside the main door, went into the kitchen, grabbed rubber gloves, a cloth, and an all-purpose cleaner, and went to the bathroom. I scrubbed the bathroom, top to bottom, wiping all my prints away. I did the same in the bedroom and repeated the process in the lounge and in the kitchen area. I rinsed out the cloth and put it back in its place by the sink. The bottle of all-purpose cleaner I put back in the cupboard under the kitchen sink. The gloves I kept. Looking around, I was pleased at what I'd achieved. Opening the door to leave, I stopped when I heard a phone beep. I took Stephanie's mobile from her handbag and read the message with a grim smile. Lily was right. Stephanie should have been careful.

A light came on outside. The neighbours? On their balcony. I wasn't sure if it was coincidence or if they had heard something. I held my breath until the light went out again. I gulped, patted my pocket, and took out the phone I'd hidden there. Scooting to the centre of the room, I dropped the phone on the rug in front of the sofa. With my toe, I carefully drove the phone under the sofa, then I popped Stephanie's phone in my pocket, picked up my bag, and opened the door, shutting it quietly. I strolled down the steps to the front door and unlocked it, letting it slam shut behind. I removed the gloves, slipping them into my pocket, and then strode to my car, where it was parked in the street. I took one last look to make sure no one had seen me. Then I drove slowly down the street.

John Maitland stepped out of the shadows. He looked up at Stephanie's windows. The flat was in darkness, but he knew at last for whom he'd been dumped. He thrust his hands into his coat pocket and started to walk away. He stopped suddenly. His coat had caught on something. He tried to turn around but was prevented by a large hand squeezing his shoulder blade.

'This stops tonight,' said a voice in his ear. 'You leave the lady alone now. Understand?'

'Who the hell are you?' John asked, trying to twist around to see his attacker.

'Just a friend of the lady. Leave her alone and you won't get hurt. Keep annoying her and, well... we know where you work and we know where you live. Tell me that you understand.'

John drew in a sharp breath as the pressure on his shoulder increased. He nodded. 'I understand,' he grunted.

'Good.'

The pressure on his shoulder released and John whirled around to face his attacker, but he was alone in the street. Only the sound of footsteps walking away let him know that he hadn't imagined the entire encounter.

CHAPTER THIRTY-EIGHT

Lily

I kept looking at my phone, expecting a reply to the text I'd sent to Stephanie. Now, although I'd uncovered how Topher had known everything all along, I wasn't sure how to react. I felt sick, realising that everywhere I went in the house there was a camera watching me. But I still had to know what else he'd been doing. I locked the back door and ran upstairs to the master suite. I scrabbled in the bedside cabinet and dug out my laptop, sat on the edge of the bed and slid to the floor, resting my back against the bed. I switched on my laptop and got the papers out of my pocket. I started copy typing some of the diary into Google translate. I put a hand to my mouth. No. This couldn't be true? At least I'd been right about the juice and milk cartons. It was all part of the gaslighting that Topher had inflicted on me. I read how he relished it when he'd hidden my keys, my ID card, and my glasses. The journal listed all of the hiding places he'd thought of to make me think that I was going out of my mind. I knew why he was doing this. He was terrified we'd leave him. Scared of being alone again as he was after his parents died. If only he could see that controlling wasn't the same as loving and protecting. However, at least now I had an idea of where all the cameras were; now I knew, I could reposition them so I had some blind spots to work in. I leaned my head against the bed, feeling, for the first time in a long time, as if I were fully in control of my mental capacity. My heart pounded as I heard Topher's key in the lock and his footsteps on the tiles in the hallway downstairs. He stood at the bottom of the stairs and called up to me, but I was too scared to reply. I texted Stephanie a quick note. *He's come home! Why has he come home?* I sat looking at the phone, waiting for an answer but none came.

After a while, Topher came upstairs and I saw he was pleased with himself. By the time he'd got into the bedroom I was in a nightdress. My laptop was tucked away and I had a book in my hand. I even made sure it wasn't upside down.

'Did you have a good evening?' he said.

I bit my lip before replying; surely he could see I was trembling? 'Yes,' I said finally. 'I came to bed early so I could finish my book.'

'You've left quite a mess downstairs. You know I don't like an untidy house, Lily.'

I sensed him staring at me. I tried hard to appear as if I was reading intently. He didn't appear angry, but that was usually the worst time of all. I felt like a rabbit caught by bright lights. I saw suspicion on every feature of his face. Presumably, he already knew what I'd done. *Has he checked the cameras before coming upstairs?* I didn't know. I was just waiting for the bomb to drop.

Topher stripped, put all his clothes in the washing basket and strode to the wet room. Even as I heard him in the shower, I felt his eyes boring through the wall. It was as if he knew I was watching him. I heard the shower turn off and him drying himself briskly. He came to bed, and I wondered if he'd washed the smell of Stephanie off himself. I also wondered if they had made love that evening. As he settled the duvet around himself, he leaned over to kiss me. He lay down and turned off his light. I felt him edging towards me. He placed his hand between my legs and, feeling that I had put underwear on, he eased the material aside and pushed his fingers inside me. I tensed, holding my breath, fingers digging into my book. Frustrated, he removed his hand from inside my knickers and took the book and threw it on the floor. He pulled me down the bed so I was reclining. He took my right hand and placed it on his shaft.

'No, Topher,' I said.

'Yes, Lily,' he replied, and he ducked under the covers. He pulled at my pants, kissed the inside of my thighs, nibbling in a way he knew I couldn't resist. And then his mouth was on me, his tongue on my clitoris and, despite what my head was saying, my body gave in to him. I knew how wet I'd become. He knew it too. He eased himself up my body and thrust into me.

It didn't take long. I felt him come deep inside me. He rested for a minute and then he rolled off and curled up on his side of the bed. After a few minutes I heard his soft snoring. I lay there in the dark, his semen oozing out of me onto the clean sheets.

When I was sure he was completely asleep, I got out of bed, I picked up my pants and my phone, I fetched my dressing gown from the back of the door and I went to the floor below, where I stepped into the shower. Once the water was hot I stood under it, allowing the needles of scorching water to pound against my back. I took the shower head and put it between my legs and removed every single last drop of him from inside me. I replaced the showerhead and I sat on the base, rested my head on my knees and wept.

I sat in the shower until all the hot water in the tank had gone. I shivered as cold water hit me and I dried myself vigorously, using the towel to warm my skin as well as dry it. I peeked in to make sure the children were asleep and plodded down the hall to the guest room.

It'd been made up so all I had to do was slide between the cool sheets and lie there until morning came.

When I woke and went to the kitchen, Heather had arrived and Topher had left for his office. I shivered with relief. After last night, I could not have faced him. I felt in my dressing gown pocket for my phone. Still no reply from Stephanie. I texted her again, telling her to call me.

CHAPTER THIRTY-NINE

Lily

By the time Tuesday arrived, Topher was still giving me the silent treatment. I'd never tried to resist him making love to me before. But whilst he wasn't talking to me he couldn't cajole me into returning to the master suite. Like my mother's ploys, I was fed up with his games too.

And then there was Stephanie. I still hadn't heard from her, and she had promised me her moral support in court today. With a certain loss of patience, I drove to her apartment in N17. I parked in a visitor spot and pressed the intercom to be let in. There was no answer, so I pressed every single button until someone answered. I bleated out a random excuse and they allowed me into the building. Stephanie was on the third floor, overlooking the terraced houses surrounding her block and the tall buildings of the City in the distance. I banged on her door until my hands were sore. There was no letterbox as the post was all left downstairs. I gave the door one final kick, which attracted the attention of her neighbours.

'Have you seen her?' I asked.

'Not since Friday night,' they replied.

There was nothing else I could do. I scribbled her a note reminding her my case was being heard today, shoved it into the post box in the lobby, and left.

I met my solicitor, Cerys Quick, outside the court room. 'I'm sorry,' she said. 'Still no luck with the CCTV tape.'

'Have the police got a copy?'

She shook her head.

This was not good. 'My father has been making wild suggestions that Topher could have threatened someone to "lose" the tape,' I said.

'Could he have?' she said. 'Would he know who to approach?'

I shrugged. 'It seems a bit too farfetched for me, but my father doesn't agree. He thinks it wouldn't be beyond Topher to do something like that. I've told him that I disagree, but can you get your investigator onto it?'

'She's working on it,' Cerys replied.

I'd told Dad to keep his theories to himself, but after what I'd found in the office, I wasn't sure what Topher was capable of.

'The evidence we have is circumstantial at best,' Cerys said.

'I have an idea,' I said, showing her a photo of the list of names taken from the Mark Brown file. 'Can you or your investigator find out who these guys are?'

Cerys gave me a nod and a brief smile. I knew it wasn't much to go on, but I hoped it was maybe enough to cast doubt on my guilt over the accident.

Our case was called. I walked in with Cerys but was soon

swept into the dock, where I sat between two large, uniformed security guards. I sat with my hands in my lap, grateful that I wasn't handcuffed, but their proximity was as uncomfortable as the idea of metal scuffing at my wrists.

Dad came and gave me a wave. I was too terrified to respond. And still no sign of Stephanie. Nor Topher. Were they together? Laughing about me?

Get a grip, Lily, I told myself. The guard on my left nudged me and we stood for the Judge's arrival. Not someone I knew, but of course it would not be. Any judge I knew through Topher would have to recuse themselves. The jury trailed in and took their seats. Some stared at me but looked away when I returned their gaze.

Denise Jones took the stand for the prosecution. She frowned at me from the witness box. I thought I'd convinced her I was innocent of this crime but every glance from her was one of confusion, as if she no longer knew whether to trust me or not. Her manner unnerved me and I was glad when she stepped down.

My barrister told the court that Vinnie Craycroft, the lorry driver, was still unconscious and unable to provide a statement. The CCTV footage was still missing. Even the police had been unable to come up with a copy, and I already knew Cerys's investigator had had no luck either.

The judge called the barristers forward for a consultation. He coughed into his microphone as they walked back to their podia.

'This is a very sad and disappointing case,' he began. 'Sad because of the deaths of an entire family, including little Jennie McAllister who was only two years old.

'Disappointing because substantial evidence has disappeared, meaning that the vehicle which Mrs Gundersen claims drove her off the road cannot be traced. However, far from finding that there is no case to answer, I feel that this case should be adjourned until the CCTV or the other vehicle can be recovered. It is clear from the evidence presented thus far that Mrs Gundersen did collide with the McAlister's' people carrier. What has not been proved to my satisfaction is that she was at fault. Mrs Jessop, how long do you think you will need to find the missing evidence?'

'It is, of course, hard to say exactly, m'lud,' my barrister said, 'but an adjournment of two months would be helpful.'

'Very well, Mr Shreeves, does that suit you?'

The prosecution barrister nodded.

The judge turned to stare at me, his gaze even worse than my mother's. 'Mrs Gundersen,' he said, 'you remain under bail conditions. And you are required to return here in two months for the continuation of your trial. Thank you.'

He rose and left.

'Lily, you're free,' Dad said, coming to the dock.

'Only for now, Dad,' I reminded him. 'Only for now.'

Yes, I was free to go home, but I had not been found innocent. The case still hung over me.

Neither Stephanie nor Topher were in the public gallery. I cursed under my breath. Where the hell were they?

CHAPTER FORTY

Lily

When I arrived home, Heather had collected a pile of suits and Topher's legal collars in a heap at the bottom of the stairs.

'I'll be doing a run to the dry cleaners before I come in tomorrow morning. Have you got anything to go?' she asked.

I shook my head and then remembered the taupe silk still hanging on the back of the wardrobe. I limped upstairs to the dressing room and collected it. The handbag and the shoes from that evening were put away. Heather had taken care of it already. But a thought came to me. I opened up the box containing the handbag and tipped the contents onto the floor. A lipstick, a tissue, and a business card. I turned it over and read the name. I needed someone to talk to about Stephanie's disappearance. Perhaps Sally Trevena could help?

I took the dress downstairs to Heather, promised to collect Darcy from nursery in the afternoon and I headed into the garden. It was cold out there, but I hoped this was somewhere I could talk without any of Topher's cameras eavesdropping.

Sally's voice came down the line, strong and confident. I tried to remember when I was the same. It had been a while.

'Sally?' I said. 'It's Lily Gundersen.'

'Lily! I've been waiting for your call,' she told me.

'You have?' I frowned.

'Of course. Now, how may I help you?'

I paused for a moment and then I told her I was worried about Stephanie.

'Can you speak up a bit, dear? I'm having trouble hearing you,' she said.

'I can't,' I whispered.

'Why don't I come to the house and we can chat face to face?'

'You can't,' I said.

I heard her take a deep breath. 'Okay,' she said. 'Can you leave your house?'

'Yes. I must collect Darcy at four, though.'

'Then come and meet me.'

She gave me the name of a coffee shop that was close enough to walk to. 'Half an hour,' she said. 'I will wait for you.'

I went back into the house, collected my coat, keys and handbag, and set out.

I sat in the cafe nursing a latte for some time before she arrived. She ordered an espresso and plonked herself down opposite, bringing with her the scent of an autumn day and the flush of confidence.

'What's up?'

'Stephanie,' I said.

'Have you two fallen out?'

'Yes, well no. Maybe. Yes.' I twisted my cold latte around

on the table until Sally placed her hand over mine and halted the movement.

'Start at the beginning,' she said.

I related the entire sorry tale of using Stephanie to spy on Topher. I expected her to look aghast but not even a flicker of surprise crossed her face.

When I finished by telling her I hadn't heard from Stephanie since the weekend, she looked worried.

'I suspected something was amiss when I gave you my card. I didn't realise how deep the trouble you were both getting yourselves into was.'

'Was it so obvious something was wrong?'

'Only to me. I know the signs to look for, but I hadn't appreciated the game you and Stephanie were playing. You may have put her in grave danger. I think we need to go to the police.'

'Really?'

'We need to report her missing at the very least. Do you know if she's been into work?'

'I hadn't thought of that,' I replied glumly.

'Well try now,' she ordered.

I went through my contacts list and found Stephanie's work number. It went to voicemail and I left a message.

'Do you have her switchboard number?'

I shook my head and Sally sighed. I could see she was getting exasperated at my lack of initiative.

'What's the name of the firm?'

I told her and she Googled on her phone, then dialled the number. 'I'd like to speak to Ms Silcott,' she said. 'Yes, it is a personal call, but I am Mr Trevena's wife. I'm sure you know my husband.'

I couldn't hear what was being said, but I saw a smug smile pass across Sally's face. 'Oh, I see,' she said finally. The smile had gone. 'Very well, thanks for letting me know,' she said.

She put the phone on the cafe table and held my hand. 'Lily,' she said. 'Stephanie has not been seen since Friday. She had appointments yesterday and today. She hasn't phoned in sick.'

'That's not like her,' I said. 'Stephanie's really conscientious.'

'Exactly. I think we need to go to the police. Who was the detective you were talking to?'

I told her DC Jones's name and gave her the number.

Sally ordered more coffee and made another call. When she finished the call, she held out her hand to me. 'Come along, my dear,' she said. 'DC Jones will meet us at the station. She's extremely interested in what you have to say.'

We left the cafe and Sally ushered me into a taxi. As we drew close to the police station I found my nerves at being questioned there after the accident coming back to me. I started to shake, and Sally took my hand in hers.

'It will be fine,' she whispered.

I hoped she was right. We plodded up the slippery concrete steps — a salute to the station's Brutalist architectural heritage. The glass doors moved apart, creaking like an ancient and rickety portcullis.

We were shown into an interview room and waited for Denise to arrive. My pulse was racing. Somewhere deep in my stomach a gymnast was doing back flips. It was worse than any pre-concert nerves. Even my breathing exercises weren't helping. I glanced at my watch, knowing I was going to be late to pick Darcy up from nursery. I'd texted Heather to tell her, but she'd not replied.

Finally Denise bustled into the room, holding a plastic cup. She put it on the table, scum forming on the surface. It looked as if it were already cold. She put a folder on the table and offered us both refreshments. We declined.

'So tell me,' she began, her tone brusque. 'You believe Stephanie has gone missing. Why are you only telling me now? You know Stephanie and I are friends. You should have called me.'

Sally took over. 'Stephanie's not been seen since Friday. She's not been at work. She's missed appointments with clients and she's not called in sick. She is not responding to any communications from Mrs Gundersen and her secretary has tried to call her today. There has been no response at all.'

Denise made some notes on the sheet of paper in front of her. 'And you went to her flat, Mrs Gundersen?'

I nodded. 'Please can't you do something to find her? I'm really worried.' I looked at Sally. She gave me an encouraging smile and squeezed my hand.

'Look, DC Jones,' I began. 'I've not been entirely honest with you...'

'What a surprise,' she replied, slamming her biro on the desk. 'You'd be amazed at how often that happens.'

Sally frowned at Denise and the detective returned the glare.

'Why don't you tell me everything?' she said finally. She picked up her drink, took a sip, grimaced, and put it down again.

For the second time that day I related the whole pathetic tale to someone who looked incredulous at the situation Stephanie and I had got ourselves into.

'And you think your husband was the last person to see Stephanie?'

'We exchanged texts about my home being full of cameras.'

'Can I see the texts?'

I passed my phone across to Denise. She made a note of the text and took a screenshot with her phone.

Step by step, she guided me through the missing person form. There were many questions I couldn't answer. I had no idea what Stephanie had been wearing. Or what she'd last eaten.

Denise pushed the form across to me for my signature. 'I have to ask this,' she said. 'Do you know when Stephanie was last seen alive?'

'Friday, her neighbours said,' I replied. 'But that was early evening.'

Sally nudged my arm. I glanced at her and she raised her eyebrows at me. 'Go on,' she said.

I covered my face with my hands, dragged my fingers down towards my chin. 'There's something else,' I said. 'Stephanie was planning to spend the weekend with my husband, but he came home in the early hours of Saturday morning.

'I was in bed, reading. He threw his clothes in the laundry basket and had a long shower.'

'And what's happened to his clothes?' said Denise.

'They've been washed,' I said. I didn't tell her that it was because I couldn't bear the thought of Stephanie's perfume clinging to them in the wash basket so I had taken care of them already.

Eventually Denise pushed herself away from the grubby table. 'I'll need to talk to people at Stephanie's firm but I will take some officers with me and we'll go to her flat. I'll talk to you again later.'

I sighed with relief.

CHAPTER FORTY-ONE

Denise

Even as I prepared to visit Stephanie's employers and her flat, I felt Lily Gundersen was holding something back. I only wished I had been surprised over her revelations about her husband, but I had always sensed there was an under-the-surface tension between them.

I voiced my suspicions to DI Blaine who, to my annoyance, reminded me of the appropriate protocol. I assured her I'd follow it.

I took a uniformed PC with me to talk to Stephanie's colleagues. Sadly, no one had a spare key to her flat, and I knew she wasn't the sort of person to leave one over the top of her doorway. The more I learnt about how careful Stephanie had become over her personal safety the more I was alarmed she would have taken part in such an ill-advised plan as spying on her friend's husband. It was as ludicrous a plot as the thrillers my ex used to read. At least that was what I thought until her secretary rushed to the lift as I was about to leave.

'Stephanie thought someone was following her again!' she breathed at me, scarcely disguising her excitement. 'She was getting a lot of wrong numbers and hang-ups.'

'But she took an injunction out against John, didn't she?' I asked, but she shrugged, unable to provide anything other than a small insight into my friend's secret life.

It was only a short drive to Stephanie's flat, and we had no difficulty in procuring access to the floor where she lived. I banged hard on the door. What was I going to say to her after our last conversation?

I stood back and a uniformed officer took over. His fist thumped louder than mine and he bellowed "Police! Open up!" more loudly than I could as well.

After a few minutes, we gave up. There was no letter box to peer through, but all the same there was an unmistakable smell that filtered through the gaps around the wooden door. I pounded on the door, hoping it would give way to my bare fists. Someone or something was dead in there. I kicked the door, growing frantic, wondering what else Stephanie had withheld from me in our after-work chats. I called DI Blaine.

'Stand by,' she said. 'I'll send over a dog team with a big red key.'

'Thanks,' I replied, and I paced the hallway as we waited.

The cadaver dog arrived, sniffed around the front door then laid by it; there was no longer any doubt about what we would find in the flat. The dog handler pulled her dog out of harm's way and a burly PC took the enforcer battering ram and swung it against the door lock. A well-timed swing of the red key always had a spectacular effect, and this time was no different. The lock stayed in the door frame but the door itself smashed against the hallway wall.

The smell was stronger now. Completely ignoring all protocol and the shouts of my colleagues, I rushed in.

Despite knowing DI Blaine would take me off the case, I raced into Stephanie's flat. However unlikely it was, I wanted to make sure Stephanie was alive. But I was too late; she was dead. I found her slumped against her kitchen cabinets, eyes, and tongue protruding. The colour of her skin and her glazed eyes left no possibility of resuscitation. Holding back hot, angry tears, I called DI Blaine again and she arranged for the forensics team to be dispatched.

Later, the team had cleared enough of the scene to allow me back in. This time I was dressed head to toe in white paper clothing, designed to protect the scene, not me. Stephanie was now a victim. There was little dignity in death and none in a violent death. I only hoped DI Blaine would allow me to stay on the case. Rushing in like an idiot would be reported, and I wasn't going to lie about my personal friendship with Stephanie Silcott. But I would find her killer. I owed her that much.

One of the CSIs approached me and showed me a phone in an evidence bag. I had seen a phone just like it only a few hours before.

There was no doubt in my mind — it was Lily Gundersen's phone.

CHAPTER FORTY-TWO

Lily

Sally took me home in a taxi. I didn't invite her in, telling her I was exhausted and that I thought I needed a nap. I hadn't told her about the cameras and Topher spying on my every move. I knew I should have mentioned it before, but I was too ashamed.

I took a shower and went to lie down in the guest room. I felt safer there. I'd not slept in the master bedroom since the weekend. I'd had to go in there to change the sheets, of course. Topher had insisted — calling me a slattern for leaving dirty sheets on the bed.

That was the only time he'd spoken to me, which meant he could make no mention of my returning to the marital bed. I was glad I had thought to lock the guest room door last night. He rattled at the door but not too loudly in case he woke the children.

It was dark when I woke. I smelt dinner cooking and I looked at my phone. *Damn, it's nearly six o'clock. Topher's meal! The children!* I dressed rapidly and ran downstairs.

Heather was cooking. The children were in the garden room, playing. It was very tranquil.

'Thank you for staying,' I told her.

'I thought you might need the rest,' she said, 'but if you don't mind, I'll be off now. There's a casserole in the oven. Dumplings are in the fridge. They'll need to go in at a quarter to seven. Then you can put the spuds on. Veggies are all prepped and in pans there.'

I look to where she pointed — the carrots, broccoli, cauliflower, and potatoes were all ready to cook.

'I've made you late home,' I said, but she just smiled.

'We'll have something out of the freezer tonight,' she replied. 'We often do on weeknights. I like to cook extra and freeze it for nights when I'm tired. Or late.'

'Topher insists on fresh every day,' I muttered. I said it mostly to myself, but Heather nodded as if she had heard me. I checked my phone, but there was nothing. I decided to call Sally when Heather had gone and see if she'd heard anything.

Heather kissed the children goodbye and let herself out. At once the children began to grizzle and I told them it was bath and story time.

'But it's too early,' James complained.

'Daddy will be home soon. Perhaps he can read you a story if you're both bathed and ready?' As I said his name, I heard Topher's key in the door. The children rushed upstairs, I put my phone on the dresser and waited to greet him. I knew that regardless of our current mood with each other, it would be expected.

'Hello,' I said, as he strolled into the kitchen. He didn't even look at me. He went to the cupboard, took out a glass and poured himself a vodka. I decided to follow the children upstairs.

After they were bathed and in bed, Topher arrived for

story time. I rinsed out the bath and returned to the meal Heather had prepared. Dumplings in the casserole, potatoes on the hob, and I went to set the table in the dining room. It was a rather grand name for the small room off the sitting room but, along with a freshly prepared meal, Topher liked to sit down and eat in style. The only time the children joined us was at the weekends, when we had a formal Sunday lunch.

I put the vegetables on the hob and lit the gas before going upstairs to kiss the children goodnight. Topher rose and walked from James' room without speaking to me. I could only hope he would approve of the wine I'd set on the table.

He did, it seemed. When I returned downstairs, he'd opened the bottle and the wine was breathing. Unbidden, Stephanie's voice came into my head.

Breathe? Sod that, she would say. *I can give it mouth to mouth resuss!*

I smiled at the memory, wondering where she had got to.

I brought dinner in from the kitchen and we served ourselves at the dining table. This only happened when Topher was giving me the silent treatment; otherwise, I dished up his food for him. The casserole was delicious, but it was as dry as ashes in my mouth as all my thoughts were on Stephanie.

I jumped when the doorbell pealed, immediately followed by a fist pounding on the glass panels. The cacophony ripped through the silence at our dinner table. In an instant I was on my feet, racing for the door. Topher yelled at me to calm down and insisted I stay in my chair. I heard his footsteps thudding on the parquet behind me.

'Stop telling me what to do!' I yelled.

I didn't care. I was sick of his orders and I needed to know where Stephanie was.

CHAPTER FORTY-THREE

Lily

I wrenched the door open and Denise stood there with a uniformed police officer.

'I'm sorry, Lily,' she said. And the uniformed officer took my elbow, pulling me down the steps. I half expected him to snap cuffs on my wrists.

'Lily Gundersen,' Denise intoned. 'I'd like you to attend a voluntary interview at the station with regard to the murder of Stephanie Silcott...'

I didn't hear the rest of the caution. The police constable was distracted by a roar from Topher as he moved forward to snatch me back. The PC pushed me behind him, but I dropped to the floor. The officer raised his arms to defend himself from this unexpected attack, pushing Topher backwards. My husband's rescue attempt was stalled, and he collapsed, panting, against the front door.

He coughed and suddenly seemed to regain his composure. He rose slowly and I heard him ask where I was being taken.

The look of shock on his face was either award-winning or he was stunned I was being interviewed. 'I'll get you a solicitor,' he said. 'Don't speak to anyone until you have a solicitor there. Do you understand, Lily? Speak to no one until you have a solicitor!'

I was too shocked to take everything in. I was shoved into the back of the police car and taken to the station where I had entered voluntarily only a few hours earlier. We drove through the open gates at the side of the station, and I was ushered into what I learnt later was a custody suite. There was a police sergeant there who explained everything that was happening. He repeated what DC Jones had said when I told him I didn't understand why I was there, and repeated my reasons for being there.

Finally, the cogs in my brain began to whir and I caught up. 'Stephanie's dead?' I asked. 'Since when? What's happened?'

'We'll be asking the questions, Mrs Gundersen,' Denise snapped at me. It seemed unlike any manner in which she had spoken to me until now. Even after the accident when she questioned me she came across as warm and understanding, but perhaps that was Stephanie's influence. Now it was as if that woman had been her twin and currently I was faced with the evil sibling.

I endured the indignities of being placed in a cell. The desk sergeant told me there was nowhere else to put me for the time being. 'What about my phone call?' I asked. 'I want to call a solicitor.'

'Isn't your husband doing that for you?' Denise hissed at me.

She was so close, her spittle flecked my face and I flinched. 'I think after our earlier conversation you'd understand why I don't want anyone my husband could arrange for me!' I retorted. Finally, my brain was starting to catch up. I felt more confident and straightened my sagging shoulders. Despite my dire situation, I was preparing to stand up for myself.

When it came to it, however, I couldn't remember Sally's mobile number, but Denise, calmer now, reminded me she still had Sally's contact details from earlier in the day. A female police officer took me to the cell. I was told to remove my shoes before I entered, even though they were only my slippers. I hesitated on the threshold until I was pushed into the room. It smelt of disinfectant with an undercurrent of stale urine and sweat. I edged towards the bench with its blue plastic covered mattress. I sat, pulled my knees to my chest and, dry-eyed, I waited.

I didn't know how long I waited but when the door opened I had fallen asleep and was laying on the disgusting mattress. I felt the imprint of it on my face and tried not to think about the grime and germs I'd picked up.

The desk sergeant told me that I could make a call, but it had to be on speakerphone, and he would be listening in.

Eventually I heard Sally's voice.

'Sally,' I sobbed at her. I couldn't hold back the tears any longer. 'Stephanie's dead.'

'What? How?' she asked.

I shook my head. I didn't know the answers. 'Can you get me a solicitor? I was seeing a Cerys Quick, but I'm not sure if I should call her or not. They want to talk to me about Stephanie's murder,' I told her. 'Obviously, I don't want anyone who Topher knows.'

'I understand,' she replied. 'Now you let me talk to the custody sergeant. Leave it with me, Lily. It'll be fine.'

I nodded, hoping she was right. The phone was taken from me. As I was led away, I heard the sergeant telling Sally what I had been arrested for and where I was being held. I could only hope she would find Cerys or someone else for me soon.

Sally was a miracle worker. Within an hour, Cerys Quick was with me and I outlined my current predicament. I told her everything and she cleared up a few of my questions.

'I'm confused about my phone,' I told her. 'I've had it with me all day today. I called Sally earlier and I showed Denise — DC Jones — the text I received from Stephanie. How can it have been found in her flat? It doesn't make sense.'

'Where's your phone now?' she said.

'At home. It'll be in the kitchen. I leave it in there when we eat. Topher doesn't like the phones at the table. He thinks it stops proper conversation.'

'That's fine,' she said. 'The police will have applied for a search warrant and your house will be being searched now. If the phone is there, they will find it. Try not to worry. We'll have all this cleared up in no time.'

'And if we don't?' I said. 'What happens then?'

'The problem is that since they haven't arrested you, this could drag on. With an arrest, the police must charge you within twenty-four hours. Then we'd go to the Magistrate's Court and ask for bail.'

'So, I'm free to go? They put me in a cell, Cerys!'

'Technically, yes, you're free to go, but that may be the point at which they decide to arrest you. I'll talk to the custody sergeant; you shouldn't have been put in a cell. I suggest you answer their questions as best you can, and hopefully, we'll be out of here soon.'

CHAPTER FORTY-FOUR

Lily

After the talk with Cerys, I was returned to a room in the custody suite to await the interview. I stared at the wall as tears rolled down my face. I couldn't sit still and began to pace, berating myself for the mess I was in. It's all your fault that Stephanie's dead, I told myself. You're as guilty as if you'd killed her. I sobbed, hoping she'd not suffered too much. That she'd not been scared. But, knowing what Topher was capable of, I knew she would have been terrified.

In handcuffs I was shown into the interview room once more.

'Why is my client in cuffs?' Cerys protested. 'She's not under arrest, is she? Or is there something you've not told me?'

DI Blaine considered for a moment and then agreed the handcuffs could be removed. 'We thought she might be a danger to the officers in the custody suite,' she muttered.

'That's nonsense, DI Blaine,' said Cerys, 'and you know it.'

I sat and rubbed my wrists, watching the two women

glower at each other. Denise commenced with a reminder of why I was there, the recording and took me through the preliminary questions.

'When did you last see Ms Silcott?'

'A week ago. We'd had a party at the weekend and she came to collect a dish she'd loaned me.' When had I learned to lie so well, I wondered, but I knew it had long been my best means of survival.

'Not to drop anything off then?' asked DI Blaine.

I shook my head. I was too scared to mention the keys Stephanie had copied for me.

'For the tape please, Mrs Gundersen.'

'No, just to collect the dish.'

'Seems an odd time of day to do that. Wouldn't it have been easier in the evening?'

'I don't know,' I replied. 'She may have needed the dish for the evening.'

'Indeed.' DI Blaine looked at her notes and Denise slid a plastic bag across the table.

'Do you recognise this, Mrs Gundersen?'

'You know I do. It's my phone,' I replied, trying hard to hold back a cry of anguish. I glanced from Cerys to Denise and back again. 'But it can't be. You know I had mine earlier today. I showed you the text from Stephanie.'

'Where was this phone found?' Cerys interrupted.

'We'll come to that,' DI Blaine snapped. 'Where were you between 7 p.m. on Friday 8th November and 11 a.m. on Saturday 9th November?'

'I was at home with my children. My husband came home early Saturday morning. He'd been away at a conference, but he'd decided to come home. He said he was missing me and the children.'

'After only a few hours? He must be a very devoted

husband,' Anita Blaine remarked. Her mouth twisted into a smirk. She knew my husband was having an affair, and I surmised she had formed an idea of what my husband was like. If only she knew the whole truth.

'No comment,' I said. This earned me a frown from DI Blaine.

'You have no witnesses to being at home all Friday evening,' she said.

I wasn't sure if this was a question or a statement. 'I was with my children,' I repeated. 'I did not leave my home. I exchanged texts with Stephanie around 11 p.m. telling me there were cameras everywhere. I texted her back but that was the last I heard from her. I went to bed after midnight and my husband came home shortly after.'

'What did you understand Ms Silcott meant by her text?'

I was tempted to reply that I had no idea, but with what I'd revealed to Sally, Denise, and Cerys during the course of the last few hours it made no sense to lie or cover up for Topher. 'My husband spies on me. He uses cameras to trace my every movement in the house. Surely those are my witnesses to being home all Friday evening!' I sighed. 'I've tried to leave him a few times, but he's always found me and made me pay. You can check my medical history. He's often taken me to different Accident and Emergency hospitals. My divorce lawyer has tracked all of those down.' I glanced at Cerys. 'Can you share those with the police for me?'

She dipped her head, making notes on her pad.

'Stephanie was getting close to him to help find the evidence that he was gaslighting me. As it turned out, we both found out that my house was full of cameras. At the same time. Earlier in the evening I had searched my husband's office for evidence that he was trying to make me go mad. I found it. I printed off an online journal he's been keeping. But that print out is in my home. Topher will have destroyed it by now.'

'Your husband leaves his office unlocked?' Denise sounded incredulous.

'No, there's a spare key. I kept it in the house, behind a framed certificate. Although if Topher has been watching me he will have removed it by now.' I told them which certificate, and Denise scratched notes on a sheet of paper. She handed this to the uniformed officer by the door, who left. Clasping my hands in front of me, I hung my head. Search warrant or not, I couldn't imagine Topher was happy that the police were searching the house.

'That seems an odd place to keep a spare key,' she said mildly.

I glanced at Cerys and she nodded, so I took them through all the hiding places he'd used over the years. As I went through them, I was amazed it had taken me this long to work out what he was up to.

CHAPTER FORTY-FIVE

Denise

The Crime Scene Investigation team had almost finished at Stephanie's flat. I couldn't face going back there. At some point I would have to, but not today. Instead, I decided to make my way to the Gundersen home. Immediately when I pulled into the street, the silence fell around me like a cloak. Busy as it was nearby, the noise didn't penetrate this echelon of wealth and privilege. I wondered how much the house was worth now after the changes Lily Gundersen had made to it. I knew what they'd paid — it was my job to know — but I couldn't help wondering what its current value was. I knew it was well out of my reach. It wasn't hard to put aside the sneaking feelings of envy. Lily Gundersen's life may have looked perfect but, I now knew, it was far from that.

At the gateway I signed the log and hopped into a white Tyvek suit. I tucked my hair under the hood and walked to the front door before I popped on shoe covers and gloves. The music room was the bay-windowed room to my left, and I strolled in to talk to the technician I saw working there. All of the framed pictures and certificates were off the walls. No key had been found.

The search team were hard at work finding treasure troves in all the places Lily had mentioned in her interviews. There was, however, no sign of a second identical phone. I was beginning to warm to Lily and wanted to believe her incredible story, if only to justify Stephanie's trust in her. However, so far, nothing had been found to back it up. I had to find out if she was telling the truth or if she was a fantasist, as DI Blaine insisted on calling her.

As I stepped out into the hallway, Kendra Wilson, the Crime Scene Manager, called me, and I headed upstairs to where she was standing.

'Anything?' I said.

'Hmm,' she said. 'Follow me.'

I fell in behind her as she mounted the second stairway and we stomped up to the master suite.

'What do you see?' she asked.

'Nice room. Nice view. What are you seeing that I'm missing?' I shrugged. It all looked normal to me.

'It's not in here I want to show you,' she said.

We ambled further into the room and into a large area that seemed to be used as a dressing room. Shoes were lined up on shelves behind glass doors and there was an enormous antique mirror which seemed to take up the entire end wall. It was everything I'd ever wanted. My envious feelings were on overdrive. Kendra opened one of the cupboards and pushed the expensive suits aside.

I squinted for a moment, not understanding what she was showing me. Her torch ran over the back of the cupboard and then I saw it. A small, polished section of wood, about the size of a thumbprint, in unpolished planking at the back of the wardrobe.

'Clever, huh?' she said, pushing the mark. Silently, a small door sprang open to reveal a compact safe.

'Can we get in it?' I exclaimed.

'Just waiting on the keys from Mr Gundersen,' she said. 'He's not very happy, but since his wife is being questioned for murder and he's been arrested for assault we got a warrant to search the property.'

I left Kendra to get on while we waited for the keys to arrive. I called DI Blaine to let her know, but of course she was ahead of me.

'I want to know what's in the safe as soon as it's opened. Keys are arriving under blues and twos,' she said, referring to the lights and sirens on the police vehicle heading my way. At least there would be no hold-up. As I finished my call with her I heard the police siren getting closer. My heart raced as I recalled my days in uniform, speeding through the streets of London. A deafening clatter of heavy boots crashed up the stairs and the keys were thrust into Kendra's hands. The PC stepped back but I could see even he wanted to see the outcome of his chase through north London.

Kendra pulled the safe out of its hiding place and put it on a plastic sheet she'd lain on the dressing room floor.

My heart was still racing. The tiny door swung open and the safe appeared empty. Kendra cursed under her breath but poked her gloved hand around inside the safe.

With a squeal of triumph, she found something. She pulled it out and opened her hand to reveal a small USB memory stick resting on her palm.

I had been hoping for Lily's phone, and groaned with disappointment, until I started to wonder what on earth could be so valuable on a USB stick that it needed to be hidden in Topher Gundersen's safe?

· · ·

Kendra slid the USB into a tamper evidence bag, and it was added to the box of evidence bags for the techies at the laboratory to work on. I picked up the clipboard and ran my index finger down the list of items. The team had found Lily's phone whilst I'd been upstairs. I sifted through to box to find the evidence bag. I pulled it out of the box and held it up to the light, examining the phone through the plastic. It was identical to the phone I had back at the office. Odd, very odd.

'I'm going outside now,' Kendra said, and I followed her across the lawn to the garden office. She replaced her shoe covers with fresh ones and I did the same. She selected a key from the bunch taken from Topher Gundersen and turned it in the lock.

I think I had expected the office to be little more than a shed, but this was a perfectly styled comfortable workspace with bookshelves and filing cabinets around the walls. A battered old Persian-style rug lay on the floor under the desk chair. Pulling the chair out, I sat at it and switched on the tower unit. As the monitor burst into life, it showed a screen requesting a password. I typed randomly but wasn't able to crack the code. I hadn't expected to, but I wanted to give it a try. Silly really.

I pushed away from the desk and laid my head on the back of the chair.

'Don't worry,' said Kendra. 'We'll take this away and see what we can get off the hard drive. Even if he's deleted stuff and emptied the recycle bin, it doesn't mean he's scrubbed the hard drive. We still might be able to recover the information. But at least it gives a better idea of what's likely to be on the USB.'

'You think he downloaded everything to that little drive?'

'Letters and such like, yes. If there were any video files,

well, they take up more space so I would expect them to be on an external hard drive someplace. We might find a link to some cloud storage when the techies go over his tower unit.' Kendra paused for a moment. 'He's taken time to clear up, hasn't he?'

'Yep, almost as if he expected it. I was thinking it too, but it still doesn't make him a murderer.'

'Doesn't it?' Kendra's voice was muffled as she dug around in the office cupboard.

'I agree it's extremely suspicious. He seemed to have had information before he should have had it,' I said, 'but I'm going to need something stronger than that before I can slip the bracelets on him.'

'How about this?' Kendra asked.

I turned around. In her gloved hands, Kendra was holding up two mobile phones. One was a cheap Nokia — a burner no doubt. The other I recognised immediately; it was Stephanie's missing phone.

'Oh,' I said. 'Those will do very nicely indeed.'

CHAPTER FORTY-SIX

Denise

I drove back to West Hampstead nick in a daze. Despite our conversation, Stephanie had decided to have an affair with Topher Gundersen. Finding her phone at his house was, to me, conclusive evidence that he'd killed her. Irritatingly, a good barrister would argue that he could have come across the phone in any number of ways. I needed something more concrete.

Kendra agreed that Lily's phone would get priority at the lab, although I needed the information off Gundersen's main computer too. Resources were limited, and I had to make a choice. I hoped I'd made the right one.

I pulled into the small car park and luckily managed to wedge my car into a skinny slot. Exiting the car like a contortionist, I trotted up the stairs, hoping that the pain in my side from squeezing myself through the narrow gap would subside in a while. I didn't need a pulled muscle right now. I needed to focus.

I knocked on DI Blaine's office door and walked in. I

should have waited; Chief Superintendent Harlow was with her.

'DC Jones,' he said. 'I understand the victim was a friend of yours?'

'Not a close friend, sir,' I said. Damn, he was going to take me off the case. 'I got to know her when an ex-boyfriend was stalking her. We've been out for a couple of meals, nothing more than that.'

'I see,' he paused. 'Very well, so long as you can keep your personal feelings in check. DI Blaine assures me that you can. We need to get an arrest in this case. I don't want overly emotional officers getting in the way of a solid conviction.'

'That won't happen, sir,' I said.

He uncrossed his long legs and rose. 'Make sure it doesn't,' he said.

He stood by the office door; I was slow in realising he expected me to open it for him.

'Dickhead,' said DI Blaine as we listed to his footsteps fade away down the corridor. 'But don't you let me down. He's a bloody relic. Thinks women aren't up to the job. We need to show him.'

I sat in the chair the Super had vacated. 'Are you going to charge Lily Gundersen?'

'I want to, but I think I'm going to have to let her go.' She scowled at a report she was reading. 'It looks like the flat was wiped down after the murder. Kendra called me to say no prints have been found.'

'Stephanie's phone was found at the Gundersen house. In the husband's office.'

'You found it?' she snapped.

'No, not me. Kendra,' I said.

'Good. We've got him cooling his heels downstairs. We'll interview him as soon as his solicitor arrives.'

'Okay,' I said. 'I'll update the decision log. I'd like to be in on that interview.'

DI Blaine nodded and flicked her hand to wave me out of her office.

Back at my desk I tried to concentrate on the inevitable paperwork and not think about Stephanie's last moments. It was a relief when I got a call to say Topher Gundersen's solicitor had arrived.

I followed Anita Blaine to the interview room. Both men raised their heads as we opened the door. Peter Robinson was expressionless but Topher Gundersen narrowed his eyes with the faintest curl of his upper lip.

DI Blaine rapidly dispatched the preliminaries and the reason for Gundersen's arrest.

'I'm assuming you'll be giving my client police bail?' Peter Robinson said in his customary monotone voice.

Anita nodded, 'I'd just like to ask a few more questions related to the murder of Stephanie Silcott,' she said. 'I'm sure your client won't mind helping us with our enquiries.'

The two men exchanged a look, but she didn't wait for an answer. 'Where were you on the night of 8th November, Mr Gundersen?'

'As my wife has no doubt told you, I was on my way to a conference in Norwich.' He leaned back, his hands resting lightly on the arms of the chair.

'Where were you planning on staying in Norwich?'

'I've forgotten,' he said. 'I'd have to check my plans.'

'Forgotten, Mr Gundersen?' said Anita. 'That seems very unlike you.'

'Mr Gundersen has said he'll need to check. We'll get back to you,' intoned Peter Robinson.

'Indeed,' Anita replied. 'Tell me, where were you when you decided to return home. Just so we can check your journey times with ANPR.'

Gundersen shrugged.

'Have you forgotten that too?' Anita raised her eyebrows. 'Not to worry, even if I have to trawl through the ANPR evidence myself, I will find out. Perhaps you can recall which route you took?'

Gundersen glanced at his solicitor, who merely raised his eyebrows. 'M11 and A11,' Gundersen finally grunted.

'There, now that wasn't hard, was it?' Anita smiled at the two men. I knew that smile. She'd trapped him.

CHAPTER FORTY-SEVEN

Lily

Cerys and I were asked to stay in the interview room after Blaine and Jones left. Achy from sitting so long in one place, I began to pace. Cerys bought us a beverage from the vending machine. I had no idea if it was tea or coffee. For all I knew it could have been soup, but it was warm and I gulped it down.

'I was wondering what other evidence they have on me,' I said to her. 'I'm sure it was Topher who killed Stephanie, I just have no idea how I'd prove it.'

'He'll have to prove he has an alibi,' Cerys said. 'He told you he was going to a conference, but was there a conference? You knew it was a lie and the police will see right through it.'

'I hope you're right,' I said.

When DI Blaine came back to the interview room she looked pleased with herself; I was sure this wasn't a good sign for me.

'You'll be delighted to know, Mrs Gundersen, that the

preliminary forensics have come back from Ms Silcott's residence,' she said. 'The flat had been wiped clean of all prints...'

'So, I'm free to go?' I said.

'No, whatever gave you that idea?' replied DI Blaine. She looked genuinely surprised. 'It simply means you wiped down after you killed her.'

'Why on earth would I kill my best friend?'

'Because she was having an affair with your husband?' DI Blaine's voice sounded as if she were explaining to a particularly stupid child.

'But like I said, I'd asked her to do that so I could find out what he was up to. I needed someone to get close to him.'

'And you expect me to believe that?' Blaine sat back in her chair, clearly bemused.

'I know how crazy it sounds, I really do, but it's the truth.'

'Well, we are undertaking a search of your home now,' DI Blaine told me.

'But it will be too late. Topher will have destroyed everything.'

DI Blaine suddenly smiled and it lit up her face. 'No,' she said. 'He was arrested for attempting to assault an officer. He's had no chance to move or destroy anything since you were arrested.'

Relief overwhelmed me, and I buried my face in my hands for a moment. Then a thought occurred. 'He's here?' I asked. 'What about my children? Who's looking after them?'

'Your husband is here now. We waited until your housekeeper could get to the house to look after the children.'

'Thank you.' I slumped in my chair. All energy drained from me. I saw no end to this nightmare.

Denise leaned forward towards me. Her voice was softer and I wonder if this was the good cop, bad cop ploy Topher had told me about in the past.

'Where is your husband likely to hide things?' she said.

'I've already told you that. He has a few favourite spots for hiding my things,' I said. 'On top of the cupboards in the kitchen. There's a tall bookcase in the sitting room, that's another. The freezer. He likes to drop things down the backs of cupboards where they may have fallen naturally. Or he pulls a drawer out and hides something at the bottom of the unit. So you can't find the necklace, say, until you've pulled all the drawers out.' I gulped, tears slipping down my cheeks. Cerys passed me a tissue and I wiped my eyes frantically. My anger was growing; I had been too stupid for too long.

'And what about the password for your husband's computers?'

'I'm not sure about the laptop. It might be the same as his big computer.' I wrote the password down in her notebook. She took it back and marked a large lazy Z underneath. Blocking out the rest of the page.

Suddenly, the interview was over and I was free to go home. Cerys stayed with me for a while.

'This is good news,' she said. 'At least they're not holding you on remand whilst they carry out investigations. You can go home to your children.'

'And Topher? What about him?

She gave me a short nod. Her lips were in a tight line. 'We have to show he is the killer rather than you,' she said finally. 'That means looking at phone records and getting copies of CCTV of the possible journeys he could have taken from Ms Silcott's flat to your home. It's going to take some time and you will need to be brave whilst we do. I will keep hassling the police and I will get my own people onto it, but it's not a quick job.'

'Are they likely to release him as well?'

'Probably,' she said. 'Have you got somewhere safe to go to?'

I thought about Fran's suggestion of the refuge. If I went to my mother, she'd only tell Topher. 'I'll call my father,' I said. 'Perhaps I can stay with him.

'Just let me know what your plans are and you'll need to keep the police informed.'

'Thanks,' I said. We shook hands and I strolled outside. It was already tomorrow. The sky glowing pink with the rising sun. I had been in the station overnight. My clothes were crumpled; I was sure I smelled rank, but I did manage to hail a cab to take me home.

Of course, I had no keys or remote to open the gates and had to press the speakerphone. Heather opened the gates and was on the steps with my purse when the cab pulled up at the front door.

'You look all in,' she said. She gave me my purse and, cab driver recompensed, I followed her into the house.

Darcy was in her playpen with a tea set, happily serving tea to her dolls. She screamed with delight when she saw me and demanded to be picked up. I bent over and hauled her out of the pen, burying my nose into her soft hair, breathing in the delicious baby smell. She pushed me away.

'Mummy smell bad,' she said, wriggling to get away.

'Thanks, baby,' I said, and swapped her with Heather for a very welcome cup of coffee.

'There's plenty of hot water,' Heather said, tactfully.

I pulled a section of my roll neck sweater closer. I didn't smell good. 'I think I'd better take a shower.' I took my coffee up to the first-floor landing and took fluffy towels from the airing cupboard.

Once I was in the family bathroom, I locked the door behind me before stripping off my clothes and stepping into the shower. It was bliss. Warm water flowed down my face and I shampooed my hair three times to eradicate the stale stench of the police station off my body.

I scrubbed my skin until it was red and sore. I turned off the water and began drying myself. I froze when I heard Heather talking to a man downstairs. I crept to the bathroom door, unlocked it, and opened it a crack. Silence. I heard the gates open and rushed down the hallway to the window, which overlooked the drive. The postman. My heart's pounding slowed, and I tiptoed along the hallway back to the guest room. Once dressed, I went downstairs to the kitchen.

I stuck my head in the fridge and jumped out of my skin when I heard movement behind me. Heather gave me a nervous smile and Darcy clung to her leg.

'Why don't you have a lie down after you've eaten?' she said. 'I was going to take Darcy with me to pick James up from school in any case.'

Tiredness washed over me, a tsunami of exhaustion, and I hung onto the fridge door for support.

'That's a good idea,' I said. I flung a few bits of ham, cheese, tomatoes and olives onto a plate, poured a glass of sparkling water and headed upstairs. I sat at the dressing table to eat. I could scarcely keep my eyes open, eating only half the food but drinking all the water.

I slipped off my jeans and got into bed.

CHAPTER FORTY-EIGHT

Lily

I woke when I heard the front door slam. Heather back from the school run? But before I could look at the bedside clock, I heard his footsteps running upstairs.

He ran to the master suite and then his steps thudded down to the first floor and he rattled the door handle.

'Lily,' he hissed. 'I know you're in there. We need to talk. Stephanie's been killed. I need to know what you said to the police.'

I sat on the bed, arms clasped around my legs, rocking myself backwards and forwards. How was he free already? Denise had promised me he'd be at the police station overnight. I needed to tell Heather to take the children to her home. They'd be safer there.

'Lily, open the door. I'm not angry with you, but we do need to talk.'

'You killed her,' I screamed. I squeezed my eyes shut, hand clasped over my mouth.

'Don't be silly, Lily. Why on earth would I do that?' he

whispered. 'Anyway, I was on my way to a conference. You know that. Open the door, Lily. We can't talk like this.'

'You'll hurt me,' I whimpered, still rocking myself.

'I won't, I promise I won't hurt you,' he said. 'Come on darling, open the door.'

I eased myself off the bed and padded to the door. He rattled the handle once more and I jumped away again.

'Come on darling, open the door. I know you want to. I heard the bed as you got off it. You're just on the other side of this door, aren't you? Just open it up, there's a good girl.' His voice was soft, smooth and hypnotic.

As if I were in a trance, I placed my hand on the key and unlocked the door. I opened it. Topher was standing in the hallway, looking exhausted and dishevelled.

'There you are, my darling,' he said. 'I just wanted to talk to you about your chat with the police.' He stepped into the room and I moved backwards until I collided with the bed. He was standing over me.

I trembled, hanging my head, trying to make myself smaller — a smaller target — but to my surprise he dropped to his knees in front of me.

'Lily, talk to me. Tell me what you told the police.'

'Nothing,' I whispered. 'I don't know anything so I couldn't tell them anything.'

'That's a good girl,' he whispered. 'Let's make sure you keep it like that. If they had anything on me, they wouldn't have let me go. If they talk to you again, stick to the truth. I went to a conference. I missed you and so I came home early.'

'Yes, Topher,' I said.

'Now stand up and give me a hug. We've both had a terrible shock.'

I stood before him, trembling; my body stiffened when he placed his arms around me.

'For God's sake, Lily,' he said. 'Lighten up. After all, you chose to stay with me. If you'd wanted to leave, you only had to say.'

Liar, I said under my breath. I thought back to the last time I'd tried to leave him and how that had worked out for me.

My mother had the children for the weekend. Topher was away at another of his conferences and it was time for me to go. I'd not even told my mother what my plans were. I didn't dare. I knew she would side with him. She always did.

'Parents should stay together for the sake of the children,' she always told me. 'You've got a good man there. A good earner. You need that now you're totally useless.'

I used to hang my head in shame. Stephanie told me I should focus less on being ashamed and more on being angry at my mother's hypocrisy. But I chose not to cause a fight; I knew I would need her help in the coming weeks, so I simply nodded. I would rarely remind her that I too was a child from a broken home.

My suitcase packed, I made my way downstairs and into the waiting taxi. I didn't relax until I was on the train to Manchester. Topher would never think about Manchester. I'd never played there. I had no friends there. No connections with the city at all. It was a perfect choice.

Another taxi took me the short distance from the station to the hotel. Once settled in my room, I called mother to see how the children were. As I had guessed, they were fine with Granny, and James asked if they could stay a few more days.

'We'll see, darling,' I told him. 'You really should be back at nursery on Monday.'

'Okay mummy,' he said. 'Bye.' He put the phone down. I was on

the point of calling again when there was a knock on the hotel room door. Excellent, room service.

I should have used the spy hole. No sooner than the door was slightly ajar it thumped into me, knocking me backwards where I sprawled on the carpet. Topher stood over me. My mind raced. How had he found me? How had he found me so quickly?

He slammed the door behind him and picked me up by the collar of my blouse. I heard the material rip as he flung me onto the bed.

'Where do you think you're going?' he whispered.

I hated it when he masked his anger with quiet and calm. It was always worse than when he shouted. I sneaked a look at the doorway, but seeing my glance, he laughed.

'You'll not make it,' he sneered. He stepped closer to the bed and I curled into a ball. He grabbed my hair and pulled me closer.

'I promise I won't mark your face,' he said.

But it was a lie as usual. Throwing me across the room was his favourite game, and it was impossible not to hit my head on some piece of furniture as he did so. If I fainted, he would wait until I was conscious before resuming the beating. He kicked me in the stomach and I curled up again, so he kicked me on my back. Worried about my kidneys, I allowed myself to go limp. Bored with my lack of response, he knelt beside me. Taking my hand in his, he squeezed my fingers until I howled in agony and begged him to stop. That was what he wanted. Begging. Pleading.

'You're disgusting,' he said, finally. 'Go and shower and then I'll take you home.'

Pushing myself from the floor, I used a chair to help me stand. I knew better than to ask for hospital treatment. I also knew the children would be getting their extra week at Granny's after all.

CHAPTER FORTY-NINE

Lily

I returned to the master suite that night. I had begged Topher to leave the house, to leave us alone, but he refused. He threatened to hurt Darcy if I kept arguing with him and if I didn't return to our bedroom. Trapped once more, I had no choice but to obey him.

Heather stayed over. She was in one of the spare rooms on the floor below.

I shuddered as he watched me undress. I stared at the wall, trying to pretend he wasn't there. Slipping under the duvet, I tucked it tightly around my body, knowing deep down it was a pathetic armour. Thankfully, he didn't touch me, leaving for work early before the children had woken. I stayed in my bed until I heard the front door slam and the small side gate slide closed. He was gone.

I swept back the duvet and went for a shower. As I towelled myself dry, I stared out of the window at Topher's garden office, wondering what the police had taken away and what they had left.

No matter. I had plans of my own today. I emptied my underwear and some clothes into a suitcase and dragged it down to a guest room on the floor below. To hell with Topher! He wasn't going to make me share his bed ever again. Once I'd unpacked, I peeked into the guest room next door and put on the electric blanket to air the bed. It didn't really need it. Part of the renovations had been insulating the house fully and putting individual thermostats in the bedrooms. I just hoped Topher didn't have any of his cameras in here. If he did, he was in for a shock.

I closed the door, meaning to collect fresh bedding from the airing cupboard, but the children were stirring. I went to Darcy's door; she was still dozy and sleepily sucking her thumb. James called for me.

'Coming, sweetheart,' I said. I stepped into his room, looked around for the camera, and once I'd found it I moved it to face the wall. *See how you like that!* I was pleased at this new, determined Lily. I only wish I'd found her before now.

'Ready for breakfast?' I said.

He nodded and held his arms out to me. I knelt by the bed and gave him a big hug, pulling him into a sitting position.

'Come on, easy day today. Breakfast first and wash later.'

He nodded and padded his way to the door and downstairs. I noticed how adept he was with the stairgate now. Perhaps he could show our new houseguest how to operate it?

I went to Darcy again. She sat in her little bed, rubbing her eyes. I picked her up and we trundled downstairs to breakfast. Later today I planned to find all the cameras and put them out of action.

Throughout the rest of the morning, my pulse raced. I was a little dizzy and was unable to stop grinning. Heather kept asking what the matter was, but I wanted to keep it a surprise. At noon, the bell rang. I ran to the communication panel. He was here. Through his windscreen he looked older and more tired than I remembered, but it was him.

My father.

I pressed the button and flew down the steps to greet him.

Heather took Darcy to the park and I promised her that my father and I would pick up James from school.

Once the front door clicked shut, we sat at the breakfast bar — strangers.

I clasped my hands together and then we both said sorry, in unison. Hugging each other, it was the ice breaker we needed.

'I'm sorry I stayed away,' he said.

'I'm sorry I made it hard for you.'

'Did you get my letters?'

'No, I didn't get anything. Mummy told me there were no letters. Where did you send them?'

'To your Mum at first, and then when I got the address here, I sent letters to this address. But those were always returned to me.' He stared at me. 'I can't believe she didn't give you your letters.'

'I got nothing,' I said.

He went out into the hallway and there was a click as he opened his suitcase. He brought in a sheaf of papers and handed them to me. 'I typed some of the more recent ones,' he said. 'I've printed them off. The ones that were sent back to me, I kept. But not all the ones I sent to your mother's address came back... I suppose those are lost.' His light brown eyes were bright with tears.

'I asked Mum about them, but she said you weren't interested in us anymore.'

'That's not true, Lily. You have to believe me.' He squeezed my hands until I yelped. 'What happened?' he said, holding my hands gently in his. 'Tell me?'

I gulped. No one had asked me that question for so long. For a moment I thought about the usual story I gave, but this time I decided to tell the truth. 'Come into the sitting room,' I said. 'It'll be more comfortable.'

I sat back in the armchair, closed my eyes and I began to tell him the story as it happened. I was transported back to the home we rented in Arlington. I had not long learnt that I was pregnant. I was excited — thrilled — at the thought of being a mother.

Topher was with me on the trip. He was between cases and decided to take some time off. He too was thrilled we were going to be parents. 'You'll have to stop working, of course,' he said.

'Well, yes, for a while. And then I'll go back to work, perhaps with less international travel,' I replied.

Topher frowned. 'No, you will need to give up work. I want you to be a stay-at-home mother.'

I laughed. I honestly laughed. 'Topher, do you know how hard I have worked to get where I am? Do you know how many hours of practice, night after night, day after day, weekend after weekend, I've done? Entire weekends practising, missing parties and teenage fun, just so I could have this career.'

'Yes, but the baby, it won't be good for the baby.' He frowned, and I was astounded that we'd not had this discussion before.

'I will go back to work after a few months. I will stay at home with the baby for a while, a year if needs be, and then I will need to go back to work. With what you earn, with what I earn, we can afford a live-in nanny.'

'I don't want my child being brought up by a nanny!'

'Topher, I understand and know it was difficult for you when you lost your parents, but it will be okay.' I found I was whispering, trying to placate him.

'No. Not at all. I am not having my child brought up second hand.'

'It won't be second hand. I'll just work in the UK. I'll be home most nights.'

'Most nights!' He was incandescent with rage. His fists clenched by his side.

'Yes, I'll be home most nights.'

'No, no, you're going to be a stay-at-home mother. That's the end of the matter. That's what I want you to do.'

'Topher, it's the twenty-first century. You can't tell me what to do.'

'Can't I?' he said.

I had never seen such a look in his eye. I was terrified. I stepped back. I found the handle of the back door behind me. I opened it and I ran out into the night. Stupid thing to do. The storm had just started. Leaves, twigs and even branches whirled around me, some of them hitting me as they hurtled past. We'd been told tornadoes were possible, but we'd not experienced them on our little farm. I hesitated and Topher caught up with me, shook me by the shoulders and turned me around to face him.

'You need to come back inside now. It's not safe out here.'

'I know, I know, I'm coming.' Yet my feet seemed resistant to the idea of walking back into the house. 'I'm coming, and then we need to talk about the baby. I need to go back to work, Topher. I can't stay at home. I need it. My mind needs it. My soul needs it. Being a violinist is who I am.'

He sighed, his expression unreadable. My breathing ragged, I struggled to get away, but he was too strong and my knees buckled beneath me. Despite the chilly evening, I was sweating. Rivulets of cold perspiration coursed down my torso under my blouse, collecting at my waistband. His lips moved, but all I could hear was my heartbeat trashing in my ears. Topher grabbed my hand, clutching it in his. Bringing my right hand up to his mouth, he covered it with kisses, and then he bent my index finger back until it snapped. One by one, he snapped my other fingers. His ice-blue eyes were calm as I screamed in agony. I tried to snatch my hand back. Dizzy and nauseous, I wrenched at my hand. Black spots formed before my eyes, my surroundings blurry as I screamed for my lost future. My hopes. All of my dreams. As I screamed, he broke all the fingers on my left hand as well. I told him that he had to take me to the hospital, that I needed some medical attention, and he just laughed.

'No,' he said. 'If I take you now they'll see what I've done. They'll know what I've done.'

'Topher, it doesn't matter. I won't press charges. Just get me some medical attention. I need to go to hospital,' I heard my voice stay calm. All those years of stilling my queasy stomach before a performance aided me now. Helping me keep calm despite the pain I was in. 'Please, call an ambulance for me.' I heard how I was pleading with him, but it seemed to have no impact. I didn't know this man before me. He was not my husband. My loving caring husband.

'No, I can't. I can't let people see what I've done.' He looked down at the ground, too ashamed to face me and face what he'd done to me.

In the background I heard the door of the root cellar

rattling. It seemed to give Topher an idea. 'Come on,' he said, and he dragged me towards where the root cellar was. He opened one of the doors, lifting it, powering against the wind.

'Put your hands there,' he said, when he'd lifted one of the doors.

'What?' I gasped.

'Put your hands there. If you do this, then I'll take you to a hospital.' He was perfectly calm. As if this were a normal conversation. 'You need to have splinters in the wounds.'

I was faint from the pain in my hands. I knew I needed to see someone. I knew I needed painkillers and I knew I needed my fingers strapped, but there was no way I was going to do what he told me.

'No!' I yelled. 'No way!' I shuffled away from the root cellar doors, digging my heels into the ground to propel me away from the cellar.

He grabbed my wrist, twisting it and forcing me towards the doors. Topher lined both my hands up against the edge of one of the doors of the root cellar. I tried to pull away and again and he kicked me in the ribs. Breathless and broken, I lay on the ground, watching the scene as if it were happening to someone else. Then he dropped the other door down on my hands. As I screamed in pain, he raised the door up and allowed it to fall on my hands again. He raised it a third time and I scuttled away, my lungs heaving, wincing with the pain of my bruised ribs. I squeezed my eyes shut to push the pain away, but it wouldn't shift. I opened my eyes; my hands, my fingers were all mangled. They didn't belong to me, but they did, because that's where the torment was coming from.

Topher scooped me up in his arms, placed me in the car, strapped me in and drove at top speed to the local emergency room. When we got there he yelled for help and I was put on a trolley. I was almost faint from the pain. A mask was put over my face and I smelt the sweet, cool oxygen and then the gas and then, blessed oblivion.

I realised that my eyes had been closed throughout the retelling of the whole story. When I opened them again, my father sat in front of me, tears rolling down his face.

'I want to kill him,' he said. 'I'm going to do everything in my power to help you.'

CHAPTER FIFTY

Lily

After I told my father the story, he went to his room to unpack. When he came down again he wanted to take a walk, so I gave him directions to the hill and the code for the gate. I picked up his wad of letters and began to read. The first one I opened had been opened and resealed with Sellotape.

> *Darling Lily,*
>
> *I'm so proud of you. Of course, I knew that you'd get an A star for music but in English Lit and Geography too!! Well done, enclosed is twenty pounds so you can buy yourself something nice.*
>
> *Much love*
>
> *Dad xx*

I looked in the envelope, there was no sign of any money. The letter had been sent to mummy's address. At least that explained the Sellotape. The next envelope I picked up was stiffer. A card. More Sellotape.

Darling Lily,

    Happy eighteenth birthday. I hope to hear from you soon.
    Lots and lots of love
    Dad xx

Dad had kept the envelopes in order of when he'd sent them. It built a picture of my past life that mummy had taken from me. None of the letters were long, but each one had gone unanswered and still he kept trying. All along she'd told me he didn't care.

Unbidden tears tracked down my cheeks and the words blurred in front of me. Congratulations on my A levels, getting into a good university, getting my degree, the job with the orchestra. He'd missed nothing, forgotten nothing. There was a card for every birthday, sometimes mentioning how much money he'd enclosed, sometimes not, but regardless there was never any money in the envelope. Mummy must have taken it all.

There was even a card for mine and Topher's wedding and a letter afterwards.

Darling Lily,

    I am so sorry about what happened at the wedding. I had hoped your mother would be able to let bygones be bygones, but I was mistaken. I left early so that we would not ruin the rest of your day. I can only apologise that it meant I could not say goodbye to you.

    I hope you and Topher will be very happy, happier than your mother and I at least.

    Lots and lots of love

And all the very best for the future,
Dad xxx

I stared up at the ceiling, blinking. Topher and Dad had taken an instant dislike to each other, which had not helped matters at all. Mum had just created an even worse atmosphere, especially when she'd started calling him names before we'd even sat down for the wedding breakfast.

I'd fled to the toilet and Stephanie had come to comfort me. It had been the worst and most embarrassing day of my life, up until that point.

CHAPTER FIFTY-ONE

Denise

As hard as I tried, I couldn't rid my mind of the bleak look Lily had given me as she'd left the interview room. I knew I deserved it. I'd let her down. Nothing that proved her story had come to light yet, but I was still hoping on something from the mobile phone investigations.

Even though I'd seen her with her phone when she'd come to report Stephanie missing, DI Blaine refused to accept it as evidence. She was convinced the phone Lily had with her was the clone and the one we'd found at the flat was Lily's real phone.

'She's playing you for a fool, DJ,' she told me frequently. 'Don't make me think I made a mistake allowing you to stay on the case.'

Part of me thought Anita Blaine was right, but then there was something nagging away at me that told me Lily wasn't a liar. Stephanie had thought the world of her, and I knew Steph wouldn't have put up with a liar.

Now I had another mystery to solve though — how and why was Stephanie's phone at Lily's house in a safe she said she didn't know existed.

There were too many things that didn't make sense, and I found I couldn't see my way through the wood clearly. It was late, I needed some downtime, and I was starving.

On the way home I stopped at the takeaway and picked up my usual: korma, pilau and a naan. I grabbed a couple of Kingfisher beers to wash it down and headed for my flat.

I ate out of the cartons — it saved on washing up — and swigged the beer from the bottle whilst I studied my personal case board. There were some loose ends I hadn't tracked down yet. I didn't know if I'd have time or even if they were relevant any longer, but I made a note to see the headmaster at Lily's old school and also to check if I could find out how the lorry driver from the accident was faring. I had a hunch that everything was connected but I couldn't see how. Or at least not so far.

The following morning, I headed onto the North Circular to Lily's old school. I thought back to the accident and how frail she'd looked when I'd first met her. I wondered if it had been a suicide attempt. A suspicion that had become stronger once I'd met her husband. Despite his undoubted good looks, I wasn't blind; there was something about him that reminded me of my mother's third husband.

I flashed my identity card at the school secretary. She sniffed in a manner I found irritating and offered to find out if David Jacobs, the headmaster, was free.

'This is a police matter,' I told her. 'He needs to make time to see me or I shall arrest him for wasting police time.'

My threat worked. She gave me a horrified stare before scuttling to his office. He followed her back to reception and took me into his inner sanctum.

'How can I help you, Miss Jones?' he asked. I shook his hand and instantly regretted it. His was the damp, limp handshake reminiscent of a dead jellyfish.

'It's Detective Constable Jones, not Miss,' I replied. I hated men who tried to demean me, but I needed information from him and I kept my temper under control. 'I need to talk to you about Lily Gundersen.'

'Oh dear, yes, Lily. We were all very sad to hear what happened to her,' he said. 'She was a good teacher... on those occasions she chose to turn up, of course.'

'How do you mean?' I sat in the armchair by his desk, watching him leave finger marks on the manila folder bearing Lily's name. Why was he so nervous?

'Well, her husband often phoned up or she'd email to say she wasn't fit for work. It had become quite a problem. I think we would have had to let her go in the end.' He brought a handkerchief to his mouth and dabbed at his moist lips.

I tried not to squirm in my chair. It was all I could do to stay in the same room as him. 'You sacked Lily in the morning,' I said.

'Err, yes,' he began. I saw he had become very uncomfortable in his own chair.

'I know we spoke about this over the phone in June, but can you take me through that conversation one more time?'

'I had been advised she had slapped one of the older boys,' he told me.

'Which boy? Can I interview him?'

'No.' He sat forward in his chair. 'That won't be necessary. The charges were dropped.'

'Yes, you mentioned that in our phone conversation. How soon were the charges dropped? As soon as they were made or after Lily's accident?'

'I… I can't quite remember,' he said, twisting his handkerchief in his hands.

'Try,' I demanded.

'Later that week,' he said, finally. 'We discovered the accusations were groundless. The boy had been bribed to make the whole tale up. It was a pack of lies.'

'When did you tell Lily this?'

'I'm not sure,' he said. 'A little while after the accident, I think.'

'Let me help you out,' I said. 'You and I had a telephone conversation shortly after the accident. You told me the charges were being dropped and I asked you to come into the station to make a statement. You've never bothered to make the statement. I also asked for the name of the boy. You've failed to provide that too. May I also presume that you've not undertaken any investigation into the bribery allegations either?' I glared at him but, since he could not or would not meet my eyes, the effort was wasted.

'Mr Jacobs,' I continued, 'if you fail to cooperate with me now, I really will arrest you for perverting the course of justice.'

'There's no need to take that tone, young lady,' he told me.

I stood, forced myself to step closer, and towered over him in his chair. 'I think there's every need, Mr Jacobs. Now, the boy's name?'

Once I had extracted the information I needed, I called the boy's parents and explained the situation to them. The school secretary arranged a room for us to meet.

When the boy's mother arrived, the fumes from her cloud of expensive perfume performed an effective choke hold. I grabbed a tissue from my pocket to cover my nose and listened to her exclamations that her son was entirely innocent. '*He's* the victim here!' she screeched.

'Mrs Wilson,' I said sternly. 'Your son has made false accusations against a teacher. All I want to do is get to the bottom of it. I need to know who asked your son to make the accusations and why. It's not hard.'

It didn't take long to crack the boy's story.

'I don't know who he was,' Simon muttered mulishly. 'He just gave me a wad of cash and told me what to say. Mrs Gundersen had said I couldn't be in the concert, so I was pretty pissed off with her.'

'Simon, language,' his mother said.

Simon glowered at her but gave me a good description of the man, and I made Mrs Wilson promise to bring her son to the police station to look through some mug shots.

When Simon Wilson and his mother arrived to look at the photographs it didn't take them long to pick out one of our local frequent fliers. A petty thief called Mark Brown.

Simon told me he had been approached in the café after school and given one hundred pounds in cash to make up the story to get Lily Gundersen sacked. He said he'd regretted it afterwards but only told the truth after his mother had found the money in his sock drawer.

I tried not to laugh at his pathetic hiding place, especially since his mother was probably still putting his socks away for him. However, I agreed with DI Blaine to let him off with a caution. It was not his fault she'd crashed on the way home after her conversation with the head.

But although I had the next clue in the trail, I had no idea why a petty thief would get involved.

CHAPTER FIFTY-TWO

Lily

My father and I spent some time in the afternoon finding and moving the cameras. There were some that were too high to reach, so we left them where they were.

Naturally, when he arrived home, Topher wasn't surprised that my father was there. No doubt his cameras had prewarned him. The two men greeted each other sullenly and dinner was a quiet, stilted affair. I went to bed early, sleeping in the guest room, and carried on reading my father's letters.

Topher came and rattled on the door at midnight, but with my father in the next room, he soon left.

Dad came with me the next morning to visit Cerys at her offices. Topher's solicitor had contacted her. He was considering divorcing me and applying for full custody of the children.

'He can't!' I hissed at Cerys.

'No, he can't,' she assured me. 'He can apply of course, but the family court usually finds in favour of the mother. The one time misogyny works in the woman's favour.'

'Great,' I said. 'Do you have any good news for me?'

'I do, actually,' she said. 'DC Jones let me know that the assault charges have been dropped. Apparently, your accuser was bribed to accuse you.'

'Yes, they told me the charges had been dropped, but bribery? What the hell? Who would do that?' I jumped out of my chair and began pacing the office.

'DC Jones has got a lead on someone,' she said. 'His name is Mark Brown, but she can't work out why he'd be involved. He's just a petty thief.'

I laughed out loud. 'He might be, but do you know who his defence barrister is?' I said with glee. I glanced down at my father with a grim smile. 'Topher is his barrister. He's got a file on this Mark Brown in his office. Apparently Mr Brown is good at cyber-security. It might even be him who fixed up the cameras in my house.'

Cerys sat with her mouth open. 'I must call DC Jones and let her know as soon as you leave,' she said. 'She's working hard for you. I've not seen her do this for anyone else. She's got a reputation for being a good copper, but usually she pulls together the evidence and hands it to the Crown Prosecution Service. I've never seen her go above and beyond like this. It's rare. Make the most of it.'

'She believes I'm innocent?' I said. I was surprised myself. I thought she'd blame me for Stephanie's death. Perhaps I did have a guardian angel after all?

'It certainly looks to me as if she's on your side. She was waiting on the lorry driver regaining consciousness. He's back home now and when Denise speaks to him we hope to get him to testify on your behalf; we might even be able to get them to focus on another suspect.' Cerys gave me a tight smile. 'Don't give up hope, Lily. We are fighting for you.'

'Any news on the CCTV?' I said.

Cerys shook her head. 'The systems have been wiped. It's as if that day never existed.'

'That doesn't make sense,' my father said, folding his arms. 'Were the cameras down?'

'No,' said Cerys.

'And what about the cameras on the other side of the carriageway? Did they record anything?' he said.

Cerys shook her head. 'They were out of action too.'

'That's very convenient for someone isn't it?' he said. 'Lily, think about it.' He turned to me. 'You were accused of assaulting a student, and now you find out that someone bribed the kid, that someone being known to your husband. What are the chances Topher could suppress evidence?'

'But how would he do that?' asked Cerys. 'In any case, he's a barrister. He's sworn to uphold the law.'

'There was a list,' I said. 'A list of names. I took a photo. It was stuffed into the Mark Brown folder that Topher had in his office. The folder could still be there or the photo could still be on my phone. Turning to Cerys, I said, 'You need to get Denise to check.'

Cerys nodded. 'As far as I know, both your phones are still with forensics. I'll get Denise up to speed.'

'Thanks,' I said. 'Sorry, you said "both my phones"? I only have one.'

'The police found two,' Cerys assured me. 'One at Stephanie's flat and one at your home.'

'That's impossible,' I said. I turned to my father.

'Have you lost your phone for any period of time?' he said.

I sat shaking my head at how stupid I'd been. 'I lost it

back in the summer. It was in my handbag in the evening. After Topher got home.'

'That's when he could have had it cloned,' said Cerys.

'I see,' I said. 'So Topher cloned my phone and that's how he's been hacking my emails. It's also the only way it can have been in two places at once. What about tracking the phone? That can be done nowadays, can't it?'

'There are, but it takes time,' she said.

'Well, at least I won't be kicking my heels in prison,' I sighed.

I trailed after my father to the underground station. My mind was racing. Cloned phones, missing CCTV, cameras in the house. Could Topher be behind all of this? On one level, it made no sense. Topher made a fuss about programming the Sky box. But on another level, it did. If he knew what he wanted done, he could pay someone to do it for him.

'Lily!' I whirled around. Was that Topher? How had he found me? I pulled my coat collar up around my neck, but it wasn't the weather causing my chills.

I turned in the direction of the underground station to see my father waving at me. 'I thought I'd lost you,' he said, when I caught him up. He raised his gloved hand to my cheek and I flinched. 'I hate him for what he's done to my girl.' He tucked my arm in the crook of his elbow and escorted me down the stairs to the trains.

Dad agreed to attend Stephanie's funeral with me. Stephanie was estranged from her parents and her sister lived in America, but she needed family at her funeral. We'd always been as close as sisters. I dressed in dark clothing, hearing

Stephanie's voice tease me about how washed out black made me look. I dabbed at the tears and checked my make-up.

Downstairs, Topher hooted the horn of his BMW. It was time to go. I thought about Stephanie during the journey. I had no desire to talk to Topher, and my father was silent on the back seat. Of all my friends, Stephanie was the only one who'd stayed close. Everyone else from university days had eventually abandoned me. And look how I had repaid her loyalty! By getting her killed. I blinked away the tears that were threatening to form. I raised my head, partly to look at the pale grey sky through the car window and partly to ensure Topher didn't see me cry. I knew he would have something sarcastic to say.

Eventually we arrived and Dad held the door open for me. Topher came around the car towards us and I flinched as, unexpectedly, he kissed me on the cheek.

Topher moved away and waited outside with some men who I assumed were from Stephanie's office, and I followed Dad into the crematorium. I stood halfway down and, as the music started, I saw Topher bearing Stephanie's coffin down the aisle. I almost choked and Dad patted my hand, motioning at me to keep quiet. As the coffin was laid down and Topher took his seat at the front of the crematorium, I heard a rustle behind me. I half-turned and sneaked a look at the new arrival. Was this John, I wondered? He was smartly dressed in a suit and dark tie. His hair was neatly trimmed and I thought how good he and Stephanie would have looked together.

He returned my stare but, unlike everyone else who had looked at me today, his expression was not one of contempt or anger. It seemed as if he pitied me. I looked away, wondering if I had guessed his mood correctly. If I had encouraged his pity, then what more could he know? Did he know who really killed Stephanie? I was sure it was Topher, but Cerys assured me there wasn't enough evidence to link Topher. Personally, I wondered how hard DI Blaine had actually looked at Topher as a suspect. I was convinced she hadn't, certainly not once she had me in her cross hairs. I had to talk to Denise.

I saw her further down, a few rows away from the front. She was looking around at the other people there and I tried to catch her eye. I raised my hand and waved at her, but Dad batted my hands down.

'We'll talk to her later,' he whispered.

I sneaked another glance at John. He was staring at Topher. There was no pity, just puzzlement, and I wondered what he was thinking.

CHAPTER FIFTY-THREE

Lily

A few days after the funeral, Cerys asked me to come along to the police station with her to see Denise Jones.

Denise smiled at us both as we sat down. 'Thank you for the info on Mark Brown,' she said.

'It was nothing,' I said. 'How does it help my case?'

'I'm still working on it,' she said. 'But it's showing me there are links between you and Mark Brown which shouldn't exist.'

'Yes, I know, but thanks for checking up on them,' I said. A thought occurred. 'I don't suppose DI Blaine has changed her mind about me yet?'

'She still thinks you're guilty. I'm sorry,' Denise took a sip of the tea she'd been nursing. 'Who do you think it is?'

'I know it's Topher,' I said. 'He must have found out Stephanie was helping me. Can't you get his prints off her skin or something?'

'I think you've been watching too many American CSI programmes,' she laughed.

'Well, that's the reason I wiped everywhere down so carefully,' I said, resentfully.

'Don't even joke about it,' Denise said. 'It's not funny. DI Blaine would take that as a confession.'

'I'm not confessing to something I didn't do!' I hissed.

Denise seemed unperturbed. She pointed at my hands with her plastic cup. 'Tell me what happened,' she said.

I laughed bitterly. The topic of my hands had been avoided by everyone close to me for so many years, and yet here was second person asking the same question in just a short space of time.

I watched her face carefully as I repeated the events of that night exactly as I had told them to my father. Her expressions flicked from sympathy to horror to denial as I spoke. By the time I'd finished, tears shone in her dark eyelashes. She pulled her sleeve down and brushed at her eyes.

'I'm sorry,' she said. 'Why didn't you tell anyone? Why didn't you leave him?'

'He convinced everyone that I was a risk to myself and to the baby.' I shrugged. 'By the time we came home again, everyone knew I'd had a breakdown. No one would've believed my version of events.' I glimpsed at my hands folded in my lap. Perhaps I should have tried harder, but I had been on a roller coaster that was hard to jump off. Exhaustion from the birth, being a new mother, my injury, and the house. 'I was always so tired,' I said. I knew it was a lame excuse, but it was all I had.

We all sat in silence for a moment, lost in our own thoughts.

. . .

'Have you had any joy with finding the CCTV footage of the accident?' Cerys asked.

Denise shook her head. 'No, nothing.'

'And what about the list of names that I took a photo of? Have you tracked any of those down?'

Denise sat up in her chair. She frowned, shaking her head, but her eyes shone, her energy restored. 'Tell me more,' she said.

'I found a file,' I said. 'When I went into his garden office, there was a file on Mark Brown. In it, I found a scrap of paper with a few names and phone numbers on it. I didn't dare remove it from the file but I took a photo. Hopefully, he's not wiped that photo too.'

Denise looked at me sharply. 'I don't think we found anything like that,' she said.

'Mark can hack into CCTV systems.'

'But he wouldn't be able to hack into the Highways Agency.'

'Look, he's same guy who bribed the kid to say I'd molested him. I've no idea what else he's capable of.' I sat back and stared at the ceiling. Tears were forming and I tried to blink them away.

It was all coming together. I hoped I'd be the one to pull the thread which brought down Topher's tangled web of deceit and lies.

CHAPTER FIFTY-FOUR

Denise

I drove away from West Hampstead station, my thoughts focussed on Lily's dilemma and the possibility of her being Stephanie's murderer. The more I thought about it, the more I felt in my bones that Topher had killed Stephanie, but I had no idea how I was going to prove it. Topher's connection to Mark Brown was a good link, but it was still circumstantial. I needed to find a conclusive connection between the two men.

I made my way to the technicians' laboratory on the Brampton Road. After a few moments' wait, one of my favourites, Dan, walked into the reception area. He was a bespectacled man in his early thirties, but he'd retained a boyish enthusiasm when talking about his favourite subject — mobile phone technology. Fortunately, over the three years we'd worked together, I'd managed to train him to keep things simple for me.

'Nice to see you, DC Jones,' he said, blushing to the roots of his dark curly hair.

'I've told you, call me Denise, or DJ if you prefer. How long have we known each other now?' I smiled at him. *Jeez, was I flirting? I'd never been able to decide which I preferred — men or women.* 'DC Jones is far too formal.'

He blushed an even deeper shade of red. Close to vermilion, I thought, as he took me into the main lab.

He picked up a tray on which sat the two identical phones. 'I've downloaded all the data I could get off each phone. I've found something interesting in relation to the Pay-As-You-Go phone too.'

I looked up at him. He was grinning widely. 'Go on,' I said. 'I'm too exhausted to grill you.'

'The donor phone had a photograph of a list of names and numbers and — wait for it — the burner had dialled some of those numbers, but only one of them twice.'

'So not only do we have the number, but we also know who it belongs to?'

'Yep,' he said.

'And these two,' I said, pointing at the two matching phones.

'Definitely a donor phone and a clone,' he began. 'This one found at the victim's flat is the clone. And this one is the original.'

Lily wasn't lying after all!

Dan continued into some long explanation about how you need to have both the original and the copy phone together to clone one. 'It's not like in the old days when you could just copy a SIM. It's much more sophisticated now.'

'So Mrs Gundersen would have had to take her phone to be cloned by someone or be without it for a while, while someone else cloned it.' I said.

'Which scenario is most likely?' asked Dan, pushing his glasses up his nose. The lenses were covered with little smudges and, as if he could read my mind, he removed the spectacles and started cleaning them with a lens wipe taken from a tub on his workbench.

'I think she's quite used to losing things, so it could have been taken from her to be copied,' I replied, thinking about who could have done that. Only a few adults had access to the house to take her phone and return it. I didn't imagine it to be her housekeeper or her mother.

'Whoever did it was able to see all her texts, and see where she was at any time with the Find My Phone app. The clone also has an app installed to record all the phone calls made to or from the original,' said Dan. He showed me the app in practice, and I saw that whoever had this phone would know exactly where Lily was, and who she was talking to. It was the ultimate weapon in the stalking arsenal.

'Can we trace where the two phones were? I mean, if one is a clone of the other, do they show up in the same place all the time or not?'

'I can see you're getting good at this!' Dan grinned at me, and it gave me an unexpected shiver of pleasure. 'I've traced them both. They ping separately, dependent on their location. So they both show up at the same time, but they'd ping different masts.'

'Unless they were in the same area?'

'Correct,' Dan said. He pulled up a map on his screen and showed me where the clone was and where the donor was on different days.

'Can I get copies of these?' I asked.

'Of course,' Dan said.

'Good,' I replied. I was very interested to see where the clone phone appeared most often. Topher Gundersen's chambers.

· · ·

I left the lab and looked at my notebook. Topher Gundersen seemed to be the most likely suspect for cloning his wife's phone and, if that were the case, then he was the most likely suspect for leaving it in Stephanie Silcott's flat. Which would mean he must have been the last person to see Stephanie alive. Was he guilty of killing my friend? Or trying to kill his wife? I didn't know for certain, but I was determined to find out.

I called into the office and left a message for DI Blaine to keep her up to speed and then made my way to Tottenham to meet the lorry driver, Vinnie Craycroft.

The Craycroft's' terraced house was neat with a tiny front garden and pots of bright flowers behind the freshly painted fence. It had an air of hope in amongst the bleak gardens of its neighbours.

I sat in the front room and waited for Vinnie to arrive. I knew he hadn't worked since the day of the accident, and I wondered how much he blamed Lily Gundersen for his current predicament. He'd been in a coma for weeks after the accident and whilst I now had his statement, taken after he'd recovered from his coma, I needed to check how much of it he still stood by and what else he may be able to recall.

Vinnie lumbered into the room, clean jeans hanging loose around what had once been a plump belly. His brown belt was cinched as tight as it would go and, if I was not mistaken, there were some extra holes pierced into the leather.

I stood, but he waved me back down into the seat. 'What can I do for you, love?' he asked.

I accepted a cup of tea from Mrs Craycroft, and Vinnie and I relaxed together in what was clearly their front parlour. I'd not been in one since my grandmother was alive.

'The 4th of June,' I began. 'What can you tell me about that day?'

'Day of the accident, that was,' he said slowly. 'I was on the North Circular just minding me own. Lorry was empty and it was high winds that day, so the trailer was a bit skittish, always is when there's no load. This old Volvo overtook me, and it's just about to pull back in front of me when I saw a black Range Rover speeding up behind. I toots on me horn to warn the Volvo but it's too late, the four-by-four hits it. Bashes it into the barrier. I brake 'cos I think I'm gonna hit the Volvo but then the SUV smashes into it again. Must have caught it just in the sweet spot 'cos it went right over the barrier. But by then I'd got problems of me own. The cab started to tip. Me trailer had swung round, see, 'cos it was light, being empty. Me cab went right over, and I was hanging out me seatbelt while me lorry skidded along the road. Not sure what hit me.' He pulled back his overlong hair to show a scar that was still in the process of healing.

'Thank you. Is there anything else you remember about the black car?'

'Yeah, I saw it speeding off. Belching smoke, it was. Pretty sure it had taken a fair bit of damage itself. It was a Range Rover. Didn't get the number, sorry.'

I thanked Mr Craycroft for his time and left.

I really needed to get hold of the CCTV footage from the 4th of June.

CHAPTER FIFTY-FIVE

Denise

Back at the station, I retrieved my email from Dan. It was hardly a shock that the person called from Topher Gundersen's burner phone was known to us. Antonio Moretti, ironically also known as Tiny Tony, was six foot four and at least twenty stone. I obtained his address and called for backup — a police van and two large PCs.

Moretti lived in a tower block, where, to our surprise, the lift worked. I wondered how much that was down to Moretti's legendary "influence", as I couldn't imagine him walking up twelve flights of stairs. Sadly, his influence didn't stop the lift stinking of stale urine.

When he finally opened the door in response to my knocks, he filled the frame. I showed him my ID and he backed into the kitchen so that I could walk down the hallway to the main room. One PC followed behind me, the other behind Tiny.

'Tony, is this your phone number?' I asked, showing him the number I'd copied into my notebook.

'Nope, nuffin to do with me.' He lolled in his armchair. The noise from motor racing on the giant TV was deafening.

'Can you turn that down?' I asked.

He ignored me and one of the PCs strolled across the room and pulled the electric plug out.

'Oi, you can't do that!' he roared. He attempted to rise from his chair and was pushed firmly back into place by the other PC. Both officers stood over him, arms folded. They played regularly in the second row for the Met's rugby team. I was glad they were on my side.

I took my phone from my pocket and rang the number. A buzzing sound echoed from the kitchen and the second officer left the sitting room to find it. He handed it to me. 'So, Tony,' I said. 'This phone number that has nothing to do with you seems to ring through to this handset here. Is there anything you want to tell me about that?'

Moretti glared at me. I wasn't sure even a smile would look good on his face, and I was grateful not to be alone.

'Well?' I said.

'So,' he said. 'I must've made a mistake.'

'This is your phone?'

He shrugged. 'Suppose so.'

'There's only one number saved on it. Whose number is it?' I knew that it was the number of Topher Gundersen's burner phone, but I was keen to see what Tony would say. But he just shrugged again.

I signalled to my colleagues and one pulled handcuffs from his belt. Tony's eyes widened. 'Antonio Moretti, I am arresting you on suspicion of perverting the course of justice…'

'No!' The roar from Tony's mouth was deafening. He pushed the handcuffs away, causing the PC to stumble. His colleague was quicker and tackled Tony to the floor, but it wasn't until both PCs were astride his back that the big man calmed down. 'You can't arrest me,' he growled. 'I'm out on licence. If I get arrested, I go back inside.'

'Then tell me what I need to know, Tony. Simple as.'

Tony rested his forehead on the carpet and muttered, 'Okay.'

I signalled to the PCs to let him back up.

'It's in the kitchen,' he said.

I frowned.

'What you're after. It's in the cupboard hidden in a bag of Frosties.'

I left Tony and sprinted to the kitchen. I poured the Frosties over the counter-top and there, in a plastic bag, was a USB drive. I marched back into the sitting room. 'What's on here, Tony?'

'That CCTV footage you've been after. I was asked to take care of it; you know, get rid like, but I thought I'd hold on to it just in case. Glad I did now.'

I picked up my handbag and headed for the front door. 'What about him?' called the larger of the PCs.

'Bring him with us,' I said.

'You bitch,' yelled Tony. 'I thought you weren't going to arrest me.'

I popped my head back around the door. 'Oh, but I'm not arresting you Tony,' I said, giving him what I hoped was a winning smile. 'You're helping us with our enquiries.'

Back at the station I plugged the USB into my laptop, remembering to scan it for malware first. The laptop chose the video program and the CCTV footage began to play. I prepared myself for a long period of watching cars. As I watched the first few moments of the video, I rang DI Blaine to let her know what I'd found.

It seemed like hours later that I was still going through footage of cars on the North Circular. Even though I had narrowed it down to the correct time and place on the road there still seemed to be eons of footage to work through. Then I saw it. Craycroft's lorry pulled into view, the trailer swaying slightly as he'd mentioned. I saw Lily's old red Volvo overtake and pull alongside. As she indicated to pull back in, the black Range Rover shunted her from behind — once, and then a second time. I'd had the accident described to me, but this is the first time I'd seen it. Even the grainy video couldn't detract from the force which was propelled into Lily's Volvo. Sitting in my office chair I braced myself for the second collision and the following carnage.

I stopped the film, wound it back and zoomed in. Lily hadn't been lying about the Range Rover and it trying to push her off the road. It made it less likely that she was lying about the murder. Not out of the question, granted. But unlikely. At least I now had a registration number. I went to the rest room and made myself a fresh cup of tea before going back to my desk and logging onto the Police National Computer. I typed in the plate number. It was registered as being off the road, but with a few taps on the keyboard I found out who the last owners were. An exclusive car-hire company near Richmond. I noted down the address and headed back to my car.

I pulled into a visitors parking slot at the front of the single-storey building. It was slightly less exclusive looking than its address suggested. As I pushed open the door, I saw a metal box screwed to the wall with the word "keys" inscribed on it.

I smiled at the receptionist and flashed my warrant card. 'I'd like to see the manager, please' I told her.

'Sure,' she said. 'Can I ask what it's regarding?'

I nodded. 'Yep, a black Range Rover.'

'Okay, please wait here,' she said. She tapped a few keys on the computer and locked the cash desk before heading into the back office. When she returned, she was followed by a large florid looking man with thinning blond hair that hung down to his collar.

'What can I do for you, Officer?' he said. 'You want a coffee?'

I nodded and gave my order to the young woman. I followed him into the back office and sat in the chair he indicated. Once in possession of the vending machine coffee I opened my notebook.

'You hired out a black Range Rover earlier this year?' I said.

'We hire out a lot of Range Rovers. They're very popular.' He sipped his coffee and looked at me over the rim of his mug.

'You might remember this one,' I said. 'I gather it didn't return in quite the same condition as it was when it left the yard.'

He sighed and swore softly under his breath. 'Oh yeah, that one,' he said. 'Not gonna forget that one in a hurry. Complete write off it was. Had to send it to the crusher. But it was all covered by insurance.'

I cursed too. I supposed it was too much to hope the car could be examined forensically. 'Who returned the car?' I asked.

'Dunno,' he replied. 'Sneaky bastard returned it in the middle of the night. Dumped the keys in the box by the front door and buggered off.'

'You have CCTV though?' I knew they did. I'd already clocked the cameras as I walked in.

'Them was no good,' he said. 'He was all dressed in black with a baseball cap pulled down to hide his face. What I wouldn't do if I got 'old of the bastard.'

'I wouldn't advise taking the law into your own hands, sir,' I said, but I smiled at him to take the sting out of my words. 'Can you tell me how the hire was arranged?'

He pulled his keyboard towards him, tapped in a few numbers that I took to be his password and began peering at the screen. 'It were all done online,' he told me.

'So you have credit card details?' I could barely contain my excitement. I had an off-the-wall theory, but this evidence would tell me if I was right or not.

'I do that,' he said. 'Plus a copy of the guy's driving licence. Want me to print it all out for you?'

'That would be great,' I said. 'Thank you.'

I took the printed sheet from him, said my goodbyes, and left the coffee on his desk. Outside, I sat in my car and compared the credit card number on the printout with the number that Lily Gundersen had given me. They matched.

Lily Gundersen's credit card had been used to hire the car that had run her off the road.

I squinted at the photocopy of the driving licence. It wasn't truly clear; perhaps Dan or one of his team would be able to tidy it up for me. I knew it was a fake. I was convinced the person in the photo was Mark Brown.

Confirmation of the connection between the Gundersens and Brown. Just what I needed.

CHAPTER FIFTY-SIX

Lily

I heard the crunch of tyres on the gravel. Dad had offered to collect James from school today. With Christmas getting closer, it was good to have another pair of hands to help.

'Go on, straight into the kitchen,' Dad said. Not his normal relaxed tone. He sounded annoyed.

'What's happened?'

James glowered at me, dropped his bag by the Welsh dresser and made straight for the snack cupboard. He pulled out a bag of Starmix and ripped the bag open. Jellies scattered across the floor.

Dad walked in and handed me an envelope. 'He's been fighting at school.'

'James? Is this true? What happened?'

He glared at me, grabbed another bag of sweets out the cupboard and tried to dash out of the room.

I caught him by the collar of his polo shirt. 'James, we need to talk about this. Fighting is naughty and certainly means you don't deserve sweets.'

He pulled one of the bar stools away from the breakfast bar and clambered on it. He folded his arms and stared at me.

'Tell me what happened.' I sat next to him and tried to hold one of his hands. He yanked it away from me.

'Wasn't my fault,' he said. 'They started it.'

I sighed and opened the envelope. My eyes skimmed over the letter.

'Okay, so who was teasing you?'

'Peter and Noah. They said you'd killed Auntie Stephanie.'

I gasped and looked at Dad. He shrugged. 'It's been in the papers,' he said. 'I suppose people have been speculating about who killed her.'

'But neither Topher nor I have been mentioned by name.'

'She was here at Darcy's party, wasn't she? People will remember that.' He moved to the kettle, shook it, filled it, and put it on. 'People talk, Lily. That's what they do. Children listen and then repeat what they've heard.'

'Are you saying I shouldn't punish him for fighting?'

'That's not for me to say,' Dad replied. 'He was standing up for you. Boys will be boys. He'll grow out of it.'

'And what if he doesn't?' I whispered.

James remained on the bar stool, his eyes darting back and forth between his grandfather and myself.

'I'd like you to go to your room, please, James. We'll talk about this some more when Daddy comes home.'

He slid down from the stool and stomped up the stairs.

'He's not going to be like his father,' Dad said.

'How do you know that?'

'Because he has you to care for him. Topher lost everything. He was just a few years older than James is, and his life was ripped apart. That's not going to happen to James.'

'Dad, I know Topher killed Stephanie. What is it going to do to James, to Darcy, when their father goes to prison?'

'They'll still have you,' Dad said. 'Are you going to tell Topher when he comes in?'

'I haven't decided,' I replied. 'But he probably already knows.'

CHAPTER FIFTY-SEVEN

Denise

Topher Gundersen stretched across the table to shake my hand. After a moment's hesitation, I accepted the gesture. Then he sat down, unbuttoned his jacket and put his right ankle across his left knee. I knew it was done entirely to show me how much at ease he was. I was determined to rile him.

He had with him Peter Robinson, who I'd had met earlier with Lily. I'd always found Robinson rather inept myself. I didn't know if Gundersen rated him or if Robinson was merely available.

After cautioning Mr Gundersen and taking him through my preliminary questions, I asked, 'What's your marriage like?'

'My marriage? I thought we were here to talk about her friend's murder.' Gundersen looked surprised.

'Yes, but Mrs Gundersen is part of the marriage. I just want to get a sense of your relationship, especially since you've been having an affair with her best friend.'

'Is that what Lily told you?' He rolled his eyes.

'Perhaps,' I said. 'Do you deny it?'

'Why would I? It was just a bit of fun. Nothing serious. She was good in the sack, and we had my wife's permission.' He smirked, perhaps reliving the memories.

'Your wife gave you permission to have an affair with her best friend? Why do you think she'd do that?'

'Because she was convinced I was spying on her,' he sighed, holding out his hands to give the impression of a wronged man. 'She has this mad idea that I've hidden cameras around the house.'

'But you *had* hidden cameras around the house. We found them when we searched the property,' I said. 'Did Mark Brown install them for you?' He jammed his hands together, the knuckles of his fists turning white. A flash of annoyance flashed across his handsome face. For a second, I saw what he'd be like when angry. Peter Robinson shot Gundersen an anxious glance. It seemed he knew the name of the petty thief too.

'I have to keep an eye on her,' Gundersen said, ignoring my reference to Brown. 'She's always been a bit flaky, but recently it seems to have got worse. I suppose she's told you it was my fault she broke her fingers.'

I raised my eyebrows. 'That's not quite how Mrs Gundersen sees it,' I replied.

'It's absolutely preposterous,' he said. 'It had absolutely nothing to do with me. She went outside in a raging storm because she thought the cellar doors were open. I had to go after her. It's a good job I did, because when I found her, her hands were trapped. I had to fight the storm to get the doors open and off her fingers. Naturally, I rushed her to hospital. But I know Lily. She will have told you a completely different story. She has, hasn't she?' He leaned forward, resting his elbows on the table.

I wasn't sure if it was meant to intimidate me or not. I didn't move. We were almost nose to nose. 'Please sit back in your seat, Mr Gundersen,' I said. 'I have spoken to your wife about those events, and her memory of that evening is different from yours. I am waiting on the medical report from the hospital in the US. Mrs Gundersen has given me to understand that there were some anomalies with her injuries and she had a follow-up visit from the police.'

Gundersen laughed and pushed back from the table. 'It's all nonsense,' he said. 'Lily has been making up stories since she was a child. Just ask her mother. Her parents used to call her Lily liar. Did you know that?'

'Mrs Gundersen and I have had that conversation, yes,' I told him. 'But it was only her mother who called her by that name. I've spoken with her father on the phone; he gave a different version of events.'

'Him! You can't believe anything he says,' Gundersen said, dismissively.

'Is that how it is, Mr Gundersen?' I asked. 'Anyone who disagrees with you is either mad or a liar?'

Peter Robinson perked up and was about to intercede when Gundersen shushed him. 'It doesn't matter, Peter,' he said. 'It's all on the tape and we'll have a copy of it.'

Gundersen turned back to me. 'DC Jones,' he said, 'my wife is a fantasist. She makes up lies all the time. She has a very tenuous grip on reality. After the accident in the States she was committed to a psychiatric hospital for a while. I had to assume power of attorney over her affairs.'

'Your wife seems perfectly sane to me, Mr Gundersen,' I said.

'Forgive me, DC Jones, are you a psychiatrist?' He arched

his head back and sneered at me down his beautifully shaped nose.

'I am not,' I replied.

'Then you're not really qualified to tell me anything about my wife, are you?' He suddenly grinned at me. And, just as Lily had told me, the smile didn't reach his eyes.

I changed tack. 'Where were you on the night of 8th November?' I asked.

'As I've already stated, I was heading to a conference,' he said. 'I changed my mind and decided to drive back. Lily hadn't been quite herself and I decided I didn't want to leave her alone all weekend.'

'Any witnesses?' I asked.

'No, I was on my own.'

'What about your satnav?'

His eyes narrowed as he glared at me. This time I saw the emotion had reached his eyes.

'What do you mean?'

'What I mean, Mr Gundersen,' I said, 'is that if you had set your satellite navigation system for the conference venue then it would still be listed as a recent destination, wouldn't it? In fact, doesn't your model of BMW have a top-spec GPS?'

Gundersen stared at me and then looked at his solicitor. He turned back to me and I was pleased to see he'd gone a little pale under his tan.

'We'd like your permission to inspect the car's GPS system,' I told him. 'That would be a perfectly adequate alibi for you, wouldn't it?'

'Go ahead, but I knew where I was heading and so I didn't need to use the GPS. I told you last time which route I used. Haven't you bothered to check the ANPR in the meantime?'

Robinson opened his mouth, but nothing came out. He

repeated the gesture two or three more times, looking for all the world like a gaping guppy. Eventually he spoke. 'Are you planning to arrest my client, DC Jones?' He said. 'Have you any grounds to suspect him of Ms Silcott's murder?'

'I know he wasn't heading to any conference,' I replied. 'Firstly, there was no conference. I have checked this with the clerk at Mr Gundersen's chambers. Secondly, I know from a witness statement I have that Mr Gundersen was with Ms Silcott on the night she died.'

Gundersen sniggered. 'You have no such thing,' he said.

He was right of course, but I hoped to have such a statement in due course. It was just a simple matter of talking to Stephanie's stalker.

'You have no evidence Mr Gundersen murdered her, do you?' Peter Robinson started to gather his papers together. 'This is a fishing expedition, DC Jones. When you have some concrete evidence, my client and I will return but, until then, we'll both bid you good day.'

Gundersen rose from his chair and buttoned his jacket. I got the first genuine smile I'd ever seen him give, and he held out his hand to shake mine. I knew it was childish, but I refused to shake his. I couldn't remove the vision of Lily's broken fingers from my mind.

CHAPTER FIFTY-EIGHT

Denise

After I'd spoken with Topher Gundersen, I wasted no time and I got Heather Elliott, the housekeeper cum childminder, in for interview.

When I'd met Heather at the Gundersen's house she'd seemed relaxed, but here at the police station she was more nervous. Her eyes darted around as if she was looking for an escape.

I took her through the preliminaries and advised her that she was here to help with our enquiries; she could have a solicitor if she wished, she was not under arrest and she was free to go at any time.

'I won't need a solicitor,' she said.

'How long have you worked for the Gundersen's?' I asked.

'Coming up for six years now,' she said. 'Mrs Gundersen was very poorly when they came back from the States. She couldn't do much with those poor hands of hers and so I came along to help before baby was born.'

'And are you happy there?'

'Happy enough,' she replied.

'You'd not choose to work for anybody else?'

'No, no I wouldn't,' she said. 'Mrs Gundersen is a lovely lady. She has troubles, of course, like we all do. But she and the children are really lovely.'

'What kind of troubles does she have?'

'Well, they always tease her about losing things. She isn't very tidy and she's always putting things down and forgetting them.' She smiled as she thought about Lily. 'And then because she takes so long to find anything, she's often late. Her mother always teases her about Lily standard time. But I don't think she's as bad as they make out.'

'What makes you say that?'

'Well I know they all think she's a bit dizzy. But even someone who is a bit dizzy doesn't leave their keys in the freezer, do they?' Heather fixed me with a stare, and I saw that, despite her anxiety to be loyal, she knew more about this marriage than anyone.

'Does she often leave things in the freezer?'

'Well that's what I'm telling you. She's a bit dizzy, not stupid. She's fine when he's not around. Her mother makes her panic too. But I reckon it's all him.'

'By him, do you mean Mr Gundersen?'

'Yeah, I do,' she said reluctantly. 'He's always having a go at her about this or that. She can't do anything right. And then he'll ring up and cancel me for a day when I know she needs me and she's gonna be busy.'

'Can you give me an example?'

'Well it's not happened so much since her accident,' Heather mused. 'But thinking back, it was just before the car crash. They had a party at the weekend to celebrate their wedding anniversary and on the Sunday night he texts me to tell me not to bother coming in the next day. Well, I know she's got all that cleaning up to do after the party and she's got the kiddies to look after, so I knew she'd need me. When he does that, I pop round anyway and just make sure she's okay. Often as not, she'd tell me there's been a misunderstanding, or miscommunication as she likes to call it, since she does need my help after all. I mean, how difficult is it to say I need the housekeeper?' Heather shrugged. 'It's not hard, is it?'

'No,' I said. I decided to change tack. 'Is Mr Gundersen good with the kids?' I watched her face carefully. Her mouth twisted, just briefly, but the truth was there.

'He's all right with the boy,' Heather said, after a short pause. 'But little Darcy... I think she's a bit afraid of him. Sometimes when he comes in the room, she just sits there, head down. You know, it's almost as if she's trying to make herself invisible. Poor little mite. But like I said, he is good with the boy and he does take them both out sometimes. Gives their mum a bit of peace and quiet.'

'So you'd say it was a happy marriage?'

'I'm not saying it is, I am not saying it isn't. There's just something... something a bit odd. Can't quite put my finger on it. The house is weird too.'

'Weird?' I said. 'How do you mean?'

'Well, it's supposed to be one of those smart houses, isn't it? But you put the kettle on and it switches off half-way through boiling. Lights turn themselves on and off. And the heating, don't get me started.' She pushed up the sleeve on her left arm. 'Look, are we done? Can I go now? I've got to pick James up from school in twenty minutes. Darcy's with her grandad. She's really perked up since he's been staying.'

'Yes, that's fine,' I said. 'Thank you.'

After she'd gone, I sat back in my chair and I thought about the two vastly different pictures I'd been given of the Gundersen marriage.

CHAPTER FIFTY-NINE

Lily

I was working my way through more of Dad's letters when Cerys called me. Denise Jones wanted another chat at the police station.

'Am I obliged to do this, Cerys?'

'She has some news she wants to share with us,' Cerys said. 'About the CCTV footage from June.'

'Has she found it? After all this time?'

'She has,' said Cerys.

'That's great news. I'm on my way,' I replied.

Leaving the children with Dad I called a cab and arrived at the station to find Cerys and Denise waiting.

Denise showed us into a side room. 'I've been doing some more investigating,' she said. 'I found out some very interesting things.'

'What would that be then?' I asked.

'I've continued my investigations into your car accident.'

'And you've found the CCTV?' I was jittery. My stomach was doing somersaults.

'I have,' she said. 'And I've found out something else.'

'Such as?'

'Would you be surprised to hear that *you* hired the car which forced you off the road?' she asked.

'Surprised? I'd be absolutely astounded!' I replied. 'How on earth did you work that out?'

'Like I said, I've been investigating. The technical guys found the list of names on your phone. They checked that against some calls made from a burner phone, which led me to someone well known to the police. He was able to supply me with the CCTV footage. I checked it out and I've seen the car pushing you off the road. Since then, I've been to visit the car hire company.' She sat back in her chair looking very pleased with herself. 'Actually, I've got something to show you.' She pulled a printout from her briefcase and pushed it across the table at me.

I picked it up and scrutinised it.

'Do you recognise the credit card number?' She asked.

'The last four digits look familiar,' I said, shaking my head. 'But I lost my credit card months ago. I haven't dared tell Topher that I've lost it.'

'Do you have any evidence of that?' She put her head to one side, giving me the quizzical expression she used when she wasn't sure if I was telling her the truth.

'No, I can't prove it,' I said. 'But if you look at the statements, you'll see a period where spend has dropped. Until you come to the big payment, which you're now telling me was for the car hire.'

I pushed the printout away from me, but then I remembered something. 'What about the solicitors' letter?' I said.

'There was a photo of it on my phone. Didn't you find that?'

'We found no such photo,' she said.

'But I found the envelopes in his study. The envelopes the letter arrived in. Topher must have written the letter to me.' I realised now I should have taken one of the envelopes as evidence.

'We didn't find anything like that in his office.'

I sighed loudly. 'He must have destroyed them and wiped my phone. He's clever, isn't he?'

'So, if I understand you correctly'—Denise leaned forward, her palms flat against the table—'you're telling me that not only is your husband trying to make you go mad, but he's trying to kill you too?'

'Well, it makes more sense than me hiring a car so somebody can push me off the road to kill me. Doesn't it? There must be easier ways to kill myself,' I retorted.

'There are,' said Denise nodding. 'But suicide is one explanation.'

'I would never leave my children alone with only their father to look after them.' I said. 'I think he paid someone to kill me. It's not as if he hasn't threatened me before.'

Denise looked at me with a strange expression on her face. 'Is that something you can prove?'

'Have you checked his bank accounts?' I asked. 'Large withdrawals and such like.'

'Of course, we have, and there's nothing suspicious.'

'Have you checked his Danish bank account?'

'Danish account?' Denise was clearly startled.

Yes,' I said. 'When his parents were killed all the money went into a bank account in Copenhagen. He came to live with an aunt in England. The house in Denmark was sold, then there was the insurance money, and I'm not sure what else. All his school fees, his university tuition and living expenses, even a lump sum for the house in Muswell Hill came from there. I don't know if he still has the account or not.' I spread my hands out, palms uppermost, and shrugged. I had forgotten about the Danish money.

CHAPTER SIXTY

Denise

Of course, everything Lily said to me made sense, but I couldn't work on supposition. I decided to drop in on the technical team and catch Dan for a chat before I returned to the station.

'DJ,' he said. 'Great to see you. Coffee?'

'I couldn't manage another one. I'm too wired,' I said, pleased to notice that he'd dropped the formal DC Jones title.

'We have herbal teas,' he said.

'Sounds perfect,' I told him.

'Anyway, what are you doing here? Is there something I've forgotten to do?'

I shook my head. 'No,' I said. 'I have a question, an idea I'd like to run by you.'

'Cool,' Dan said. He passed me a mug of some foul-smelling concoction.

I sniffed at it and pulled a face. 'What the hell is this?' I asked.

'Raspberry leaf tea,' he said. 'Dr Whitney was drinking it

all the time before she went off on maternity leave. Is it any good?'

'You try some,' I told him. He leaned towards the mug and sniffed. My heart thumped and the hairs on my arms stood on end. What the hell was happening to me? If he got any closer, I'd no idea what I'd do. I thought back to my fateful pass at Stephanie and pulled away from him. Now was no time to work out my confused sexuality.

'See what you mean,' he said. He went back to the cupboard. 'Let's see what else we've got.' He pulled packet after packet from the shelves. It was a surprising selection of herbal teas, presumably left behind by Dr Whitney before she left to have her baby. I selected one. Dan boiled the kettle again and, armed with fresh decaffeinated tea, we went to his office.

'Sit yourself down,' he said. 'What can I do for you?'

'I'm not sure if you can help me,' I began. 'I don't even know if this is possible.'

'Come on, spit it out.'

'Okay, so, if I make a payment by credit card, how can I prove I am who I say I am?'

'Well,' Dan said, 'there's a number of checks and balances in place. First off, there is the CVC number. That little three-digit number on the back of the card. You'd need to have that, plus you need to have the start date and the end date as well.'

'Yep, so I've got all that. Is that it?' I said.

'No. There are some more checks that the banks and credit card companies put in place. Such as the BIN number and the IP address.'

'BIN? IP?' I stared at him, eyebrows raised.

'Yes,' said Dan. 'The BIN is the bank's international number, so the company we're shopping from checks with the bank. In turn the bank knows which country the card issuer is in and what country the payment is being made from. So, if your bank account or your credit card is registered with a British bank and you're making a payment from Uganda, say, or if you're on holiday in Spain, the credit card company would know the payment was being made out of country. That's why sometimes when making payments abroad you have to speak to the card company.'

I nodded. 'And the IP address. What's that all about?'

'That's the Internet Protocol address of the computer. Every device you use has its own unique address. In this situation, the card issuer would know which computer was being used to register the payment and, if there was something iffy about it, then they'd decline the payment.'

'So I could go to the credit card company and ask them exactly which computer was used to make a payment?' I said.

'If you've got all the details. Certainly. The bank should have no problem finding the information at all.'

'Dan, you're an absolute star,' I said. 'I could kiss you.'

'Steady on,' he said, and he resumed his more familiar shade of vermilion.

I got Dan to promise to email me the details of what he'd outlined so that I could explain it to DI Blaine when I returned to the station. There was no way I could do it from memory and get all the nuances right.

He was as good as his word and when I got back to West Hampstead nick there was an email waiting.

'Guv?' I said. 'I need to run something by you.'

She looked at me over the top of her glasses; the action intimidated me as always. Did she do it on purpose, I wondered. 'What is it?' she asked.

I outlined everything that I'd done in the last few days. I'd posted everything on the board to keep the whole team up to date, but I just wanted to reiterate and let her ask questions.

When I came to the part about the traceability of credit card transactions, I saw her eyes begin to glaze over, but she did allow me to ask for the warrant. It was quickly agreed, and I called the credit card company to make an appointment to see someone in their fraud department.

It was a short meet as when I got there the fraud person had already looked up the transactions and gave me the IP address of the computer used.

I checked my records and was disappointed to note that the IP address matched that of Lily Gundersen's laptop. Damn.

It seemed as if I was never going to get a break in this case. I went to the kitchen and boiled the kettle for a cup of tea. I looked around at the mess, but seeing it was my name on the roster to wash up I quickly scrubbed some mugs and wiped down the surfaces. As I rinsed out the dishcloth it suddenly occurred to me that I should check Lily's timetables.

I ran back to my desk and found Lily's teaching schedule. There it was: when the Range Rover hire transaction was taking place, Lily was teaching violin to a class of sixteen-year-olds. It looked as if she would have ample witnesses to her location. But surely her class plans would be on her laptop? Damn, one step forward and one step backwards.

CHAPTER SIXTY-ONE

Lily

Cerys called me a few days after our meeting with DC Jones. It wasn't good news. Denise had been able to confirm it was my laptop that had used in the transaction to hire the Range Rover.

'I don't understand,' I said. 'How can that be?'

'It's pretty technical,' she said. 'I'll detail it all to you in an email.'

'Can you send it in a letter?' I asked. 'I'm still scared Topher can read all my emails. I'll keep an eye out for the postman.'

'Okay,' she said. 'The transaction took place in the week before your accident. According to your timetable, you should have been teaching at that time. 30th May. Can you remember what you were doing that day? It was a Thursday.'

I closed my eyes, holding the phone against my face and sat with my head back. Think! Think, I whispered to myself. I steadied my breathing and took myself back to the week before the accident. The days blurred one into another. I remembered buying an antique desk set for Topher for our seventh anniversary. Was that the Wednesday or the Thursday? Then it came to me.

'I took the day off,' I said. 'I went to find a present for Topher. I was browsing stalls in Portobello Road market.'

'Would anyone remember you?'

'No, I don't think so.' I thought back to that day. I had wandered down to the vintage clothing store, looking for something unusual. Wood or wool is the theme of a seventh anniversary. I'd found a silk smoking jacket, but it wasn't quite right for a health nut like Topher. And it smelt of smoke. 'I did have a long chat with the owner of the vintage clothes store about cleaning a silk jacket. But it's such a long time ago I'm not sure she'd remember me. Then I walked back into the market. It was starting to rain, and the stall holders were packing up. That's when I saw the perfect gift. It was an antique desk set. Wooden. With an old fountain pen and an inkwell. I chatted with the guy and I bought the desk set. He gave me a receipt, but it's not time stamped.'

'I'll see if the police can find the receipt. It might have the stall holder's name on it. Denise can certainly check the time it started raining. Tell me,' Cerys paused, took a breath and said, 'Does your husband have access to your laptop?'

'Yes, he uses it all the time. He'd send emails to the school as if they were from me to say I was sick and wasn't coming in. He'd cancel appointments and not tell me. He did it all the time.' I said.

'Didn't it occur to you to change your password?' Cerys sighed, as if changing my password was the most obvious and simplest thing in the world.

I hung my head. 'He didn't like me doing that,' I said. 'He thought there should be no secrets between husband and wife.'

'But you didn't have the passwords to his computers?'

'No, I didn't. He said it was an entirely different situation. He had client confidentiality to think about.'

'I see,' Cerys said.

But I knew she didn't understand at all. I hardly understood it myself. Topher ruled my life; I was powerless to stop him.

'Has Denise talked to Stephanie's ex yet?' I demanded.

'No, not as far as I'm aware.'

'He was still stalking her,' I said. 'Even after she took out the injunction.'

'Okay,' said Cerys. 'I'll call her when I leave here.'

'And he was at the funeral. I bet he knows something. I'm sure it was him. He was staring at Topher. Glaring at him, in fact.'

Cerys assured me she'd tell Denise everything that I'd said. I bade her goodbye and replaced my mobile in my pocket.

The post had arrived, containing a letter from my mother. It was not good news.

Lillian, she wrote.

I have been talking with Topher and we agree that with all this going on the children should stay with me for the time being. Topher tells me that James is very upset and has started wetting the bed again. Darcy is too young to know what's going on but she's upset too. Having your father in the house is only causing more upset.

I cannot believe the stories you're telling or even what drove you to kill Stephanie. I am astonished that you've not been arrested and put in prison. Topher tells me the police have all the evidence they need but are not acting upon it.

I have told the police how difficult and depressed you were as a child and how depressed you were when you became pregnant. I know the accident with your fingers was a terrible thing to happen, but you still should have made more of an effort to cuddle James when he was a baby. I did what I could to make up for your short-comings, but it should have been you. You've always been selfish and self-centred. I suppose that's why you were so jealous of Stephanie.

Topher also says you're seeing some sort of psychoanalyst. I'm sure they're telling you it's all the fault of your upbringing. But I won't have that. I was a good mother and have done nothing to deserve such an ungrateful child as you.

I don't want to hear any more of your lies.

Best wishes,

Mummy.

I screwed the letter up into a ball and threw it in the bin. How dare Topher go behind my back and spin this tale to her. Mummy was right about the psychoanalyst, however. And now I was able to see my relationships with both of them so much more clearly.

CHAPTER SIXTY-TWO

Denise

'Okay, thanks for letting me know, Cerys. Did you ask her about the laptop?' I said. But the reply wasn't what I'd hoped for. Knowing that her husband had access to the laptop anytime he felt like it was good news. But it was the information about her taking a day off when she could have had a ton of alibis that wasn't good. Finding the stall holder was going to take a lot of shoe leather but I could get uniform to track him down.

I missed what Cerys said next. 'What was that?'

'Lily was asking if you've spoken with the ex-boyfriend yet?'

'No,' I said.

'She thinks he was at the funeral and he was glaring at Topher. There might be nothing in it, but it feels like he may have information he's not sharing. Lily said Stephanie still thought someone was stalking her.'

'Damn, I did spot him at the funeral,' I said. 'But Stephanie hadn't mentioned to me it was still going on. I'd hoped he'd stopped, but because I'd warned him to leave her alone there's no way he'd come forward now.' I checked my file on John Maitland. I was on the point of calling him, when I decided that a surprise visit at his place of work might be more effective.

I presented myself at the reception of Granville Insurance Brokers later that day. After a short wait, the manager presented herself and took me to her office.

'How can I help you, DC Jones?' she said.

'I need to speak to one of your employees,' I said. 'A John Maitland. Is he not here today? I did ask for him.'

'He went out for lunch, but I think he's back now,' she said. 'I'll get someone to fetch him. Will the staff area be okay for you to talk to him?'

I nodded. 'Yes, that's fine.'

I sat in the small kitchen waiting for him to show up. When he did, I remembered how Stephanie had described him and what had attracted her in the first place. He scowled as he walked into the room but offered me his hand.

'Hello John,' I said. 'Remember me?'

'Of course,' he replied. 'What do you want with me now?' He didn't look at me but at a spot somewhere over my right shoulder.

'I saw you at Stephanie Silcott's funeral.'

'So what?' he said. 'She was dead. I couldn't be accused of stalking her once she was dead, could I?' He looked at me for the first time; I saw the pain he was in.

'How long did you keep following her after you were warned off?' I said.

'You know that already, or you wouldn't be here,' he said.

'I was pretty upset after she dumped me. I wanted to know why.'

'And when she took out an injunction against you, how did that make you feel?' I watched him carefully, knowing I'd get my answer from his actions rather than his words.

'No comment,' he said, but his knuckles gripping the arm of the chair told a different story.

'You kept on stalking her.' It was a statement, not a question.

'No! Well, it wasn't quite like that. Anyway, she had someone scare me off.'

'Do you know who?'

'Nope, I was outside one night, and the blond bloke left in his Beemer. Then someone grabbed me and told me to leave her alone. So, I did.'

'When was that?' I asked, barely able to contain my excitement. A blond man with a BMW — there was no doubt in my mind who that was. Don't lead the witness, I told myself.

'Early November.'

'Friday the 8th of November?' My heart was pounding. I couldn't believe that I finally had the truth in my grasp.

'Yeah, probably early hours of the Saturday when matey frightened me off.' He shrugged. 'Why?'

'Didn't you see the news. Didn't you see the appeals for help?'

'I'm sorry, no. I don't watch the news. It's all bad, isn't it?'

I wanted to throttle him. 'How did you find out about the funeral?' I asked.

'Someone here must've mentioned it.'

'And whilst you were stalking Stephanie Silcott, did you happen to leave a box full of maggots on her doorstep?'

'Maggots? Hell no! I was angry at her but I'm not a psycho!'

'Stalking is generally considered to be psychotic behaviour, Mr Maitland. You would've saved us a lot of time if you'd come forward with this information earlier.'

'Yeah, but you might have arrested me for stalking her after the injunction,' he said.

'I still might, Mr Maitland,' I said. 'I still might.'

I got him to tell me once more as much as he could remember about the man leaving Stephanie's flat and the BMW he was driving. I'd need a full statement in due course, but all I could think was, *Gotcha!*

I ran from the building to my car, trying to call DI Blaine at the same time.

'Slow down, DJ,' she said.

'We've got him, Guv,' I panted. 'Gundersen — I have a witness who saw him leave Stephanie's flat on the night in question. He did it! He bloody well killed her.'

'I'll have a warrant by the time you get back here,' she said. 'Well done.'

CHAPTER SIXTY-THREE

Lily

'I've read all your letters, Dad,' I said. 'I'm so sorry.' I patted the seat beside me on the sofa in the garden room.

'It doesn't matter,' he said, as he sat next to me. 'I guessed your mother was behind it. I didn't blame you. Your wedding was my chance to get my little girl back. I messed that up too.'

'I'm not a little girl anymore, Dad. I have children of my own now.'

'I've missed so much,' he sighed, and stared out into the garden. A robin perched on a bush near the window and stared with its bright eyes. Dad rose from the sofa and the robin flew off.

'We can catch up now.'

'Can we?' he said. 'I've missed you growing up. I've missed your babies growing. At least I made it to some of your concerts.'

'You did?'

'Yes,' he said. 'I kept out of the way in case your mother

was around. I sat in the cheap seats, but I could see my little girl playing her heart out.'

'Thank you.'

He turned from the window, his eyes shining. 'It wasn't enough, though. I should have tried harder. And now you have so much hanging over you.'

'I know.' I got off the sofa and stood by him, looking out of the bi-fold doors into the garden. I rested my head on his shoulder. 'I wish it were all over.'

'Have the police said anything more about suspects?'

'Stephanie had an ex-boyfriend, John, who was stalking her. Then there's me; we argued. There's also Topher, who was having an affair with her.' Dad put his arm around my shoulder and held me.

'She had an exciting life,' he muttered.

'She had another client do something similar a few years ago,' I said.

'What? Another stalker?' Dad said. 'Do you know who it was?'

'I can't remember his name,' I said, biting my bottom lip whilst thinking. 'His surname was something like Meyhick, Maychic. I think he was a gangster she was defending. That was a horrible time for her.

'Then recently she had a delivery a few days before she was killed. It really upset her. She thought it was a delivery of flowers from Topher. But, when she opened it, it was full of rotten food and maggots. She came to see me and we talked about it. And then she said I wasn't to worry about it and she'd found someone to help her.'

'Any idea who that someone might be? Is it worth telling the police?'

I shook my head. 'I've told them everything that I know. Personally, I think it was Topher. That's why I asked you to come and stay. He won't do anything while there's someone else in the house.' I jumped as the robot vacuum cleaner burst into life. 'Bastard!' I yelled, and grabbed the machine, holding it off the ground until it stopped whirring. I turned it over and switched it off.

'What the hell was that?' Dad said.

'Topher,' I replied. 'This is a so-called smart house. Everything can be controlled remotely. So Topher can turn the lights on, change the temperature, even put the kettle on from his mobile phone.'

I saw Dad's jaw tighten but before he could say anything the phone rang. I saw the caller ID. Cerys.

'Lily,' she said. 'Thank goodness I've caught you. There's been a development.'

'A development?'

'Yes, Denise has got a statement from John Maitland and a warrant to arrest Topher. Have you got somewhere you can go so you and the children are safe?'

I opened my mouth to reply, but nothing came out. Dad snatched the phone from me, and I heard him questioning Cerys.

'No, don't worry about it. We'll pack and leave now. Thanks, talk later.' He put the phone down and turned to me. 'Lily, Lily sweetheart, we have to go.'

'Where? Go where?'

'It doesn't matter. A hotel... anywhere. We can't be here in case Topher comes back. He's already killed one woman. Do you want to be next?' He raced out the room and I heard him on the stairs calling to Heather to pack clothes for the children.

I was rooted to the floor, unable to move. I twisted around to stare at the camera we'd discovered in one of the roof lanterns. It was too high up to remove so it had stayed.

Does he know what's happening? Has he worked it all out, I wondered.

The camera blinked as I stared at it. Was he watching me now? I wanted to run from the room, but I calmed my nerves and walked away. I trod each step of the stairs quietly and purposefully. I was not going to let him see me panic. Although my heart pounded, blood racing though my ears, I was going to own this situation. He'd see us leave, but he would not see us frightened.

I was not going to allow him the satisfaction.

Heather packed toys and clothes for the children while Dad and I packed a few items each.

Heather and I sobbed as we said goodbye. She promised to leave the house as soon as we'd gone and not come back until I'd told her it was safe.

CHAPTER SIXTY-FOUR

Topher

Topher Gundersen thanked the caller from Judge Mayhew's office, placed his mobile phone on his desk and leaned back in his chair. Despite knowing the danger he was in, he remained calm as he watched Lily and her father on the camera application dragging suitcases down the stairs. Pushing himself out of his chair he went to the bookcase, casually swept the law books aside and retrieved a cash box concealed behind them. He unlocked it and took out a Danish passport and a bundle of Euros. These he placed in his laptop bag. Back at his desk he booked himself a train ticket, shut down the laptop and placed that in the bag with the passport and cash. He put his jacket and overcoat on and walked into the anteroom where his secretary sat.

'Are you okay?' she said. 'I thought I heard a crash.'

Ignoring her question, he simply said, 'I'm going out. Cancel this afternoon's appointments.'

'Yes,' she said. 'When will you be back?'

'Later.' He buttoned up his overcoat and looped the soft

woollen scarf Lily had bought him for his birthday around his neck and strolled from the building.

Once out in the fresh air he hailed a taxi.

'St Pancras,' he said. He relaxed in the back seat of the black cab and watched the streets of London crawl by. Looking at his watch, he saw there was still plenty of time. He'd need to pick up a change of underwear in any case.

At the station he paid the driver in cash and merged into the crowds. He wandered into a bar, ordered a beer, picked up a newspaper and sat down in a corner. After a short while he was joined by a younger weaselly-looking man.

Topher said nothing, and simply finished his beer and left the newspaper and his overcoat behind. Mark Brown picked up the paper, removed his jacket and baseball cap, swapped the envelope inside the newspaper for the car keys and put on the overcoat. He too left the newspaper on the table.

Approaching the boarding desk, Brown presented his ticket and his passport.

'Thank you, Mr Hendriksen,' said the conductor. 'Have a pleasant trip.'

'I will,' said Tajo Hendriksen and strolled down the platform to take his seat in first class.

Topher Gundersen pulled the baseball cap down low over his hairline, covering his bright blond hair. He picked up the car keys and strolled out of St Pancras. He'd have to lie low for a few days, but not for long. He wanted his son with him.

* * *

Lily

It was light when I woke. Could I really have slept all night? There was a soft knock on the door.

'Come in,' I said. It was Dad with a cup of tea. I hoped there was no sugar in this one. He was old school and believed that sugary tea was beneficial for shock. Last night's cup of tea had been horrid. I smiled my thanks for this one.

'How did you sleep?' He placed the tea on the bedside cabinet, pushing the cold tea to one side.

'Really well, thanks. I didn't think I'd get any sleep at all. I was so scared last night.'

'I can imagine,' he said. 'Do you have any plans?

'I don't know. I guess wait until Topher's been arrested, then perhaps I can go back to the Vicarage.'

'What if they give him bail?'

'They won't for murder,' I replied.

'Okay, so what if they don't charge him?' He put his fingertips under my chin and looked deep into my eyes. 'It is possible.'

'I know,' I said. 'But I have to stay in London, I know we can't stay here. This suite is costing a fortune.'

'It is,' Dad said. He should know, he was paying for it. 'What about if I take the children back home with me? Is there anyone you can stay with in London?'

I shook my head, but then I thought of Sally Trevena. 'Perhaps,' I said. 'I'll have to call her and ask.'

He gave me a hug and left me to drink my tea. I rested back on the pillows. My limbs felt empty, I had no energy to pick up the teacup. I expected to be relieved, but I was exhausted. Just one last hurdle and I'd be free. I closed my eyes, shaking my head. The last hurdle was the biggest one of all. I could only hope that we'd make it.

There was another knock on the door, but before I could

say anything the door burst open. I squealed in fear, until I saw the intruders were James and Darcy. I hoped they hadn't heard me.

They were full of energy and looking forward to an adventure with Grandad.

'Please can we go?' James begged.

It was a relief to see how resilient they were. I hoped they'd stay that way when their father was in prison. Breakfast arrived and they raced into the sitting room to enjoy the excitement of room service. I showered and managed another cup of tea before calling Sally.

'Of course you can stay, Lily. Stay as long as you need. I'll make up the spare room. What time will you be here?'

'Later this morning,' I said. 'Are you sure it's okay? Dad is taking the kids back with him, so it'll just be me.'

'You could still bring them if you want. There's plenty of room.'

I said no. Was that relief I heard? Hers and Ralph's children were grown up and had long left home.

I packed mine off with my father, making them promise to be good on the journey and to call me on my mobile as soon as they arrived. I stayed in the suite until Reception told me my taxi had arrived.

My own journey was terrifying. Each time the cab stopped and the doors clicked open I was terrified that Topher would leap in and drag me out into the street. It was a relief to arrive in Sally's quiet street.

'Lunch will be ready when you want it,' Sally said, placing my suitcase on the floor. 'Towels are there on the chair and the bathroom is at the end of the corridor.'

'I'm starving,' I said. 'Do you mind if I eat first? I should have had breakfast at the hotel but I was too scared to eat.'

Sally laughed. 'Good, come on down. It's just soup and a sandwich.'

I nodded. 'Anything would be wonderful. Do you have any coffee?'

Sally smiled. 'Of course. I'll put the kettle on.' She left me to my own devices and I took a look around the room. Should I unpack? I had no idea how long I'd be staying.

I decided to leave everything in the case for now. My tummy rumbled when I smelt the soup and I quickly popped to the bathroom to use the loo and wash my hands.

'DC Jones just called,' said Sally, as soon as I entered the kitchen. 'She's going to drop by later to bring us up to speed.'

'Okay, that's good,' I said. 'Has she arrested Topher yet?'

'I don't know, my dear. We'll just have to wait until she gets here.'

Denise arrived when I was on the phone to Dad; he was at a service station and only half-way home, but he still sounded jolly and the children hadn't fought in the car — at least not too much. I cut the call short, explaining my hurry and raced downstairs to hear what Denise had to say. She was in the kitchen, drinking coffee. She looked dreadful, with dark circles under her eyes. Her hair was lank and lifeless. A stark contrast to the pretty woman I'd met earlier in the year.

She rose and gave me a hug.

'Have you arrested him?' I said.

'No, he's gone missing. We've put out an all ports warning for him, but we have his passport so he can't leave the country using that one,' she said.

'Good. When can I go home?' Sally and Denise looked at each other warily.

'I don't think it's a good idea just yet. He may come back to the house. You could still be in danger.' Denise looked at Sally for support.

'Denise is right. You can stay here as long as you need to,' Sally told me.

'I just want to be free of him. Free of the fear.' I collapsed into a chair at the kitchen table. I was exhausted.

'I understand,' said Denise. 'I still need to be searching for Topher, otherwise I'd be happy for you to go home. Can you think of anywhere he would go? Does he have a boat? Friends with a boat? Friends who would harbour him?'

'I can't think of anyone,' I said. 'All his friends are lawyers and barristers. Some judges, but not the kind of people who would shelter a wanted man.'

'No, of course not,' sighed Denise. 'It was worth a try though. We're trying to track down his car as well. We know he went into work on the day before yesterday, but he didn't drive in and the car's not at the station or at your house.'

'You think he may have abandoned it somewhere?'

'It's possible,' said Denise. 'Who knows what he was thinking? We've put out an appeal and are waiting on results from that. Right, I must get back. Thanks for the coffee, Mrs Trevena.'

I followed Denise to the front door, gave her a hug goodbye and watched her get into her car. Just as she started the engine, she took a call. I heard her voice. She started to drive off, thumping the steering wheel as she went.

CHAPTER SIXTY-FIVE

Denise

As soon as I waved goodbye to Lily and sat in the car, I got a call from DI Blaine.

'Not good news,' she said. 'A taxi driver thinks he picked up Gundersen from his office and drove him to St Pancras.'

I thumped the steering wheel, but as Lily was still watching me I drove away. 'Any sightings once he got in the station? If he went in the station, that is,' I said.

'We're pulling the CCTV now and I've got half a dozen uniforms down there flashing his photo around,' she said. 'DJ, is he the kind of person who could get a false passport?'

'Of course he is. He got a false driving licence for Mark Brown to hire the Range Rover. He knows the right people and he's not short of money so he could afford a decent one.' I thumped the steering wheel again. 'I should've asked Lily.'

'Would she know? She didn't seem to know much about his work life,' DI Blaine said.

'Perhaps not, but I should have asked, Guv.' I didn't thump

the steering wheel a third time since my right hand had gone numb.

'Indeed,' said DI Blaine. 'Come and see me when you get back.'

With that, the line went dead, and I was left with a droning sound and an empty feeling in the pit of my stomach, considering the bollocking I was going to get when I returned to West Hampstead nick.

I grabbed a sandwich and a tea from the vending machine and strolled into the squad room. DI Blaine waved me into her office as soon as she saw me.

'We've had a lead,' she said, a gleam in her eyes. She'd never lost her enthusiasm for the chase. I half expected her to shout, "the game's afoot", but she didn't.

'How?' I mumbled, through a mouthful of cheese and tomato. I grimaced as my tongue encountered the soggy bread. *I should have gone for something else.*

'Barman remembered him. Never leave a pub's newspaper in a puddle of beer. It annoys the bar staff and they remember you.' She rubbed her hands together and smirked. 'I've got uniform bringing in the CCTV footage from the station. It'll be easier for you now we've got an idea of time.'

'I'm sorry I didn't ask Lily about the passport,' I said.

'Oh, this isn't a punishment,' she said. 'I just thought you'd want to nail the bastard for your friend.'

'I do,' I said. 'Thanks.'

I finished my sandwich as I waited for the video footage to be brought in. As soon as it arrived, I signed the chain of evidence log and practically snatched the DVD out of the PC's hands. I trembled putting the DVD in the drive on my laptop. I fired up the program and clicked on the day and time in question. There he was. Unmistakable with the short blond hair and his height. I followed his progress to the bar. I couldn't see inside but that footage was on the other disc the PC had brought in. After twenty minutes he left, and I watched him walk away to the Eurostar Terminal. Bastard. He did have another passport after all. I flicked back to the footage of the pub again. Just in time to see another man leaving and putting some keys in his pocket. Pulling his baseball cap down over his face, he headed to the underground. I was going to need the other footage too to see where he went. Damn, but it was going to be worth it to get that smug git Gundersen for Stephanie's murder.

I called DI Blaine at home. 'We've got him, boss,' I said. 'Gundersen is on CCTV going to the Eurostar Terminal. He doesn't come back again so he must have had another passport hidden away somewhere.'

'Get onto Eurostar and find out what name was used for the ticket,' she said.

'Yep, on it, boss,' I said. I dialled the number for Eurostar ticket enquiries and spent several minutes on hold. I spoke to someone, repeated my question, and was put on hold again. After thirty minutes of my life that I would never see again I finally got to speak to someone who could understand my question.

'I'm looking for a ticket which was booked online only a couple of hours before the train left. One person. Travelling alone. Yes, male. You have? Brilliant.' I clutched the handset, scarcely able to breathe. I'd got him. I was sure of it. And then he slipped away. 'Three single male travellers? And all booked online shortly before departure?' Damn. 'Did they all take their seats? Only one. Good, and his name? Hendriksen. Tajo Hendriksen. Thanks, yes. You've been very helpful.'

I slammed the handset in place and slumped back in my chair, exhausted. Hendriksen was the name Mark Brown had used to collect the hire car rented to kill Lily. So, who was travelling on the false passport? My guess was that it was Gundersen on the Eurostar to Brussels. If I was right, he was heading for Denmark. I called DI Blaine again. Getting the Danes to arrest one of their own was far above my pay grade.

'Good work, DJ,' she said. 'I'll get the Super onto it. The Commissioner will need to call the Danish Embassy. But well done. Looks like we've nearly got him.'

I put the phone down. There was no point in mentioning she'd never suspected Topher Gundersen. Not even once. But if he was out of the country and not likely to come back voluntarily, it was safe for Lily to go home. I couldn't wait to tell her.

CHAPTER SIXTY-SIX

Lily

Sally passed me the handset with a smile. 'Good news,' she whispered.

I nodded, but I was still anxious until I heard Denise's voice. 'Hi. We've tracked him down. He's on his way back to Denmark,' she said. 'We know the name he's travelling under, so he'll get stopped by the Danish Police. You can go home, Lily.'

I knew it was inadequate, but all I could think to say was *thank you*. I passed the phone back to Sally and collapsed at the bottom of the stairs. My heart pounded. I was free. I was really free.

'The children,' I said to Sally, and she passed the phone back to me.

'I'll go and get us both a drink to celebrate,' she said. She bustled to the kitchen and I heard glasses and a bottle opening. I dialled my father's number and waited for him to answer.

'It's me,' I said.

'Who else would call me from London, sweetheart?' I smiled to myself at how different the responses were from my parents. With Mummy I could always envisage the telephone lines freezing as she spoke.

'They've not been able to arrest Topher,' I said. 'He's left the country. Heading back to Denmark.'

'Really,' he said. 'That's a pain. I wanted to see him punished. I know it's great news for you, though. I'll drive back in the morning with the kids.'

'Thank you, Dad. I couldn't have done this without you. Thank you for believing I'm innocent now I can go home to be with my children,' I said. I was shocked at how firm my voice sounded. Gone was the usual tremor. Had I finally grown up? 'The police seem confident that they'll get him back.'

'Good,' Dad said. I heard the smile in his voice. 'Have you told your mother yet?'

'No,' I said. 'I'll let her know when it's all over.'

'Very well,' he said. 'Goodnight darling.' The single tone sounding in my ear told me he'd put the phone down. Tears pricked my eyes but instead of biting them back I let them fall and sobbed. All of the pain of the last few months flowed out of me and, for once, I let it.

Denise

I sat back in my chair, resting my feet on the desk, and clutching a hot coffee in my hands. Not the outcome I'd hoped for. Slipping handcuffs on Topher Gundersen's tanned wrists had begun to fill my dreams. Wiping that smug smile off his face. I sighed; it was not to be.

The St Pancras station CCTV was still running, and I watched as Mark Brown strolled away, tossing car keys in his hand. Time to bring you in as well, I thought. He walked towards the exit as I sipped my coffee, struggling to keep my eyes open.

My head lolled onto the chair back and I gave up on the struggle with my eyes, allowing them to close. Above my head the fluorescent light shimmered, causing a pale orange flicker against my retina. Just five minutes and then I'd request a warrant for Mark Brown.

I took in a deep breath and released it. And another. With the third breath I knew I was going to fall asleep. I gave myself a shake and placed the coffee mug back on the desk. Reaching forward to switch the laptop off, I swore softly. Why had Mark Brown come to meet Gundersen at the station? Not to bring him his car if he was now walking away with the keys. What the hell was going wrong? Then I saw it. I swore loudly.

I flicked to the footage of Gundersen going into the bar, then I watched him leaving. When he left he was a foot shorter and his overcoat was baggy.

The baseball hat guy, on the other hand, had grown taller and the jacket was too small for him to do up.

'Guv,' I yelled. 'Problem!'

DI Blaine was by my side in moments. 'What?' she said.

'Look.' I pointed at the screen, rerunning the footage of Gundersen entering and leaving the bar.

'Oh, fuck,' she said. 'Go. Go now. I'll call uniform. They'll meet you there.'

I ran for my car, taking the stairs two, three at a time. Placing the blue light on the car roof, I hit the button and squealed out of the station car park like a boy-racer. I could only hope I wouldn't be too late.

CHAPTER SIXTY-SEVEN

Lily

I stepped back into the house and noticed the stale smell. It had only been locked up for a few days but it was still stuffy. Dust lay on all the polished surfaces, making them dull. Taking Denise's advice, I only opened the small windows at the front of the house. I opened up the roof lanterns at the rear and ran up the stairs to fling open all the windows, allowing light and fresh air to flood the first floor and the master suite on the top floor.

I changed all the towels in my bathroom and put fresh sheets on the bed. It looked strange with only one set of pillows, but I would never need pillows for someone else in my bed ever again. When Topher was found he would go straight to prison and I would divorce him and keep my children.

I made my way downstairs and had a cup of tea before tackling the children's rooms. I collected their clothes together and took them downstairs to be washed. Then I changed their bedding. They'd be home soon and I couldn't wait to see them. I heard the front door open. I frowned; they'd made good time. I hadn't realised my father had kept a key for himself and I rushed to the landing to greet them. I was halfway down the stairs when I realised that it was not my father in the hallway. It was Topher. Scruffy and dishevelled, but it was definitely Topher.

'Ah, my darling wife,' he growled. 'How good it is to see you! It's been far too long.'

'What are you doing here? You can't be here. The children are coming home any minute.'

'Yes, then we can all go away together.' He smiled at me. That slow treacherous smile that never reached his eyes.

'I'm going nowhere with you,' I told him. 'I'm calling the police. They'll arrest you and send you to prison for killing Stephanie.' I turned to go to the bedroom and the landline. All at once I was face down on the stairs. Topher had hold of my foot and was dragging me down the stairs.

I twisted around and tried to kick at his hand, but he only gripped tighter. I dug my fingernails into the stair carpet and heaved, desperate to escape from his grasp. I felt my ballet pump loosen and my foot was free. Without looking around I raced up the stairs into the master suite. I locked the door and looked around. Damn, I'd trapped myself in the bedroom. I went to the open window, but it was too far to jump down onto the extension's roof. I picked up the phone and dialled 999, but before I heard an answer Topher was pounding against the door. His fists and feet thumped the wood, and the door was vibrating under the torrent of abuse. I knew it would not be long before he was through the door and it would be my flesh meeting his fists and feet, not wood.

I looked around frantically and then I remembered. I scrabbled over the bed to the side that had been Topher's and, pressing my index finger on the hidden button, I opened the eaves cupboard. Hoping against hope that the police hadn't found it and taken it away.

I reached in and laid my hands on the cool, smooth metal, breathing in the unmistakable smell of gun oil. I pulled the shotgun out of the cupboard but, as I looked back inside the cupboard for the box of cartridges, the bedroom door finally gave way.

Topher burst into the room and stood in the doorway, heaving. Breathless and angry.

I picked up the gun and nestled the stock into my shoulder as Dad had taught me.

Topher stepped toward me. 'Oh, don't be bloody stupid, Lily. Give me the fucking gun.'

Trembling, but with the gun still resting under my cheekbone, I backed away from the bed so he couldn't dive across it at me. Topher took another step forward. I sidestepped to the end of the bed.

'You killed Stephanie,' I said. 'You killed my best friend.'

'I am your husband,' he said, holding his hands out towards me. 'You should not need any other friends. You should only need me.'

His brave words, didn't terrify me today, I'd seen him take a step back. His smile was strained. Eyes wary. I edged forward. He took another step backwards.

'I've called the police,' I said.

'I doubt it,' he said. He cocked his head to one side. The grin was unbearably smug. 'I cut the line before I came in and I'm sure you haven't a clue where your mobile is.'

Damn, I knew he was right. My phone should have been in my handbag in the kitchen. I wilted momentarily and then smiled as I realised I did know where my phone was.

Topher frowned. 'Why are you smiling?' he asked.

'Because I do know where my phone is, Topher,' I said. 'It's in my back pocket.'

He blinked. A flicker of disbelief washed across his face and I moved closer to him. He glimpsed behind and backed out of the bedroom. I eyed the door. Could I barricade myself in here until the police arrived? But that would mean dropping the gun, and he'd be free to roam the house.

'Come on, Lily,' he cooed at me. 'You don't want to do this. I'm your husband. You love me. We're happy together. We make a great team.'

I heard his words but it wasn't a version of our marriage I recognised.

We continued the strange dance. He stepped back as I moved forward. Like a waltz with roles reversed.

'I'll change, Lily,' he said. 'I'll go to counselling. Everything will be better. You'll see.' I shook my head. Partly in denial and partly to remove his insidious voice from inside my mind.

At the top of the stairs, he wobbled for a moment and clutched at the newel post. I moved forward and Topher lunged for the barrel of the shotgun. He wrestled with it, twisting it in my hands as I tried to hold onto the gun. I slipped two fingers into the trigger guard, hoping I'd be strong enough to hold on. If I let him get hold of the gun… I gritted my teeth and gave one final pull. Topher fell backwards down the stairs.

The smell of cordite and blood mixed in the air, assaulting my nostrils, and I vomited. My ears still ringing from the sound of the blast, I collapsed in a heap, clutching my fingers, sore from where the gun had been wrenched from my hand. I leaned my head against the cool wood of the banister as I sobbed. I cringed, expecting Topher to run up the stairs, to pull my hair and kick me but, when he didn't, I took a peek at him. He was still lying at the foot of the stairs. The barrel was still in his right hand, but what was left of his chest was bloody. Blood dripped down the wall behind him.

I sat at the top of the stairs, reflecting on what Topher had said about intruders not taking the gun from us. Funny, the mistaken assumptions we make.

I sighed, and then reached into my pocket for my phone and called DC Jones.

CHAPTER SIXTY-EIGHT

Denise

I arrived at Lily's house under blues and twos. The ambulance had already arrived. Although Lily had assured me that Topher was dead, paramedics could pronounce life extinct and give a time of death. Once Kendra had finished at the crime scene they would be able to take Topher's body to the morgue.

Inside, I beckoned Lily down the stairs and we went into the kitchen. She had blood splatter on her face, which Kendra needed to photograph. She had the grey face of someone in deep shock, and I called a paramedic to take a look at her.

'I'm fine,' she said. 'Just a bit dazed. I thought he was my Dad back with the children. You told me he wouldn't come back. What happened?'

'He tricked us,' I said. 'It wasn't Topher who left the country. He got Mark Brown to bring his car into central London and then take his place on the train. They swapped coats. A simple trick but it had me fooled for long enough. Brown has now disappeared in Belgium.' I was on the point of telling her how sorry I was when there was a commotion at the front door.

I had started to learn to recognise the dulcet tones of Lillian Stanton.

She burst past the police officer on the door and bustled into the kitchen. 'What the hell is going on here?' she demanded. 'I saw about Topher on the news. I've come to take the children home with me.'

'The children aren't here,' Lily said. 'They're with Dad.'

'What on earth have you done that for? Have you lost your mind?'

'Be quiet, mother,' she said. 'There's been an accident.'

'What kind of accident? Why have you got blood on your face?'

'I can't tell you,' Lily said.

'I'll do it,' I said. I took Lillian by the elbow and marched her into the rear garden. In the kitchen I could see Lily sat dazed. Kendra had come into the kitchen and was photographing her face. Taking blood samples. Lily wandered to the sink and washed her face.

'Well, Sergeant, I'm waiting,' said Lillian. 'What kind of accident?'

'Mr Gundersen has been shot,' I said.

'You mean Lily's murdered him!' She turned to the scene in the kitchen and began to stride towards the woeful setting inside.

I grabbed her arm and she yelped. 'I'm sorry, but you need to listen,' I said. 'Your son-in-law came back here tonight, assaulted your daughter and was shot when he tried to wrestle the shotgun from her.

'So you're just taking her word for it?'

'No, we've obtained access to an application on Mr

Gundersen's mobile phone. The footage on there backs up Lily's version of events.'

'Version. Yes, that's a good word for her constant lies.' She rubbed her arm where I had grabbed it. 'I only came to collect the children.'

'I think they'll be fine with their grandfather,' I said. 'We need to interview Lily and check the footage.'

'I don't understand about the footage. Where did that come from?'

'Mr Gundersen had cameras installed in the house to spy on your daughter. You didn't know about them?'

That was the catalyst. Lillian Stanton stumbled and collapsed onto the low wall surrounding the patio. 'So it was true!' she whispered.

'Sadly, I think everything she's said about her marriage is true.'

'I didn't believe her.' Lillian held her hand over her mouth, shaking her head.

'I know, but all the same, I don't believe she's lied about any of it.' I patted my pockets to see if I could find her a tissue, but she pulled a lace-edged square from her sleeve. I watched her waft the useless piece of material around, occasionally dabbing it at her eyes. I'd already noticed there were no tears.

'Well,' she said. 'I can't sit here. I have another long drive ahead of me. You'll let me know what happens to Lily, won't you? If she's charged with this murder as well, I don't know if I can cope with the children.'

'Lily said it was self-defence,' I replied. 'I'm inclined to believe her. But I'll keep you posted.'

I stayed in the garden and watched Lillian walk away. She held herself upright and, when I saw her profile, her chin jutted out. If I'd bet on her kissing Lily goodbye, I would've lost my money. Lily stood and said something. Lillian looked shocked and I wondered if Lily was finally standing up to her domineering mother.

'Oh Stephanie,' I whispered. 'If only you could see this.' A soft breeze rustled the bamboo grasses near the hedge and as Lillian stormed out the front door, I walked in through the back door.

EPILOGUE

Lily

I opened the front door and said goodbye to the viewers. They loved the house, they said, but… and there was always a but. The Old Vicarage was the murder house.

The children waved bye-bye to our visitors as they crunched towards their car, and we wandered to the kitchen where I unbolted the stable door to the garden and they rushed out into the sunshine. It was still cold, but spring was in the air. I could feel it. I closed the bottom half of the door and leaned against it, marvelling at how resilient they were, although there were moments, at bedtime or during the night, when James cried out for his father and I had to explain, once again, that he wasn't coming home. His cries woke and upset Darcy, but all the same I could see how she was blossoming into much a happier child.

Cerys and Denise came to tell me they'd worked through all the videos my husband had recorded of me. Every single moment of our life together. They offered, but I declined to watch any of it myself. I didn't think I would ever forget the last time I was with him. Even now when I walked into the hallway the smell of cordite lingered. No amount of air freshener seemed to eradicate the stench. I thought it would be several years before I could cope with fireworks again.

I was happy to be free of Topher and the grip he had over me, but he was my husband, and a small part of me had loved him.

I was distracted from my musings as a click from the kettle told me the water had boiled. I made tea in a new china teapot; one Topher would never see. One he would never throw at the wall. One that I would never have to sweep up and put into the dustbin.

I dragged a bar stool across to the half-open door and I listened to the children playing. My mind drifted to Stephanie. I missed her so much, especially at times like this when life was peaceful. Countless times in the past weeks I'd found myself picking up the phone; I'd be halfway through dialling her number before I remembered, and my tears would flow again.

Then the reverie was over. Darcy came racing towards me, floods of tears, arms outstretched.

'Mummy, Mummy. He hurted me!' she cried.

I leapt from my stool, wrenched open the half stable door and swept her into my arms.

'What's up, my sweetheart?' I asked, burying my head into her hair, breathing in the sweet baby smell. 'What's happened, poppet?'

'Look, look! He hurted me,' she pulled off her coat and held out her podgy arm, still with dimples around her elbows.

I breathed in sharply and looked at the dark bruise

forming on her arm. Already the red was turning purple and darker still in the middle.

'That's going to leave a nasty bruise,' I said, and I looked at James as he sauntered back towards the house. I kissed Darcy's arm and, as I did so, I reflected that, if his father were here, James would learn to leave no bruises at all.

A NOTE OF THANKS

Thank you for picking up The Love Trap. I hope you enjoyed reading Lily's story. If so, pop me a review on Goodreads or Amazon. It's a way for other readers to find my work.

Amazon

Goodreads

If you are interested in hearing about my work, please feel free to join my mailing list where you can access some of my short stories (available only to my subscribers) hear my latest news, what projects I'm currently working on or even just ask me a question.

https://contact.carolinegoldsworthy.com/contact

AUTHOR'S NOTE

Why would anyone write a book about domestic abuse and violence? This was a question posed to me by another writer in an online group and I did have to think about it for some time. This story has nagged me to be written for a long time, however. Early summer 2020, when the UK and most of the world was in Lockdown, I gave in and began writing.

Sara Cox, my editor, immediately hit the nub of the problem with Lily's life – *why doesn't she just leave* – was her question. And it's a question often asked about abuse victims. I've asked it of myself.

So, as is normal for me, I found several articles and began to research. Distressingly, what I discovered is, that leaving the abuser is often the most dangerous time in the relationship. A Guardian article from a few years ago, put the figure of women killed by their abuser after leaving, at 75%.

The Femicide Census (2020) is more conservative in its figures, but during 2018, 37 of the 91 women who left their abusive partners were killed by that partner. 11 of them were killed in the first month after leaving. These figures are **only** for England, Wales, and Northern Ireland.

Domestic abusers isolate their victims from family and friends, meaning that the person does not have a support network to fall back on. There's also the shame associated with being in an abusive relationship. It sucks at and destroys your confidence and many of these people have little or no control over their own money. Some are even prevented from having a job that might give them financial independence.

I don't think *The Love Trap* will be the only book I write on this subject. Another idea has begun brewing. If only there were more hours in the day.

Thanks
Caroline
Ipswich (December 2020)

ACKNOWLEDGMENTS

Bringing a book into the world ready for publication is always a team effort and it's good to be writing the last sections which make up the published product.

Even in the middle of a global pandemic a writer doesn't work in complete isolation. So, here's the shoutout to the team.

Sara Cox, my fantastic editor. Due to her efforts The Love Trap is a great deal better than the initial draft. Thank you so much. What you have taught me about writing over these last few months will stay with me the rest of my writing life.

To Susannah M – who read through the manuscript and gave me some feedback on my approach. Thanks xx

Finally and by no means least – thanks to Andie (found via FiveSquid) who created such a stunning cover from the image I found on SelfPubBookCovers.com/ACBookCovers.

It's beautiful – thank you so much.

ABOUT THE AUTHOR

Caroline Goldsworthy is an emerging author of a gritty urban police procedurals – the DCI Ronald Carlson series and an increasing number of standalones. This is her fourth novel.

Caroline's debut novel, *Tangent*, was inspired by the Ipswich murders, which commenced shortly after she moved to Suffolk in 2006. It was shortlisted for the Selfies Award in March 2019.

More information about events and new books may be found at:

www.carolinegoldsworthy.com

 facebook.com/CarolineGAuthor
twitter.com/CarolineGolds63

ALSO BY CAROLINE GOLDSWORTHY

Printed in Great Britain
by Amazon

86395477R00189